Received On

SEP 2 2 2021

Magnolia Library

NO LONGER PROPERTY OF
SEATTLE PUBLIC LIBRARY

THE
INDIGO
PRESS

D0954264

LESSONS IN LOVE
AND OTHER CRIMES

LESSONS IN LOVE AND OTHER CRIMES

ELIZABETH CHAKRABARTY

THE

INDIGO

PRESS

THE INDIGO PRESS
50 Albemarle Street
London W1S 4BD
www.theindigopress.com

The Indigo Press Publishing Limited Reg. No. 10995574
Registered Office: Wellesley House, Duke of Wellington Avenue
Royal Arsenal, London SE18 6SS

COPYRIGHT © ELIZABETH CHAKRABARTY 2021

This edition first published in Great Britain in 2021 by The Indigo Press
Elizabeth Chakrabarty asserts the moral right to be identified as the author of this work
in accordance with the Copyright, Designs and Patents Act 1988.

First published in Great Britain in 2021 by The Indigo Press

A CIP catalogue record for this book is available from the British Library

This is a work of fiction. Names, characters, places and incidents are
products of the author's imagination or are used fictionally and are
not to be construed as real. Any resemblance to actual events, locales,
organizations, or persons, living or dead, is entirely coincidental.

ISBN: 978-1-911648-22-2
eBook ISBN: 978-1-911648-23-9

All rights reserved. No part of this publication may be reproduced, stored in a retrieval
system or transmitted, in any form or by any means, electronic, mechanical, photocopying,
recording or otherwise, without the prior permission of the publishers.

Design by houseofthought.io
Typeset in Goudy Old Style by Tetragon, London
Printed and bound in Great Britain by TJ Books Limited, Padstow

MIX
Paper from
responsible sources
FSC
www.fsc.org
FSC® C013056

CONTENTS

AUTHOR'S NOTE

This novel is a work of fiction. The characters and places within it are products of imagination, and any resemblance to actual persons, living or dead, is purely coincidental. However, all the examples of hate crime and acts of day-to-day racism portrayed within this novel happened to the author.

AN AUTOBIOGRAPHY OF LOVE AND RACISM

Racism: (n) 1. The belief that each race has certain qualities or abilities, giving rise to the belief that certain races are better than others.

2. Discrimination against or hostility towards other races.

(Pocket Oxford English Dictionary, 2013)

My earliest memory is of my Indian father going missing. I was about two years old, so I have only a non-verbal memory of that time, but now I can write it: how the world drowned through my tears. Even remembering, writing it now, that feeling returns: gutted, life ebbing away, desolation. Sometimes it returns at times that chime with that loss, feelings of abandonment – love gone wrong, death and racism.

I have other memories, happy ones too, that might not be memories but what I've been told, and they have become memories as I've grown older. What's happened and what I've been told have merged, though it's easier to tell what's really happened now I'm an adult. Yet I know the world I live in doesn't always want me to tell reality from fiction.

1.   It's the 1960s and it's sunny. I like drawing pictures on big sheets of paper drawing-pinned to the coffee table in the sitting room.

I draw ships, like the one Daddy and Mummy and my sister came to England on. I know some words: Mummy, Daddy, and my sister's name. I feel things: the sun's warmth on my face through the window as I draw the rays of the sun in the sky; our father's joy as he plays with us on the swings, when he takes us out in the park on Saturday afternoons; and our mother's soft hands as she tucks me into bed at night and, long after she's closed the door, the sweetness of her perfume.

2. One afternoon, Daddy and my sister don't come home. I'm with our mother, and I start to cry. I don't stop crying for weeks, and then months. One day, when I have no more tears, I stop crying. They never returned. Now it's just my mother and me in our flat, surrounded by other flats, and streets of houses all with families and fathers and sisters who come home every evening. I look at the black-and-white photos of when we were all together. There's Daddy, my sister and me, and our mother too, her skin colour different from ours. When we are outside in the town, her pushing me in my pushchair, I see her skin colour is similar to the other people here, but she is more beautiful and she is warmer. Look how she smiles at me.

3. I'm in my pushchair in the English spa town where we live, and I'm being wheeled past the big white building with statues outside, and green wreaths of twisted branches and red poppies. I point at a stuffed snake in an antique-shop window. In the reflection, a white man appears. He looks from me to my mother, like he's trying to work something out; like me adding up on my abacus. My mother listens; he says something about his time in India in the British Army during World War Two, and seeing snakes there, like the one in the window, then something I don't understand. My mother quickly turns away, taking me home. Inside, she closes the door and she cries.

4.   At infant school at lunchtime, I am sent to sit at the slow eaters' table. I don't understand why. I don't eat slowly; I never eat there at all. It's not food, so I don't eat. On the white plate in front of me is a whitish-greyish mound, something greenish that smells like it's gone off, and something brown that smells dead. At home I eat from a thali arranged with little bowls: melt-in-my-mouth rice, and mustard-coloured egg curry, fragrant with herbs and spices. We – the boy and girl with me – are forbidden to talk, unless we eat. None of us eat. An adult tells us about the starving children in Africa, how ungrateful we are for what we're given. Shrieks break the silence, the other children larking around in the playground outside, where we're not allowed to go until we've eaten everything on our plates. We three brown-skinned children, our eyes watering a little, look at each other, not sure what we've done wrong. Every weekday, we sit silently for the whole hour not eating the uneatable, while the kitchen staff push past, slopping disinfectant around us with mops, grumbling about us being in their way. When the bell rings, we're shunted off to lessons, like the contents of the plates are shoved into the other leftovers, squashed down and wheeled away to the rubbish bins outside. We don't talk or look at each other outside of the slow eaters' table; we've done something wrong and we avoid each other's wrongness, even when we're seated next to each other for silent reading. I don't talk about it when I get home; I'm hungry and quickly eat what my mother has prepared. Hunger and silence are part of school, like lessons, which I don't talk about either. I can already read and write – I can't remember ever not being able to – and in lessons I haven't learned anything new. My mother asks if I've made friends, and I answer no, we just do lessons. She looks puzzled, but then she asks what I've learned. I tell her we chant times tables, and copy letters of the alphabet along a straight line. She stops what she's doing on the kitchen counter and closes her eyes. I've said the wrong thing, but I'm not sure what

else I've learned at school, other than learning to be silent. In bed, I cry under the covers, like I used to, that missing feeling. My mother cries too, in the room next door. I listen, and I dry my tears on the handkerchief I keep under my pillow. When silence comes it's easier than the sound of tears.

5.   In the 1970s in the morning when I get to my secondary school, I go to my house. The school has about two thousand pupils divided into eight houses. My house is named after Winston Churchill, who I've learned in History is important because of World War Two, which we're told – besides Hitler, of course – was started because some European countries didn't have so many colonies as others. School is difficult as I have to listen to these things that I know aren't quite right, that there's more to it than we're taught. What I know from my mother is these larger countries like India, which were called colonies, wanted independence from the smaller British and other European countries who had taken control of them as they built their empires. At home in the evenings my mother is writing her dissertation on James Baldwin. There's a pile of his books on her desk; I turn over the top one and his face looks back at me. I feel an affinity with him, his face, like he's my father. There's a poster of the socialist and pacifist Bertrand Russell on the wall above my mother's desk. I don't know why I know that it's him, but I do; like I remember my mother pinning a CND badge onto my cardigan as I was sitting in my pushchair at a demo when I was little. Each morning at secondary school in Churchill House, I take off my coat. Chosen by my mother, it's a yellow coat, the colour of sunshine. I hang it up in the open cloakroom allocated to my tutorial group, where there's a peg for each pupil. At the end of each day I return there, put my coat on and walk home, sometimes with pupils I know, sometimes alone. In between I walk around school like everyone else, in my uniform, or rather the girls' uniform: a white polyester blouse

and grey viscose skirt, red jumper, black nylon blazer, and a black and scarlet tie that serves no purpose but is compulsory. The uniform is uncomfortable, not warm enough in winter, and the fabric next to my skin is scratchy, provoking my eczema all year round. The days are long; every hour we move between lessons, carrying our books, my shoulders hurt from the weight. Then the sitting in one position, staring ahead, listening, not just to the teacher talking at the front of the class but also to what people are saying behind me, words I don't like, whispering about me, like passing worksheets around the class. I try to concentrate on the teacher, but that makes it worse, provoking more whispering, teacher's pet and swot added to those horrible words. I'm glad when it's four o'clock, time to get my coat, go home – until one day I'm later, after picking up books in the library to take home. I need books: after lessons, I swallow books and they fill me up, while other kids stuff chewing gum, crisps and sweets into their mouths, then vomit horrible words that spread like cold germs from one to another. That day, when I think school can't get worse, I find the cloakroom is empty of coats, apart from mine. It's drooping from the same peg I left it on – but as I take it down and go to put my arm in a sleeve, I see something and stop. Inside my coat, on the soft silky lining, written in blue felt-tip marker pen, there's that horrible word, 'paki'. I don't understand what, who, why, how could. I can't touch it I can't drop it but now I'm wide awake with my heart beating in time with my fear. I look around; there's no one but silence. I don't know what to do; I just want home. I'm cold; I don't want to, but I put on my coat. At home I hang it on its peg in the downstairs cloakroom. I don't know whether to, or how to tell my mother, I don't have the words, and if I told her it would be like it was happening all over again. Later she's tidying up, she notices it, and she's really upset. The next day she comes to school with me and confronts the Head of House about it. He insists I tell him who did it, but I don't know. I can't remember much after that, if anything was announced about it. No one was ever found out, or owned up to doing it. Everyone forgot about it – I mean the school forgot. I never forget seeing that horrible word inside the coat I put on to go home alone in the cold. Inside I know, and whoever did it does too: the thought of that still makes me shiver, like feeling the draught of a door opening and closing behind me, but when I look there's no door, just a wall.

6. At school I make friends. We do better than the pupils who mess around in lessons; we concentrate and do our homework, and take turns in getting praise from the teacher. Before our English Language O level exams in the summer, we stand at the front of the class and practise our speeches one by one. I think mine was about being mixed-race, and about India. By then I was interested in all things India, from the elephant ornaments on the bookshelves at home, to the sweetmeats that Mummy's friend bought in a café we visited on the other side of the city. There were more Asian people living, working and shopping there, and the cafés and shops sold embroidered and sequinned fabrics, and jars of orange and red spices, the colour of the paints my mother used in her sketchbook, burnt umber and sienna, deep rich colours that sound like the music playing in the café where I'd savour golden gulab jamun or creamy rasmalai. When I finish my speech I go back to my desk, and another student walks to the front. The girl next to me leans closer, whispering, 'I don't think of you as Asian.' I don't know what to say. She is, I suppose, a friend, but the invisible thread of friendship snaps as she smiles like she's being nice. It doesn't feel nice, though. Wasn't she saying being Asian isn't something she thinks about, because being Asian isn't nice? At break I walk as far as I can down the playing fields. I stare up through the branches on the trees, searching that nothingness of grey English cloudy skies for a glimmer of golden sun. After that day, friendship became a jigsaw puzzle, working out whether pieces fitted together: people

could be nice, inviting me to parties on a Saturday evening, or asking me to walk home from school through the park together. But the walking together through the park was because of a recent school assembly when we'd been told not to walk there alone; after school one day something awful happened to a girl there. In the mornings I come out of the house, and there's an unspoken rule to walk with the children of the neighbours through the park, but when we get to school we go our separate ways. We are busy, I suppose, revising for our O levels, preoccupied with making choices about what to study at A level, those of us who are going to stay on into the sixth form. After school I walk up the steps to the house we live in now, with its front garden of flowers and a weeping willow tree in the centre of the lawn. At the kitchen window my mother has put up a Labour Party poster for the council elections, which reminds me of a few years ago, another poster about the referendum on joining the EEC. At school we had easily changed from imperial to decimalization ages ago; it was more logical counting in tens rather than groups of odd numbers. I like the idea of Europe, it is holidays and sunshine, and other languages, and Britain is geographically part of the continent of Europe anyway. At school other pupils don't feel the same: 'We're an island, it's safer to stay that way.' The girl who didn't see me 'as Asian' now sits next to someone else in our shared classes, someone who isn't Asian. Now I often sit next to a boy in class: the one pupil whose skin and hair colour are nearer mine. His mother is Spanish and his father English, so we have being mixed heritage in common. When we get to know each other more, he tells me about the racism his mother experienced at the golf club where his dad likes to play. I feel sad for his beautiful mother, who waits for her children near their front door, welcoming them when they're safely home. I like him, I feel safe sitting next to him in school and walking home afterwards.

7. It's the mock exams. I enjoy the silence of writing timed essays, with just the scratching of biros on exam paper booklets until the invigilator calls out, 'Time's up.' When the results are out, I read them at the end of the day, in the form room I've been in for registration every day for five years in Churchill House. I've done well: a string of A grades, all high percentages. The results are printed on white paper. The last result is Maths, A: 100 per cent. Pleased, I fold the paper back into the brown envelope to take home for my mother – but then something weird happens: my form tutor calls me to his desk as the others leave for the day. He tells me they have ordered the re-marking of my exam paper, that I couldn't have got 100 per cent. I'm not sure what to say; was he saying they thought I had cheated? He looks down at the list of numbers on his desk, and gestures for me to go. Deflated, I walk home, the envelope in my satchel. The next day I am told my Maths result is 'left as it was'. I nod, and say, 'Thank you,' though I'm not sure what I'm thanking the teacher for, it's just how I've been brought up, to say please and thank you. I think of the word on my coat, and the girl who'd commented on how she thinks of me, meaning what I look like; there are things that are said or written or done that make me feel like a zero. I feel out of breath, though I am only walking slowly back to my seat. I count in my head from one to ten, to calm my breathing, but that doesn't help now numbers aren't as straightforward as they used to be. I rethink my option choices, whether, rather than Maths A level as planned, to swap to French instead. Yes, better to do English, French and History, with the teachers I feel comfortable with.

8. Two years later, our A levels are over, and there's the sixth-form disco to celebrate leaving school. I get my hair cut short for the first time since I was a little child, and that evening a friend meets me on the way to the disco, another boy I feel safe with. He says, 'Gosh, you look so much better, less Asian, now.' I look

ahead, don't say anything, and change the subject. What I've learned to do is cry later; hold it together. I don't want to lose friends, and friends sometimes think and say things that are terrifying, that try my heartbeat. Like running a race, I have to carry on, keep calm. When we're at the disco, and in the darkness of the common room, we drink illicit cider rather than Coke, then I start to feel lighter. I watch people dancing. The doors open out onto the quad, and I find myself swaying to the music outside. Above me the sky is dark, but I can imagine the wide world out there, and gradually I see the stars. Someone touches my bare arm, and there's the Spanish boy. John Lennon's 'Imagine' is playing, we dance, and when the music changes we move closer together, and kiss. Afterwards he walks me safely home. I think about how I like girls too; he seems to know that just like other friends do too without me saying anything. We pick up things about each other from how we look at each other and how we look at other people. It doesn't seem to matter to him, we like each other just the way we are. When we leave school, and both move to London for university, we continue our friendship. We lose touch with everyone else; we don't try, and they don't either. We stay in touch with each other, without trying. Now it's just us.

9. At university in London, I'm enjoying studying Drama and English, all day in workshops and lectures, or reading and writing in the library. One day in the library I find a shelf of feminist post-colonial texts, and I start reading one standing there. I borrow these books, and back in my room I refer to them in my essay, critiquing a long poem from the English Literary Canon. I've been getting good grades, and I enjoy writing this essay late into the night, eating digestive biscuits instead of dinner and drinking coffee to stay awake. I hand it in the next day, and the following week I'm looking forward to my tutorial to get feedback. When I knock on the office door, there's a curt

'Enter', and inside the office, the tutor, an old-before-his-time white man in a tweed jacket, looks up and launches into an angry tirade, throwing the essay towards me. I can see the grade as it hits me: an E; my first. I don't hear what he says as much as see it, his skin reddening with anger and his voice high-pitched; he's holding in more than he's letting out. I learn my lesson: I keep the feminist post-colonial books for my private reading; to pass exams I will have to critique literature as a text, without critiquing the culture of its production. That feels odd now I've discovered these books that make sense of the world, but it's what I have to do, if I want to do well and avoid people throwing words and paper back where they've come from: me. As I return the books to the library, before going to the Drama department for my seminar, I'm aware of how I have to act a character, an acceptable version of me, but this is my real life. On the Drama department noticeboard the week before I'd put up a newspaper article about race and theatre, next to the other notices about auditions, visiting theatre companies and guest lectures. This week as I wander through the foyer the article I put up isn't there; around the gap last week's other notices remain. A theatre technician walks in and stops next to me, the whiteness of a back-to-front rolled-up poster under his arm. He makes no eye contact, but emits a grunting, huffing and puffing sound as he flexes his elbows, getting some pins out, rattling the canister, readying to pin up whatever it is. I get it: he needs space. I move aside, but I wait. When he stands back, I see it's advertising auditions for a student production of a Chekhov play. That's exciting; we've been studying Chekhov this term, perhaps I'll audition. The technician moves in front of me, putting a notice in the space where my article had been: 'All notices must be given to the theatre technician before displaying on the noticeboard.' His white hand presses the drawing pin, fixing the white page in the gap. He glances down at me sharply, like stabbing two drawing pins in my eyes, then he goes into his office and the door slams shut. In the silence I reread the Chekhov poster. Later I go back to the library and take out the play, and read the speech. In my study bedroom, preparing for the audition, I lose myself in the words of the young woman. She's like all young women: she feels love and hope, she's constrained by where she lives and the people who control her life. I'm in my room but the room becomes a room in Russia, and then in my mind it's a room in India and I'm grappling with fathers and daughters, the desire to go to the big city, make my own life. When I've finished, I rest, give my heart time to go back to normal, let the beads of sweat on my forehead cool me down. A week later at the auditions, I'm waiting for my turn in the dusty darkness of the corridor outside the student-union hall, in a line of white women, one after the other going through the door and coming out ten minutes later. Finally I'm alone on the hard bench, by the closed door. I'm wondering whether they've forgotten me, whether I should knock, remind them I'm here, when the door creaks open, a slither of light slicing the corridor, a sign for me to enter. A white guy and a white woman, students from the year above me, are sitting with their backs to the door, but she swivels round and nods me towards the stage. I climb the steps and centre myself, give myself a moment eyes closed, then when I open my eyes I start the speech with the smack of the words, how I feel, just like I did in my room but I'm onstage, and my voice soars, my heart echoing with the desire for love and to be where I must be. At the end I stand still, my heart beating fast, waiting. Out of the darkness, like in a cave, a voice says, 'Thanks.' There's whispering, the scrape of chairs on the wooden floor, then the guy says, 'That was good, but of course we can't cast you, you don't look right.' I manage to ask, 'What do you mean?' He says, 'Well, you're, um …' I reply, 'Yes?' He says abruptly, 'It's Chekhov, isn't it?' I think of Russia and India, how it's all connected in one massive area on the world map, on the wall near my mother's desk at home. I think of her black Russian shawl with its red embroidery draped around her shoulders, a gift from one of her friends. He gave me the wooden Russian doll, with its one doll inside another and then another, sitting on my bedroom shelf at home. For some reason I remember those Tiny Tears dolls, and their pale plastic skin. How their blue eyes opened and shut and how they made a crying sound but without any actual tears in their eyes. The white guy says, 'Thanks for coming,' like I've been round for tea. They're whispering to each other as they leave without looking back, the door creaking closed behind them. Alone, for a moment I breathe in the stage, then I climb down and leave. A day later the cast list is pinned up on the noticeboard in the Drama foyer: a list of English names, unlike my own. I breathe, I return to my books, I write my thoughts in my journal; the writing travels, sprawling over into the margins, and the letters morph into nothingness when my tears hit the page. Unlike the dolls, I cry real tears.

10. At the women's group, the discussion is on abortion and everyone's white and straight. I don't go there again. I meet other women at the student union who are studying social sciences and social work, not the arts. Together we set up a black women's group; black is a political term that answers the endless chasm between what we're all feeling about racism, especially the things we've been made to feel we're not supposed to ask about but which we want to: from the names of writers on the reading lists to the use of blackface on the stage. We become allies, our similar experiences in the struggle to just be, and to become what we want to be, struggling with the difference between the ideas we're taught and the reality of our lives. We make banners and march against apartheid in South Africa and for gay equality in the UK; we debate late into the night about how our bodies are commodified in the media just like in pornography. We trust each other and become comrades and friends, and some people pair up and become lovers. I have lovers, and then a girlfriend, and

then another one. They're mostly white, I'm not sure why, but they're who I find myself with, these women who want to make love with me and who I want to make love with too. When we talk, in the moments when people do, at bars and after that, after sex, we sometimes discover silence in our conversations. Racial difference hovers between us, my experience of life is different to theirs; it's so different to the rapport with my comrades. With my lovers I can only make love, but love feels easier than day-to-day life, making love on my private stage, in an intimate play between the sheets, when I'm naked and feel good I let go of everything else – until I wake in the morning and my latest lover is getting dressed, then gone. Like sleep at night, love is a temporary feeling. When I sit down at my desk for the day, I'm back to facing the opposite of love in the books and plays I have to write about in the arts, an intellectual gymnastics masking my feelings. Critical writing is a kind of performance, acting what's expected: an essay reflecting the dominant cultural ideology. Abstract words. Depressed, at night I succumb again, searching for another escape, an answer my mind and body crave: but she's still seemingly somewhere else.

11. Years later, now working in London, I get an invitation to the school reunion organized by a woman in my old school year; she's got breast cancer, she wants to see the people she grew up with. I'm not sure that I do want to. I procrastinate, but my mother's still living nearby, and it's a weekend, so I go. The guy who said I look less Asian is there, and so is the woman who said she didn't think of me as Asian. People look older, they mention jobs, and marriage, partners and kids. They wear the clothes of people who have dressed up for a social function, the men sweating in their too-warm suit jackets and the women cooler in printed frocks with statement jewellery. Someone by the drinks table says to me, 'Oh look, there's Gillian,' pointing to a woman dancing with a video camera in her hands on the almost empty dance

floor. I say, 'She looks familiar?' The person by the table says, 'She won the Turner Prize? Thought you would have known each other, she was a bit weird too.' I turn to her, not sure what she's getting at, but she smiles, saying, 'She used to bunk off school all the time; was a punk or something,' perhaps trying to be humorous. I don't recognize her, or what she says about me, and I don't recognize Gillian from school, though I've seen her work at the Tate in London and remember reading she couldn't wait to escape where she grew up, like me. Then there's a hand on my arm, it's a woman saying quickly, 'I just want to apologize to you for how I was racist to you back then.' I look at her, and have no idea who she is – was – she looks older than me, with full make up and her hair styled in waves, above an immaculate white blouse and black skirt. I find my courtesy; I reply, 'Thank you, but I can't remember you.' Her eyelids quiver; she wasn't expecting that. I don't know what else to say, but I'm saved by the speeches which I don't hear as I'm thinking back, who was she, what exactly is she apologizing for: whispering horrible words as I passed through the corridor of this school, or as I sat in the same class, or was it something she wrote on my coat when no one else was around? I have a mobile phone now it's the late nineties; I call my mother and say I'm coming home. I walk back with some of the same people I walked home with as a teenager, a gay guy and a woman who left school before A levels. I don't swap numbers or even speak of keeping in touch, how people do. I'm never going back. Alone, I turn the corner. The light is on, and my mother's in the doorway. I need sleep, and then I want to go home to London, get on with my life and never look back.

12. I move from job to job, in the cultural industries, film, TV, the-atre, and then in academia. My career develops, to a point. I'm in a professional job, but when I reach up to the next rung of the ladder, my hands reach not the glass ceiling that feminists,

or rather white feminists, talk about; instead I get grazed and crushed by a ceiling made of granite. It isn't that I don't get shortlisted, or invited for job interviews – but afterwards, even when my presentation to the board, and panel interview too, seem to have gone well, with lots of interesting supplementary questions, and smiles, afterwards, usually a day later, by which time I know the job has gone to someone else, my phone rings. 'Thank you for coming,' like I've given a guest lecture, not been interviewed for a permanent position. 'The panel want me to commend you on your fascinating research,' and speedily onwards to the usual brief ending, '… but sadly, we felt you were not quite the right fit.' I don't really listen to the sign-off, 'Good luck with your search,' knowing the call is almost over and it's time to start another application. It's that word 'fit' with all its meanings from athletic, good-looking, shaggable, to the one they mean at job interviews: I don't look right on the first line of the application form, and not facing them in the interview room either. Though I con myself that if I've been shortlisted it means I have a chance, I know it's all generally a performance of equality. I see it sitting, waiting in corridors, like auditions. I can't help noticing the other people, like I do as I sign in at reception and see the list of names upside down, and then while I'm waiting, that we're all wearing black suits, you can hardly tell us apart, well, from the neck down and if you don't look at our hands. Just like when I come out of the interview I check my watch, and I'll have been in the interview room for the allotted time like the interviewee before me. Afterwards I look at the website, see who's got the job. Usually it's a white man, or a white woman; it's rarely a man or a woman whose skin colour looks like mine. I learn to move on; keep applying.

13. I stay in my job for another year. And then another. Like each job I've had before, there is the usual indirect or direct racism that I'm used to. Sometimes I even joke about it with friends in the

evening over drinks, like when I was once asked in a new job in trendy lefty Islington, 'Have you had an arranged marriage?' 'No, I'm a lesbian,' I thought of saying, but obviously didn't. Then something strange, or rather strange for me, happens. After all the years of being shortlisted and going through interviews, then still being stuck in the same job, I get shortlisted, interviewed and finally offered a new job. It's going to be an adventure, a change. I read the contract, then sign on the dotted line and post it to the place where a few months later I start work. But then everything starts to go wrong. It's not even what I'd come to see as normal direct or indirect everyday racism, it's beyond anything I've ever experienced. It's not a 'words can't break my bones' moment, quite the reverse; for the first time in my life I'm scared to go to work –

HOW TO WRITE ABOUT THE TRAUMA OF RACISM

Abject: (adj) 1. Very unpleasant and humiliating.

(Pocket Oxford English Dictionary, 2013)

I don't know how it's going to end. Even now I'm home here in London, it's unfinished, so when I think about it even for a second I'm back there: the most unpleasant, humiliating, frightening experience I've ever had. I don't know who was behind it, what they wanted. I don't know whether they're still out to get me.

I haven't told anyone my absolute fear, can't say it aloud: I'm frightened for my life. I thought being at home would make it go away, but it hasn't. Fear follows me like a shadow. When I open doors, I go carefully, worrying who might be waiting there, what might happen next. When I hear footsteps behind me in the dark, I walk faster, clutching my mobile in my pocket, ready to dial the police once more. Then my heart beats faster and faster, like it'll break through my skin, my body telling me I'm alive I'm alive, despite what's out there, who's out there.

Who's out there? That's still the question.

Waiting for whatever happens next, the unknown, curtails how I live. Early on I was told to be careful about revealing where I am, especially on social media. But that was going to be difficult: I'm a writer and performer, I have to publicize what I'm doing, events in public places.

The police officer said, 'Well, just use it in a limited way, do what you have to do. Make sure friends know your whereabouts.' Then, 'Do you have a partner?'

'Um, not at the moment.'

I understood why she asked, but my answer made me feel worse. I had been dating but nothing that had gone anywhere.

She asked the obvious question: 'Is there anyone who might have a grudge against you, a colleague or an ex-partner?'

I've had my fair share of difficult relationship endings, but no one I know would treat me like this, at least I hope not. What's happened has even tainted my memory of love, like love is a kind of mental illness.

I shook my head.

'Are you sure?'

'I'm not sure about anything at the moment. It's difficult to trust people, but I can't think of anyone I know who would do this.'

I wish I had someone, someone who makes me feel safe, to love and be loved by, but I don't. I'm on my own. What's happened has made meeting even beautiful strangers fraught. The idea that some-one who has seen me around, probably spoken to me, could do that makes me wary of people even offering me a drink when I'm in a bar, or asking me out. But now friends say I have to get on with living, and love is what's missing. Love might annihilate the memories. Perhaps.

When I came back to London, I called the police officer to let her know, and to find out what would happen to my case now.

'We'll keep it live. It's an ongoing case as we haven't found a suspect or suspects.'

'What does that mean?'

'If anything happens again, call me, or if I'm off duty, quote the crime number, and obviously if you feel in danger, call 999.'

It's still weird to link dialling the emergency services with being at work. When I first told friends about the incidents, some found it shocking, but others didn't, having experienced so much racism themselves in various workplaces. Some white acquaintances listened but didn't say anything, perhaps not knowing what to say, or not under-standing, never having experienced racism, how it feels: degrading, frightening and soul-destroying, and inextricably linked with living in this country.

It continued for years. I stopped talking about it. People can only stand so much of others' trauma before they change the subject and talk about things that are inconsequential when you're experiencing serious racial harassment. Sometimes talking about it is like repeating it all over again, re-traumatizing, increasing my fear over when it might happen again. Not talking about it is a kind of coping mechanism, though that means dealing with it alone.

In this era of social media, even if I don't constantly post where I am, it's easy to track people down with Google. When I say 'people', in that abstract way, what I mean is me. It's funny how I find myself doing that: thinking about my experience in the abstract, like I'm writing an academic paper, with all the distance of not using the word 'I'. Yes, I have a compulsion to write about, or rather through this, what I'm living. I think about it almost all the time, like I would a relationship. That feels weird.

When the incidents were happening to me, management, col-leagues and my union did the right thing to monitor and protect me as much as was possible at the time; however, for me it is a con-tinuum of my experience of racism over a lifetime. Racism is what happens to ethnic minority employees in the workplace, just like in our everyday lives.

Reading back what I've just written reminds me of character types in TV crime series, from the whistle-blower who, even after they've left an organization, is haunted by whoever is out to get them, to the police officer on the victim's side. That's strange after all these years on demos to stop war or protest against racism, when the police were often the enemy, rushing at peaceful demonstrators or dragging us into police vans. Yes, now it's strange I have the police on my side.

I have followed the expected trajectory, from school to univer-sity to work, but no one brought me up to deal with racism, the fear and anxiety, not being able to sleep, not knowing what to do. I'm probably repeating myself, but the experience of racism repeats, so it becomes a pattern, and that forces me to think about it even in my day-to-day life. The unknown follows me around, even inside my home. Like I'm a character in a crime novel, and the person out to get me feels close by.

I remember I was offered counselling, but I turned it down. I was anxious as a result of what had happened, but me being counselled wouldn't stop it. I wondered whether whoever was behind it needed counselling, how disturbed they might be; how far they might –

I try to switch off the nightmare of that thought, though it's difficult. It reminds me of something useful I was offered when I was still working: someone to walk me to the bus stop when I worked late, when there would be fewer people around and it was dark. Fortunately it was someone I instinctively trusted, though it was odd being walked to a bus stop by another adult, like when I was a kid, walking home from school through the park.

Now I'm alone, and home and hopefully safe in London, I'm giving myself breathing space before hunting for another job. I can't face that yet.

When I wake in the morning I'm relaxed. I put the coffee on, and while I'm waiting for it to brew I look outside, past the buildings taller than mine, all the million- or billion-pound buildings of the moneymakers, like brutal scars cutting into a blue-skied day: the Shard, and what Londoners call the Walkie Talkie and the Cheesegrater the other side of the river. Sometimes the buildings disappear on a misty day, and the city goes quiet, blanketed in white; then I'm alone in my garret flat, suspended above a silent city. When I turn on the radio to listen to the news, the world returns, all Brexit and Brexit-related, all doom, but at least it's doom outside of me. I eat muesli or toast, but once I've washed up the breakfast things and turned off the radio, I sit down at my tiny desk in the corner of the living room, between the sofa and the windows overlooking the street.

There's something about sitting down at a desk, even at home: it all floods back. I distract myself: open an email, start a reply, dealing with domestic admin, then procrastinate on the Web, but eventually I close the browser and open a new document. It stares back at me, like the blank wall above my desk when I look up; like the anxiety-inducing infinity of the unknown.

Anxiety consumes time, and I have a lot of time on my hands now, so the anxiety expands. When I look down, the laptop has gone to sleep, its blank page a black hole of what's happened, and what might happen in the darkness of the future.

A siren shrieks outside. I half get up, then the siren gets absorbed into the noise of traffic; I sit. I touch a key; the screen wakes with its white rectangle of a new page without writing, like the blank face of a stranger whose features I might gradually learn to see.

Could I do what friends have suggested: write about what happened, and try to make sense of it from this supposed safety? Or should I carry on with my work in progress, what I usually write about – love? I toggle between the two, between love or, what would I call it, hate? Or could I connect the two, write about love and hate? Isn't that exactly what I know?

I've often had to remind students that the creative-writing mantra 'write what you know' doesn't mean write what's happened to us, but to use the emotion of an experience and recreate that emotion in a fictional context. Emotions are the fuel igniting the engine of conflict, and conflict is what drives fiction, just as conflict drives life. Microaggressions, the beats of myriad conflicts that measure our lives, also reveal fractures in seemingly perfect surfaces. There are always fractures, despite the outward-looking faces of people, or institutions, because humans are fallible.

Humans are complex creatures, and real life isn't like blockbuster movies, where good characters survive, just like bad people don't always get what they deserve, except in crime fiction.

I've been thinking a lot about crime, spending time with the police and that active crime file. Besides browsing the shelves of my local bookshop, when I wander in between the tourists and the office workers on their lunch breaks, and where I found myself buying a couple of the latest crime novels. Reading them, one after the other, late into the night to get to the end, the funny thing was although I felt relieved with justice served, the longer I thought about them, the less satisfying I found them. Not because the bad people got their comeuppance, but because that doesn't feel real, at least not to me right now. Real is the nightmare of waiting for someone's next move, even when I'm miles away, here at my desk in the daylight. This precarious safety isn't justice.

Writing can be a kind of justice, but there are different sorts of justice. The central text of my doctoral thesis was Shakespeare's *Hamlet*: a father's ghost demanding his son avenge his murder is what sets the play in motion, but the play is mostly about how when we're troubled our relationships are destabilized too. When the world feels wrong, we see those around us as though under a microscope, and we don't know who to trust, then we seem like, or feel like, we're going mad. I remember that there were moments I felt myself losing it, even though my workplace did everything they could to support me through the racism I experienced. Once you know fear, it's all-pervading. Fear is the most destructive emotion.

I digress. I want to try to stick with the point about writing, about intention and its subversion, about the subconscious. We start writing about the thing that forces us to our desks, pressing our pens into our hands, but as I write, something else takes hold of my fingers and starts spelling out the emotions quivering around me. The angry anxiety-inducing emotions on the lips of people chatting behind me in the queue at the ATM, or by the bar as I wait for a friend: whatever the latest political battle is, especially now, like Brexit, it's no longer straightforwardly between left and right but between multiculturalism and nationalism, economic logic and racist paranoia. So even the love that I usually write about – someone standing in a bar waiting for someone who may become a lover – becomes tainted with the uncertainty poured out alongside the drinks. How is it possible to write about love in this era of hate?

Often in a tutorial, encouraging a student to get more deeply into a character they're writing, I mention Keats's 'Negative Capability' from his *Letters* (December 1817), and paraphrase it. How we have to feel our way towards what we don't know, the human pulse of the character we hate, as much as the character we love. To be human is to be a mess of feelings and contradictory actions: there is humanity, humanity's inhumanity, and acts of inhumanity that sometimes result in more humane acts, despite tragedy.

To further the point with a student, I'd turn to the bookshelves and take down a book to illustrate my point. Many of my books have old annotations in fading pencil, as the key texts haven't changed much since I was an undergraduate: the Canon, or rather the Western Canon, and it's Shakespeare I return to again and again. Now we're in a golden era of renewing Shakespeare for the contemporary era: all-women casts, black kings, women falling in love with women, but –

Something that's odd is how in contrast to the diversity of restaging Shakespeare, keeping the Canon and English Literature alive, there's a diversity lacking in most contemporary literature. I mean, white fiction, not that they call it that, and 'they' being the professionals who speak and write about literature, who are, of course, mostly white.

When I first read the classics, although I was conscious the characters were all white, I empathized with the hero or heroine and read past the whiteness to the human within: Lizzy Bennett and Jane Eyre, Juliet Capulet and Hamlet. I've been an independent young woman, in love and confused; I've mourned, but been conflicted over my father. Like I am conflicted over the whiteness of the Western Canon.

I stand and stretch. Across the room, there are the classics, back home in London, like me. After the dusty shelves in my office at work, here they're jostling with other books, in the confined shelves built into the eaves, wedged in next to, or lying on top of, the contemporary novels and plays I read now I'm not working and can read what I want. Recently though, I've been dissatisfied with how often white characters are imagined so differently from ethnic minority characters. White characters are humans: they live and love and are central to stories, whereas the ethnic minority characters usually serve the whiteness of the narrative, sometimes quite literally. As unnamed nurses and doctors, or serving in bars, restaurants and shops, serving, meeting and greeting for the accumulation of white capital, ethnic minority characters are useful until they've served their purpose: for consumables, sex, drugs or the post-9/11 cliché of terror or war. And even if they are imagined by a liberal writer, somehow the ethnic minority characters are ones we never really know beyond their skin colour and ethnic-sounding name. They appear only in relation to a white character who they marry or date or work with; they are rarely leading characters within a tree of interconnected relationships. Or their first and only appearance is as a corpse to be dealt with by white characters, and their relatives are absent or never mentioned, existing off the page only in the minds of readers like me.

It's stuffy; I open the window, breathing in the fresh air. Down on the street below, women and men of different ethnicities walk along, living real lives outside the pages of the walk-ons, clichés and corpses of contemporary white fiction. There's an Asian woman in a short skirt with a black man in a suit, talking as they stroll past a group of white women and men reading the menu outside the pub, as other people cycle by. It's London, and I'm home.

In the kitchen I fill the espresso pot and put it on to brew, the same pot I've had for years. I remember working from home when I lived in the countryside, and making coffee in this same pot. I'd carry my cup and stand by the window, looking out at the calming flow of greenery: fields, hills and the woods. No houses or humans in sight, just the timeless space of the natural world, it could have been any time. Then I'd remember the latest headlines. The selfish irony of a so-called tolerant nation with its 'this island is full up' headlines, when other front pages show photos of drowned asylum-seekers washed up on Mediterranean beaches, our fellow humans trying to escape from Western-backed wars in the oil-rich Middle East. The beautiful greenery of wooded hills stretched across the horizon. In the sky above the only movement, from the military base hidden by the hill, the hovering of heavy black helicopters' vibrating wings would often wake me at night, start my heart beating fast. In the day there would be the swoop of large birds, their wings in flight against the mingling of blue and white, the clouds never far away. The elegance of a bird's flight, swirling, hovering, and suddenly swooping down; then my realization: when birds swoop like that, they're going in for the kill. There are always smaller, more vulnerable creatures.

My mobile sounds a WhatsApp notification, a friend asking to meet for a drink later, after a 'Bad day at work'. I reply. Her name appears again: 'See you later.'

With my coffee I return to my desk and, sipping, face the whiteness of the blank page. I think about my friend and what we've shared over the years, our mutual experience of racism at work.

There are truths hovering closer, in the gap between fiction and real life.

There's my pile of library books on the coffee table nearby. The reviews of the novel on top raved about its portrayal of America. The reviews didn't say white America, or white families, but on the book cover there's a young blonde woman sitting at the steering wheel of a car; she drives the narrative, supported by a few shallowly portrayed ethnic minority characters. Once started, I read on; I hope to see more of these peripheral characters, but as major characters. I want to see what a character does when he or she experiences racism, and what characters do despite it, how they cope, how they love despite hate. That would mean portraying white characters as we experience them in real life, when characters are shown dealing with racism, or their ups and downs of life with a white partner or colleague. I rarely read white characters acting like many white people do around people like me, when racism is involved.

I can't forget the sharp tone of the white person who once said to me, 'I wouldn't call it racism.'

How easy it is for people to twist what happened until it appears as something benign; how would I write about that? How would I fictionalize the unintentional racism of apparently well-meaning people?

And what about the actual person, or perhaps persons, behind the attacks on me? How could I write about my antagonist, when I know nothing about them? Apart from the fact that, given what they did, they are most likely white, and more likely a man, as academia is male-dominated; how might I imagine that person? And what about the people who they love, and who love them too: would they know what they're capable of, that level of hatred?

Even characters of hate must fall in and out of love. I don't want to treat white characters how white writers treat ethnic minority characters. And yet what I want to say about ethnic minority characters must show how the fingers of hate sometimes strangle the fragile beginnings of love: that there's a near impossibility of love when hate is out to get you. Hate, like fear, fragments love into a mosaic of anxieties; it disturbs and destroys. What I want to explore about white characters and hate is as important as what I want to say about ethnic minority characters and love.

Yes, that's it: what I want to explore about white characters and hate is as important as what I want to say about ethnic minority characters and love.

I start to write, thinking about what's happened, happening, will happen: the conjugation of infinite racism.

Those peripheral ethnic minority characters in fiction, what are they about? Not just love of white lives, isn't it the opposite too, a deep-seated hatred of others?

What happened to me could have happened anywhere. So it's not about any one individual, or institution, it's about British culture, and how a character with a psychological chisel is able to gradually work away at the seemingly calm professional façade of another character, a fellow employee.

When I have lectured, it has inevitably been almost always on white fiction, not that it was ever called that, of course, I mean fiction predominantly involving white characters. Preparing to teach those texts, the more closely I examined them it was strange how fictive this fiction appeared. I'm thinking about behaviour and speech, what white people are really like when you watch and listen to them, how they betray their values.

'White people' I know is a difficult term for white people more used to skin colour being about others; white skin is the default, always assumed. In fiction race is mentioned only if it's not white, even if indirectly, like the ethnic clichés of 'almond-shaped eyes' or 'coffee-coloured' skin. The UK is a majority white land, as I remember being spelled out in red, white and blue leaflets, the nationalist UKIP election papers posted through my letterbox during the European and local elections. The national context of what started then has hardly been explored, even all these years after the event, but it all began when UKIP did incredibly well at those elections, precipitating the roller coaster of politics moving swiftly towards the EU referendum. Day by day I noticed how white people walked and talked, taking up more space on pavements and in conversation, while ethnic minority people like me would shrink back a little, not sure how to deal with the xenophobic atmosphere in the press and daily life. I was worried, seeing 'go back home' graffiti on walls and along the bus route to the train station, on posters Sellotaped to windows, 'Our Little Island Is Full'. My home has always been here on this island, where race marks those who belong and those who don't, from public life to the professions – not that I have ever felt totally comfortable or equal here, or as though I belong.

In my social world and that of my interests, in the arts and politics, I'm often the solitary person with a darker skin and a foreign-sounding name, the peripheral ethnic minority character in others' social worlds; like an ethnic minority character adrift in the white fiction or policy-making that people make their living from.

Like other ethnic minority writers, I've grown up in a world where we're seen not as potential cultural producers but as a small part of the audience consuming white characters on the page, stage or screen. When I'm leaving the theatre, collecting my coat from the ethnic minority person working in the cloakroom, I weigh up the lessons learned from consuming the products of white imaginations. It's not just the infrequency of ethnic minority fictional appearance but the violence of how we're treated: the bare carcasses of characters, inferiors to be manipulated then disposed of, how we're so often destined to appear as dead bodies in the minds of a white imagination.

How could I explore this in writing, what form might it take? Not autobiography; it's an active crime investigation, and also I don't know how it's going to end. Racism is so much bigger than any individual or institution. Fiction would be a means to explore the machinery, machinations and impact of racism, and focus away from the specifics of my individual experience.

Although it could happen in any workplace, I will set it in the world of the university. It could have happened anywhere, from a world-renowned university to one of the ex-polytechnics. Rather than the minutiae of what and where it all happened to me, I will focus on the theme of sustained serious racial harassment in a university through fiction, exploring what intrigues me: what I don't know, who and how.

So instead of dredging up all the memories that make me anxious even now, I could use only the specifics of the racist crime I experienced, and explore the theme of racist crime in a genre-fiction way? Have a detective or a character eventually finding out who's behind it, and perhaps even get the perpetrator arrested? Then I could use the theme of love despite hate to counter the crime plot, a relationship keeping the protagonist going, despite what's happening in her workplace.

The ethnic minority characters will be in the foreground: the victim; people who care about her, and that she cares about too, like a best friend, a parent figure, and perhaps siblings; and the love interest? Or will the love interest be white, like the majority of people she comes into contact with in her professional life? Yes, a white love interest would complicate the racial dynamics, not to do to white characters what white writers do to ethnic minority characters.

The other white characters would be: a faceless aggressor; colleagues; and a character blurring the themes of love and hate?

Perhaps a seemingly helpful white-saviour figure, a well-meaning manager, plus other minor white characters encountered in a professional setting.

So, the main character won't be me, though she'll be a bit like me for what happens to fit the character. She'll be looking forward to a new job in academia, but she's not naïve, she's experienced usual day-to-day racism – she just won't expect what's about to happen to her: the crime.

Then there's the question of how it ends, and whether there might be justice.

Now, where to begin? A title, a chapter heading and the opening: that's often a teaser of what's to come, implying where we'll get to once we know the victim and the aggressor, and that there will eventually be a body.

But to begin, the title, something like:

LESSONS IN LOVE
AND OTHER CRIMES

1

LOVE IN THE DARK

In the future, there *is* a body. She's looking at it now, even though she really doesn't want to. The thing is, it's not the body anyone would have imagined – isn't it the least likely person?

AUTHOR'S NOTE

And the antagonist?

My antagonist knew me, and my movements, and what would really get to me; that's how it felt. What can I imagine about someone like that?

Most places I've worked men have been in the majority. If my fictional antagonist is a man, he's focused, not the type to leave his office door open, invite people in, or chat as they pass. His door is shut.

Alone, sitting surrounded by his books, he faces his screen. A mug of coffee in one hand, his other hand on the computer mouse. His desk? No family photos, or thank-you cards from former students; just him, focused on his screen.

I imagine glimpsing him through the screen, not his face though, just the black corduroy of a jacket, close up. He's half standing, close to the screen. Now there's an out-of-focus whiteness, his fingers clutching the camera, tilting it away from him.

What's he doing?

He's used to a virtual learning environment, rarely seen in the real world, he's concealed behind PowerPoints and podcasts. Having thousands of students globally, his overheads are low – a computer, the internet, one salary – he's popular with management, leaving him to get on with his work.

Behind his closed door, he has time: no clocking in and out, with twenty-four-hour access. Academics aren't monitored, with freedom of expression enshrined in their contracts unless they draw bad publicity to the institution. He'd be careful, using encryption for his other work: his research – but what would that be?

Like one of his virtual students I examine what I see through the screen. The blur of dark clothes as he moves aside, then the familiar academic background the camera is directed towards: well-ordered bookshelves, the arm of a black executive-style desk chair, and – that blur of movement again, coming into frame – the jacket sleeve leaning down on the armrest, the only evidence of a human body hidden beneath the fabric. He notices this too: the sleeve is withdrawn from sight, leaving the image of an academic office, a wall of books lined up on white shelves.

A red light starts flashing in the corner of the screen; he's recording. Text appears, typed across the centre:

'LESSON ONE: AN INTRODUCTION'

So it's the beginning of a new module.

There's a pause; there always is, just before a lecture starts, drawing listeners' attention before the first key line.

What is his subject? What lessons does he teach? That book-lined background, rather than a lab, feels like it's not Sciences, but which Humanities subject? One of the Arts, Social Sciences, or could it be Law?

His voice, a confident middle-class English accent, starts to speak:

LESSON ONE

'In the twenty-first century intercultural communication is subtle but powerful. Advertisers use it all the time, that's how they turn a profit across the spectrum of social groups, harnessing their aspirations and playing on their fears. Politicians love it: all the shaking of hands, or kissing babies in ethnically diverse areas during elections. Now think about it in reverse, from your own personal perspective. When small digs have felt lethal, haven't you been culturally psychologically wounded about your class, gender or race? Our identities are tied up inextricably with culture, so when we're wounded it's a kind of death. You can't forget it, can you?

'You've probably guessed by now that in this particular module, corpses are for losers, so you'll treat the victim with kid gloves. Your aim is for the victim never to forget what's happened to them, without drawing attention to yourself. The question is: how?

'Successful victim-related crime is all about the three Cs: conceal-ment, continuity and caution. Without a corpse there are no worries about evidence – DNA, fingerprints and dental records – cutting out the middleman: the police aren't interested in crimes without evidence, and evidence for them means bodies or bodily matter.

'Even without a body, there may be clues left at the scene of the crime. Non-human material evidence may be traced eventually, so the more ordinary it is, the more difficult it is to see it as evidence. So choose disposable items: modern multicultural or mass-market products work well, and have the advantage of meaning something different according to who the victim is, particularly the ethnic minority victim.

'So, no corpse, and a powerful piece of intercultural commu-nication: the victim is alive, but starting to feel uncertain, perhaps scared. They won't be able to stop thinking about you. Enjoying that power, you'll be thinking about them too. Crime is closely related to obsessive love, it's addictive and all-encompassing. Enjoy it, but tread carefully.'

AUTHOR'S NOTE

Now the protagonist.

Like me she's mixed-race, but younger. She's moved back to London after what's happened, trying to get on with her life, difficult after trauma. We meet her where she's more relaxed, at home, when things are starting to feel like they're going better. She's got a stake in the present, she's started dating someone, so it's the opposite of hate, to begin with.

What's she called? A short ethnic-sounding name, with none of that describing of coffee-coloured skin …

OK, I'll start, and see where she leads me.

TESYA

Now of course it's months before Valentine's Day, too early even to be thinking of such things, but she does as she closes her new front door, after Holly's red hair and white silk shirt disappear and the downstairs door slams to behind her. Their dates are like the cliché of Valentine's, flowers, alcohol and sex – or rather love. This, whatever it is, is too early for the L word, though their dates feel like what she thought love could be, if she ever found it. But it's only been a short time, and their dates are always over before they've got started.

She surveys what's left of their few stolen hours across her newly rented loft space, between the bookshelved study area – the stack of unpacked boxes – and the kitchen through the archway. She picks up her bra and shirt, draped over the sofa arm – she'd just slipped her t-shirt and jeans back on while Holly got dressed, after her mobile sounded: what always happens. Having kids, Holly has to leave her phone on, just in case – if only next time they could have longer.

On the coffee table there's a cork in its bent-back cage of wire, two champagne flutes stained with their different shades of lipstick, and the bottle of Moët – Holly's so generous. Tesya pours the last of the bottle into a glass and, sipping, slumps down on the sofa among the faded mirror-work cushions with their musty dusty smell of home. All the places she's lived with these cushions, since student days. Leaning back, there's Holly's perfume, sweet and floral. She closes her eyes, conjuring Holly up.

That euphoric rush when she arrives. When Holly pulls her into her arms and unravels her through kisses and caresses, then takes her by the hand and they lie down skin against skin, making love in the dark. Nothing else matters – not what might matter with another person, their different skin colours – in the darkness of her bedroom they are only shadows and pulses of exquisite pleasure. And then afterwards, after desire, the most intense pleasure of all: to be held.

Across the room, through the open door to the bedroom, the duvet trails across the floor, the pillows are askew and the alarm clock's red digital numbers quiver back at her.

Ever since she's known Holly time has been between them.

The little she's learned about Holly's life through picture-messaging and texting, it all sounds wholesome, chaotic and rather lovely, like Holly herself. She's perfect.

Living back in Shoreditch is perfect too. Sometimes she forgets what happened, until something reminds her. Like that pile of unopened boxes: the contents of her last university office still waiting for her in the corner by her desk. She'll have to get round to taking them into her new office, book a minicab, or ask –

Her mobile vibrates on the coffee table. She picks it up; it's Jazz. Always Jazz.

In a while she's walking into the packed bar, and it's buzzing with a happy Friday after-work crowd. A waitress delivering a burger and vinegary chips cuts in front of her. Good she's out, otherwise she'd have crashed and woken with a hangover from drinking without food, after Holly left; what always happens, they've rarely eaten together. Jazz drinks, but she doesn't forget to eat, even if it's just chips on the way home.

Jazz's favourite bar, off Hoxton Square, is in between the women's sex shop and a trendy cinema, and the crowd mirrors the locale: sexually charged, gender-ambivalent. She loves this vibe, even though it's a million miles from Holly's grown-up elegance, and she loves her too. Love isn't straightforward, or at least it never has been for her.

She weaves through the crowd, hearing snippets of conversation and glasses chinking in the echoing cavernous bar. She steps between arms and elbows, past the absorbed eyes of dating couples, and the darting eyes of singles. Not long ago, that was her and Jazz together in clubs, catching up on each other's news while girl-watching, then standing rather coolly by if one pulled and the other didn't – but always checking the other got home safely; what friends are for.

Emerging at the end of the bar, she sees Jazz standing by the window overlooking the smoker-packed city garden. Jazz has changed out of her work sports gear into one of her slogan t-shirts, the Black Lives Matter one she'd got on the demo they went to a few weeks ago. Her hair is tied back in a braid, so her silvery earrings glint against her skin, shiny with the heat.

Jazz turns and sees her. 'So, she let you get away?'

'Jazz, don't!' She smiles but inwardly tenses, needing Jazz to stop teasing her or whatever it is she does that makes her feel prickly about mentioning Holly.

She recognizes by sight Jazz's work colleagues around the table. One of them gets up, rolling a cigarette. She moves aside to let them pass, and then sees the bottles of wine lined up. That's a surprise: her comprehensive-school colleagues usually drink bottled beers on the evenings she's joined them.

'Celebration?'

'Sonia's leaving do – the art teacher.' Jazz gestures towards the smokers through the window, then picks up a glass. 'Red or white?'

'White, thanks.'

Once she's drinking again, and buzzing with the vibe, she's happy to be out listening to Jazz and her friends chatting excitedly – it's half-term, a week without school targets and students.

Earlier she'd asked Holly about their next 'date night', as she calls it. She'd replied, 'Darling, it's half-term,' and kissed her, slipping off her shirt as they'd moved into the bedroom. The question of when they'd see each other next was forgotten, under the covers –

Now she aches for Holly – isn't Friday night for lovers?

'What's wrong?' Jazz looks concerned.

'Nothing – just …'

'Holly?'

'It's half-term for her kids too.'

'Right. So she still hasn't introduced you, not even as a new "friend"?' She does that thing with her fingers to show the quote marks.

Jazz is angry for her – but she doesn't want her to be. 'No, she hasn't, but I get that, it's only been a few months –'

'And she lives out in the sticks in the white fascist home counties –'

'Jazz! I told you the kids' dad died only a year ago … Look, it's late, I should be –'

'Tesya, sorry, I'll shut up. You know it's just because I haven't even met her. I do worry about you, you know?'

'No one's met her – I hardly do, but we're together, and I –'

At that moment, returning from the bar with another bottle, Sonia looks concerned, overhearing them.

She drops the topic and tries to 'Behave,' as Jazz whispers to her, which at least makes her smile and mouth back, 'Sorry.'

Jazz smiles and mouths back too, 'You know I love you?'

They smile and chink glasses. Then someone orders nachos, and the evening morphs into a hazy Friday night out with friends.

For a while she forgets about Holly and the banter with Jazz and even why she's back here in London, but then Jazz asks, 'What are you up to next week?'

'So much work, and I must get round to taking my boxes –'

'You want me to drive you in one day?'

And as usual Jazz eases what she'd been putting off: unpacking boxes that would take her back to her last office. Now she's working in a Red Brick Victorian university in central London. Weird to think just over a year ago she'd been so happy to start a new job at a New Build university in the gorgeous countryside, not far from the coast. Even Jazz had been optimistic once she knew she'd end up seeing her often; it was en route from her beloved weekend rowing club in Norfolk.

But she's trying not to think about it, now she's escaped.

'I said which day?'

'Sorry … what suits you? I need to go in most days …'

'How about we load the car one evening, and then I bring it in the end of the next day. We could catch a movie and dinner afterwards. How's Thursday?'

'Not Thursday, I might be –'

'OK, I know, don't tell me … Well then, how about Tuesday I'll pick up the boxes, and Wednesday drop them off in the afternoon, movie later?'

So it's sorted, and they switch conversation, Jazz talking about the ballet she'd booked for later next week at Sadler's Wells, and soon it's closing time; time to walk homewards.

They say goodbye outside her apartment building. She unlocks the door to the shared hallway, walks past the pile of bills for inhabitants long gone to new homes without leaving forwarding addresses, and soon she's upstairs, drinking water thirstily next to the unwashed champagne glasses in the sink.

She walks around picking things up and putting them where they're supposed to be, tidying the general disarray after Holly leaves – not just the glasses and the bedclothes, but her mind. When she drinks, at first it relaxes her, she loses her doubts, but when she starts to sober up – or tries to – her anxieties flood back. Like they've never spent a night together – she hasn't told Jazz that, she knows what she'd say – but that's what makes her feel sometimes, where's it going? Even though she loves everything about Holly, and she hasn't stopped feeling how she did the day she first met her.

Apart from Jazz, she hasn't told anyone how they met, on that internet dating site that everyone they know uses, so you have to be careful to avoid people you've already dated, friends' exes and, of course, friends. It was Jazz who'd suggested it – 'You need to get out there on the scene, or even on the Net. Do something rather than stay in on the sofa, stuck in the past. Start having fun again, Tesya?'

They had been getting ready to go out to a bar, and they had fun, they always do – but when she came home to her empty bed, late that night, she acted on Jazz's suggestion. She put herself out there, albeit in brief: just a short dating-site profile, and a photo that didn't give too much away so she'd be recognized – she had been careful, of course. Only enough to give a flavour of herself: it showed her as a tiny figure dwarfed by tall trees in a forest – taken by Jazz on a summer ramble in Epping, not far from London.

Soon she started to receive notifications: people liking her profile, and even short messages – nothing that tempted her, only the red flag of overly keen people or just not her type – until one day her profile was liked by mysterywoman.

She looked at her profile, and instantly liked hers too; she got a good feeling. Their profiles echoed each other; neither of them had said much, but what they said chimed: both busy working women who would love to enjoy more downtime, browsing bookstores and discovering hidden-away old-fashioned wine bars. It wasn't really much to go on, she knew that – the other thing though, what really drew her, was mysterywoman's photo. Like hers it didn't show much, less even, but she couldn't stop herself clicking on it, to see her again, and again.

Back to the camera, a head of shoulder-length shiny red hair looked out of a window, the only other colours the delicate white fingers on the window ledge and a glint of greenery in the distance. Mostly she was in shadowy silhouette, caught against rays of sunshine. There was something about her silk-like hair, the soft outline of a slender body, the curve of her waist –

She lay awake that night in bed, hugging the duvet around her, wondering what if, the being held and holding, closing her eyes and seeing the love and safety she craves in those hands – then feeling silly and ridiculously like a teenager again. She switched on the lamp, lighting the overladen bedside table, her phone balanced on top of her diary, along with a pen and a pile of paperbacks – the other side, the table empty apart from its rarely used lamp. She turned off the light again; in the darkness the head of red hair was still there – she wished she could reach out and touch her shoulder, and that she'd turn towards her, and see her face and –

The next day a message came, 'I'd love to meet for a coffee, I hope you would too?'

And Tesya's immediate answer, 'I'd love to. When would be convenient?'

Just a few days later, it turned out, not long until they'd meet. The time went quickly, deciding and re-deciding what to wear, and hours staring at herself in the mirror with the red hair of the woman she was going to meet ever-present, though especially so in the last few hours while getting ready, applying her lipstick, blotting it on a tissue, and seeing the copy of her red lips against white, and wondering, hoping … Yes, that was it: the colour and shape of love and hope.

Tucked away down a side street, and then a narrow passageway, the hidden-away Hoxton café-bar mysterywoman suggested was one she'd not heard of, not far from her new home. She hadn't revealed where she was living, so it was slightly odd she'd suggested meeting so near, but as they had revealed similar likes, her choice of place felt right when she opened the door to the smell of freshly brewed coffee and open wine bottles.

It was an old Victorian warehouse, a labyrinth of interconnecting rooms, with bare floorboards, and filled with stripped wooden tables, mismatched chairs and the shelves of second-hand books, chess sets and board games of the hipster district. There were some slick-suited people holding meetings over their laptops, high-energy talk bouncing back and forth. Others sitting alone were looking busy on their phones, and there were couples – it was late afternoon, when couples meet between work and home, deciding where to go next. She continued on looking for mysterywoman, who she only knew by her username, though she had signed off their last message exchange – confirming where to meet – revealing her own. Not that her name mattered, she would know her by her red hair.

Apart from her hair colour, she knew she was a businesswoman and had kids, probably why she hadn't written much in her profile – like herself. She'd been warned last year to be careful with social media, not to give away personal information on Facebook, but that was sensible for anyone, especially someone with kids.

Where was she? She walked into the last of the maze of rooms. It was quiet, and darker, lit only by lamps glowing on low tables set between deep sofas and high-backed armchairs. There was no one. Perhaps she'd missed her – or she wasn't going to show up.

She turned to go when there was a sound behind her. She glanced back. In the furthest corner, from the shadows of a large bookcase, someone stepped forward. Clothed in a black skirt suit, with a closed book in her white hands, she leaned down and put it on the nearest table. Under the lamplight her hands were pale, and her hair shone red –

She hadn't noticed Tesya, her footsteps hidden beneath the classical music playing through speakers in each room, and she was in the doorway, in the shadows too. Was it her? 'Hi?'

She looked up, and said quietly, 'Tesya?' with a smile, but like a question, though she must have recognized her from her profile photo.

There was something poignant about her uncertainty, appearing out of the darkness a delicate ethereal creature that pulled her in – 'Yes –'

Then she answered with her name. 'I'm Holly.'

On someone else the name might seem old-fashioned, but on her it was exactly right: she was blue-eyed, pale-skinned, while her lips were blushed like winter berries – finding her was like finding the evergreen of holly in the middle of a white winter.

They sat in the dark velvet armchairs, and drank espresso in tiny cups, and they started to talk –

Tesya asked, 'Have you come far?'

Holly gestured to her laptop bag. 'No, from a meeting in the City.' She told her about her IT consultancy business. Tesya reciprocated briefly by mentioning her new job, then changed the subject, suggesting, 'Another coffee, or perhaps wine?'

'White wine would be lovely, just a small glass?'

But when she returned with their glasses, Holly was on her phone, texting.

She looked up. 'Thank you, but I'm sorry, I'm going to have to go soon, I don't like to leave the kids for long, since their father …' She stopped, her eyes dampened. She reached for her bag from the floor, and took out a tissue.

Tesya sat, not sure what to do, asking, 'Holly, are you saying that –'

Holly dried her eyes and looked away, then almost in a whisper said, 'Sorry, it's difficult to talk about, it's a year ago now, but the children still feel the loss, as though it was yesterday …'

Everything about her suddenly made sense, her aura of fragility, her black clothes: the father – presumably her late husband or partner – must have died. She felt awful; she said, 'Holly, I'm so sorry.'

Holly reached for her hand, Tesya leaned towards her and then they were holding hands. Holly closed her eyes. Her past was obviously that, over; she wouldn't ask her more. Some things are best left unspoken – like Tesya won't tell her about the painful things that happened to her last year.

Holly moved closer, whispering in her ear, 'So good to finally meet you.' There was the caress of her breath on her neck, the flicker of her fingers on hers as she passed one of the glasses, then picking up the other one, she said, 'To us' –

Oh yes – she reciprocated, 'To us' – they felt the same, it was so good to finally meet in person rather than through the anonymity of typed words on their screens. The caress of her words, the touch of her hands, her breath on her skin – her closeness breathed hope into the darkness.

The hopeful promise of that moment was cut short. Holly stood, picking up her bag, retying a scarf around her neck. As though she guessed what she was about to ask, Holly said, 'Maybe ... next week? I'll check my diary.'

'Come to my place, it's near here?'

'That would be wonderful.' She kissed her, and said, 'Must dash. Until next time.'

Then Tesya walked home, while everyone else seemed to be going out for the evening in the heat of the rush hour. Where was Holly dashing back to? She'd not asked her in their flurry of messages online, or in the flush of real time they'd just spent together.

That had become their pattern: hurried rendezvous at Tesya's, arranged and curtailed by messages from her phone, despite the childminder, the children, or things she had to do 'en route back home that might take time ...'

She can't expect more, and yet Holly always leaves her with hope – 'Next time we'll have longer, I'm sure.'

But when they're together it feels right – despite how it feels when they're not together and she might not hear from her for a few days. Then it feels like something's wrong, and the longer she doesn't hear from her she thinks the worst – that something awful has happened – but right at the last moment, when she can't bear not knowing what's become of her for another second, Holly texts or calls. The following week she turns up to their rendezvous and everything's perfect – until she leaves to go home.

That was the one thing that had made Tesya pause, that first time Holly came to her flat – the answer to her simple question, 'Where do you live?'

Holly was buttoning her shirt by the side of the bed, and laughed. 'You'll never have heard of it, it's hardly a village, just a hamlet in the middle of nowhere, an hour or so east out of London.'

She wouldn't have noticed her silence, it was such an innocuous question and answer – and Tesya hadn't mentioned she'd been working and living out that way last year. But eastern England is a massive area, and Holly's small domestic world was nothing to do with her world of academia – it was just not what she wanted to hear.

So over the past few months they've been dating she's felt almost glad Holly's never invited her to her home; as Holly says, 'It's easier here, no interruptions, just us.'

And it's meant Tesya doesn't have to go back there, even though at some point she'll have to face it, but if the journey's to see Holly it'll be OK – even after what happened out there, before she met her.

But when there's something you're not doing – because you're not invited, or because you're scared – that you normally would do in a relationship, it hovers in your mind. Which is why she tries to distract her thoughts from circling around and around, like she does now: filling the dishwasher, then remaking the bed, where Holly's lingering perfume on the pillows taunts her with what she really wants tonight: to fall asleep in her lover's arms.

Earlier as they lay there, in the dark, she'd said, 'I wish you could stay tonight.'

Holly was silent, then pulled her closer. 'Darling, I promise a night soon.'

She didn't push her; the way Holly holds her she cherishes every moment, making her forget what she'd asked for until later –

Now she pulls on her nightshirt, switches off the light and tries to sleep – but when the alarm clock is telling her it's one in the morning, her mind is buzzing in a panicky everything-going-wrong way. Drinking hasn't helped. Neither has talking about moving the boxes with Jazz, which she can't face, even though it's over and she must be safe now. Surely?

Everything that happened there still haunts her.

She shouldn't have, but she's come back into the other room. She stands by her desk, facing the boxes unopened since she moved here. Perhaps she should try now, get it over with. She tears back the brown sticky tape and opens the cardboard leaves of the box on the top of the pile. Just office paraphernalia, a stapler, pen tidy and other items from her old office desk, shoved into a box and sealed up fast – on that last dreadful day.

There's a little bundle wrapped around with black ribbon. She's not sure what it is until she unravels it, then, of course, it's her staff pass hanging on a lanyard, like the plastic rectangle of a credit card, her name typed in black on white. Why on earth did she keep that?

Time is supposed to travel forward, but the horrible mundanity of what happened sucks her backwards, dragging her down into its black hole –

To when someone in a spotless suit was helping her pack, passing stuff, but she was dropping things, her hands hot and sweaty, just wanting to get out of there – but a cool hand was taking over, packing her things away then sealing the boxes. There'd be no trace of her – a whole year of her working life.

Life.

Now she's crying hot salty tears, clutching the plastic lanyard, and inside it, her name.

It's the middle of the night. Time passes. Then a siren starts shrieking outside; a sign of life, of a sort. She drops the lanyard back and reseals the box – but even as she does so she feels stuck inside it. Squeezed of the oxygen of self, she's just the letters of her name imprisoned in indestructible plastic, slowly suffocating again: what it felt like then – and moments like now. It's the early hours, but she couldn't sleep, even if she manages to get herself to bed – she can't sleep, not how she feels now, alone, her heart beating. Just like it did when even in the light of day she could feel somewhere out there the eyes of hatred. How those invisible eyes silenced her being, dominating every waking moment.

AUTHOR'S NOTE

That's how it is, was – takes me back to that push-pull of love and fear, being in the dark, the asymmetry of everything, and so the drinking – easing the desire, until the desperation returns. Yes, that takes me back.

2

FIRST IMPRESSIONS

THEN

The walk took forever. Rather than the bus, she had chosen the novelty of walking away from her new town digs, downhill, towards the greenery of the countryside on the horizon. Her shoulders were relaxed despite the weight of her work-bag slung across her body, ready for her first day. There was something about closing the door on her last job in the Golden Spires, saying goodbye to the ancient college buildings – once she'd got over the history and romance of the place people aspire to, all the *Brideshead* clichés, she saw it for what it was. Like the rest of the UK, the Golden Spires were built on the wealth of slavery and colonization, and under the surface still steeped in a racist view of people like her. She was never going to feel comfortable there. Not that anything major had happened, only everyday racism – or rather, everyday middle-class or upper-class racism. Only.

The problem with academic jobs was there were so few you were forced to move to where the job was, and make a new life, but if something went wrong everything fell apart. Her dream job had withered away slowly, but looking back it felt like a nightmare – she shook off the thought – no, nightmare was a bit melodramatic. It was just a disappointment, professionally and personally. The usual asking about her name, and where she came from – and people not liking her answer, 'London,' expecting somewhere more exotic. Ethnic minority Britons aren't supposed to identify as coming from Britain, but somewhere that Britain colonized, countries that most have never even visited.

Just the usual racist stuff, as Jazz would say. Although it was the usual stuff she got less of in London, where people are more aware of indirect racism, or they experience it themselves – the majority of Londoners. Not like where she was now – and definitely not the Golden Spires.

What else was a disappointment there? Her abortive attempts at research networking: despite the university encouraging collaboration, providing research sandpits to play with blue-sky research ideas, and her colleagues appearing to listen to her ideas, as she had theirs, her follow-up emails remained unanswered. And when she said hello when bumping into one of them in the quad, and recognizing another of them near the library, they forgot they'd ever met her – that she was a colleague – mistaking her for a foreign student, an Admin temp, or a tourist wandered off the High Street into the picturesque grounds to take a selfie.

They recognized each other – she'd watch from a distance, pairs of people shaking each other's white hands or patting each other's similarly gowned backs – though they rarely recognized her. Ethnic minority people all look the same to them – difficult to tell us apart.

It wasn't just race, but class too. She wasn't born into that public-school Golden Spires trajectory, so it was a world she flailed in – all those ritualistic dinners, under ancient ceilings. People talk of a glass ceiling, but in the Golden Spires she found that ceilings and walls were not just made of impenetrable stone but skin and speech too. Who you were, how you spoke, who you knew, all dictated who talked to you, whose door was closed to you, and how far you might rise, or whether you'd sink without trace. It reminded her of school playgrounds, and the biting ice of forever-wintry mornings despite the season for the girl who gets called racist names, who no one plays with during the ironically named playtime in British schools; name-calling is a kind of playing, but not for the victim.

The racism of the world of work was subtle; it wasn't about name-calling but other forms of sidelining people. She had arrived there with happy optimism only to become increasingly unhappy, alone at her desk, struggling to concentrate. Then at lunchtime in the refectory they were supposed to eat together, conversing in an intellectual collegiate community, though she felt increasingly adrift in a foreign country: if early, she'd end up sitting alone, while people coming in later would bunch up together at other tables; when she came in later, setting her tray near people already seated, they would politely rebuff her attempts to join in the conversation, and as they left she'd be alone with their breadcrumbs and dirty dishes – as though she wasn't meant to eat at the same table but be cleaning up after them.

Despite the excitement of multicultural twenty-first-century Britain, paraded and televised around the world during the 2012 London Olympics, outside London the ghosts of those ugly ancient divisions were alive in the accents and assumptions echoing under the shadows of college cloisters, and deep inside the minds at work within those beautiful walls. Like the people working in the farms or factories outside the city – who she'd see on the High Street on a Saturday, in the supermarket or one of the pubs, where it was like any other place in the UK – how had she ever imagined herself fitting in? She wasn't born into that world but had grown up in a children's home. The world she'd dreamed of was limited for people like her: after a long recruitment process, it had only been the offer of a short contract anyway, as flimsy as the white paper it was printed on. Limited like her one-to-one communication with colleagues – almost non-existent: brief instructions about registers and stationery supplies. Limited until she'd fallen for Aisha, and thought she felt the same way – until she'd discovered Aisha had moved on to someone far more useful than Tesya, who was after all just another ethnic minority tutor on a brief contract like herself.

Why does she always remember Aisha when she last saw her? The back of Aisha's long dark hair looking into a man's eyes – the pale grey-haired lecturer she'd seen her with. He looked like most of the lecturers with permanent tenure: white, older and more established than either of them – although now Aisha's career might blossom.

Perhaps she was being unfair? Didn't that moment she last saw Aisha say more about their shared dream of the Golden Spires than their shared difference?

In a way her dreams – career and romance – had turned into a sort of nightmare, an equal but opposite reaction, like she was taught in Physics lessons as a teenager. OK, she's exaggerating, but funny how those formulas stick in the mind: an equal but opposite reaction; from dream to nightmare – like love turns to hate, when you fall out of love.

She stops, adjusting her work-bag strap on her shoulder, like she adjusts that thought. Surely she didn't hate – but, well, what she felt when Aisha left was the opposite of what she felt when she fell for her. How she had willed that first embrace when their eyes met across a candlelit table in the stuffy college dining hall, during an excruciating, slowly served conference dinner. When it ended, they left together, and once they were further away Aisha kissed her, then they went back to hers in a rush of searching, getting to know each other's bodies –

Until the momentum of lust was over – and that mundane twenty-first-century technological first sign of an ending: the build-up of unanswered texts and calls. Then the second sign: her battling against the logical side of her mind – perhaps Aisha's phone was broken, or something awful had happened to her? The third sign – like the triangulation of sources in her academic research, three different methods producing a reliable thesis – was the confirmation, walking across the High Street the following Saturday afternoon. Aisha with someone taller and male: a couple; he put his arm around her shoulder as they disappeared into the crowd out enjoying a sunny day.

And what was left? Not love, but something else. The object of desire becomes an object of despair when she becomes something to be turned away from. Not hate, not really despair either. She hadn't played the spurned lover – the character in soap operas screaming across the street. She walked home, and closed the door. It had hardly been a relationship, just an affair. She let her go, what you have to do. She'd called Jazz, who had come to pick her up, driving her away that weekend to Brighton's cheery seaside and accompanying her later on the beach, where she walked away her fluctuating feelings, like the tide's coming and going. That night, Jazz said to her, 'Plenty of fish,' as they stood facing a sea of strangers in a bar – though they ended up talking to no one but each other, while drinking far too much.

It was months ago; she'd dated a few people since, no one special, but still – why had Aisha resurfaced in her mind now? She waited at the lights then crossed the road. Perhaps her mind was just sifting what was left, what minds do. She was over Aisha, but she needed, no, she wanted, to meet someone else. Someone she could relax with and have a proper grown-up relationship with, not another brief affair.

It was going to be good to be somewhere new. Almost there: through the greenery ahead were glimpses of the New Build university's concrete buildings. She speeded up, enjoying the crackle and crunch of treading down on dry autumnal leaves, the dead stuff under her feet.

Downhill, four-wheel drives zoomed past, their occupants hidden behind glass reflecting the landscape – everyone mechanically going somewhere fast while she was relishing the liminal space, between leaving and arriving where she hoped to find her rural idyll. Working and writing, and hanging out in the country with the new friends she'd make. Rambles across wide expanses with the sun on her face, and the beauty of nature ahead, nothing to worry about and every-thing to look forward to – like ending the day in a country pub with the mesmerizing flames of an open fire, the warmth of a bottle of red between friends; the rounding-off of happy days.

God, thinking like a TV ad, all sunlit days and friend-filled nights – but perhaps here she might get what she craves. At a more modern New Build university surely there would be like-minded people.

Out from under the trees, blinded by a sudden shaft of sunlight, she stopped and put her shades on, then picked up pace ready for the day ahead.

Although she'd been there once before, in a taxi for her job interview, when she arrived this time walking onto the campus, she was shocked by what she hadn't taken in before: the ugliness of the harsh lines of high concrete towers mounted with decorative metal cage-like structures, and the lower walls a mosaic of tarnished rust and dirty off-white concrete, punctuated by slabs of opaque glass. The whole effect was a monstrosity at odds with the soft green undulating countryside at the edges of her vision.

She checked the map she'd been sent with her induction pack, and then made her way to the Faculty of Arts. She circled the concrete tower block until she found what appeared to be the entrance, a square panel of glass with a swipe-card terminal. She didn't have a staff card yet, so she hovered until a student entered, slipping in behind them, but was then immediately stopped by a security guard, barking at her for her ID. After her induction letter was inspected, she was buzzed through the foyer into the office of the Faculty of Arts administrator, her passport and degree certificates were photocopied and then filed away for Human Resources. Finally, her identity verified, she was escorted along a corridor, up in a lift, down another corridor, around a corner, and at the far end of another corridor she was handed a key and abandoned at the door of her new office.

Facing her in the middle of the door, neatly typed in black on white paper, her name was inserted behind a piece of transparent perspex. She opened the door. Inside there was a strong chemical smell, polish or room freshener. She quickly opened the window, and then turned back and scanned the white box-shaped room: its empty shelves, the clean but worn desk with a pinboard above, punctured with drawing pin holes from earlier inhabitants' long-gone notices. She sat down and opened the desk drawer; a cracked empty biro rattled and came to a halt. She binned it, then started to unpack the pens and folders she'd brought with her for her new life 'out in the sticks' – how Jazz had described it when they'd arrived at her new digs yesterday.

She had booked her temporary home over the internet when she'd had confirmation of the job offer at the New Build university. She handed in her notice, and when term was over she packed her belongings and left the Golden Spires, and headed to London. She'd spent the summer at Jazz's, relieved to be back in the middle of the city and have fun days and nights out together in its noisy 24/7 sound-scape – like yesterday, when the sounds of voices from outside the pub nearby mingled with the buzz and hum of domestic appliances from neighbouring flats, as they went backwards and forwards filling Jazz's car. They'd set off through heavy traffic, from city to motorway, but as they were nearing their destination almost all the vehicles were stationary, hemming in houses either side of the long road they drove down, on the edge of the nearby town.

When Jazz turned off the engine it was eerily quiet, even for a Sunday afternoon. She said, 'God, this really is out in the sticks,' just as a dog somewhere started barking, then they both laughed.

While they unpacked the car, a few pedestrians walked by – a man with a dog on a lead, and a woman in a skirt, pushing a sleepy child along in a stroller. Like the pictures of women and men in the *Janet and John* books; the first books she'd found, battered and torn in a box of toys, when she was a kid in the children's home. She'd stared at the words for mother and father. Then at the image of a white woman and man, with matching girl and boy children, in front of a symmetrical house in a flowering garden; so different from her home until that moment – and right up until now too.

The row of terraced turn-of-the-last-century houses was silent. Behind the closed white-netted windows people must have been napping, or sitting in their front rooms whispering, so as not to disturb the neighbours.

The house they finally entered had bright modern blinds at the windows downstairs, and as they climbed the stairs, there were cheerful patterned curtains hanging at the windows on the landing. There was the faint murmur of a television behind one door, and as they climbed up, past the next flat, there was the thud of a bed banging against a wall, accompanied by the breathy sounds of sex in full swing.

She stopped momentarily in the dimming light on the stairs – suddenly wanting to go back to London.

Behind her, Jazz said, 'Are you all right?'

She hadn't replied, but had carried on upstairs, unlocked the flat door and sighed as she put down the box she was carrying. Jazz seemed to sense what she was feeling – by the time Tesya had found the kettle and filled it, and the water for tea was coming to the boil, the sound of Prince was piercing the silence from her mobile. They smiled at each other – and yet she found herself stretching out to lower the volume. Prince's beautiful voice felt too loud and other for this town, especially on a Sunday afternoon.

Later, walking the deserted streets in search of food – a shop to stock the fridge, or somewhere to eat – they chatted about suburbia, joking about where everyone might be –

'Swinging at key parties?'

'Dogging?'

They stifled their giggles, unnecessarily as there was no one around and hardly anything open. After being turned away from a series of chain restaurants and pubs – 'Kitchen closes at eight-thirty, love,' they were told at each place – they ended up at an old-fashioned Indian restaurant, surrounded by people desperate for food to soak up alcohol already drunk, while drinking more. The tables were close together but it was fine, familiar: the red and gold flock wallpaper, dark wood furniture, and the usual items on the menu – they ordered the British favourites of tikka masala and naan bread, and downed a couple of Cobra beers while waiting.

Over the meal they gossiped about mutual friends, two of whom had started dating each other, and a couple who had just split up, then about the week ahead – it was exciting. 'Good to be starting work again, after the summer – Jazz?'

She was distracted, her eyes darted somewhere behind Tesya. She glanced back. A group of men was squashed around the table; their military haircuts and khaki uniforms reminded her that the town was home to an army base – like the Golden Spires, where there had also been a military presence, but that city was more famous for its rowing club. Perhaps it reminded Jazz too – when she turned back, she said, 'I'll be driving past, to and from rowing out in Norfolk next weekend. I could drop by?'

Yes, the men reminded Jazz of her beloved sport, or so she'd thought –

Later, just before she left to drive home, Jazz asked her, 'You will be all right, won't you?'

'Yes, of course. Why do you ask?'

In the small square hallway off her new studio room, the light was too bright, there was no shade over the bulb, and Jazz looked tired, her eyes reddish as she asked, 'Didn't you notice, people staring at us in the restaurant?'

'No – you were facing out, I was facing you and the wall, remember?'

'But when we left, didn't you notice then?'

'No, I had my mind on returning here and unpacking my duvet. What's worrying you, Jazz?'

'Perhaps I'm just being paranoid –'

'What was it?'

'Those squaddies, tanking up like that … took me right back to the Green Zone. Soldiers are the same the world over, they have to let off steam … and they're racist as hell.'

Everyone knew what British and American soldiers had done in Iraq and elsewhere: those horrific photos of Abu Ghraib. Jazz knew more than she ever let on, it was obvious in how she was often worried about people staring when they were out – but they were at home in the UK, not in a war zone. And it was also probably the amount of alcohol that they shouldn't have drunk, not on a Sunday. Surely it was relatively safe here – she didn't want to start worrying about that sort of thing the night before starting her new job, she wouldn't sleep. She didn't want Jazz to worry either, driving home. 'People were probably staring at us because we seem to be the only "ethnic minority" people in the whole of the town.'

'Apart from the waiter and chef ...'

'Don't worry; I'll be fine. And I'll be so busy at the university, I'll hardly be here in the town ...'

'Sure?'

She hugged her in reply, but after Jazz left, and she was struggling with pulling the duvet cover over the duvet, she wondered what had set off Jazz's train of thought. How had the men stared at them? She smoothed the covers, but as she was undressing, she couldn't stop wondering again about what Jazz had never told her. What happened to her in Iraq, to make her get out of the army so suddenly?

She'd never directly broached it. Jazz made it clear it was a no-go area of conversation, telling her only, 'It was a warning of worse to come, so I got out while I could.'

She'd been unemployed for months afterwards, getting up late then slumping on the sofa, cheering up only when Tesya came back from the library – she'd stayed with her in her graduate student digs. They would go out and she'd be her normal self for a while, but she'd drink too much then get really weird. It was such a relief when she found the scheme for ex-military to retrain to teach in schools and got a job teaching PE in an inner-city comprehensive, not far from where they grew up in Hackney. Jazz was busy and healthy again now, and it suited her; she was happy again, at least in her job – and anyway she hardly ever had girlfriends that lasted long.

Lying in bed, she worried about Jazz, just like Jazz seemed to worry about her. Perhaps that's why they remained friends, despite their different interests; they looked out for each other, like family – or what they thought family might be like. In children's homes, between the turnover of staff and the kids arriving and leaving, she never got a sense of what a permanent family and family home might feel like. Children's homes were never really homes. What they both knew was long nights in dormitories, crying in the dark with no one to comfort them, except for other kids. Families were alien entities, yet also intensely interesting: where they had been briefly, before they had been sent out on their lonely journeys. Sometimes they would share tiny experiences that awoke memories buried deep but which were still there. Like the dark eyes of a mother resurfacing years later in the eyes of a stranger on a bus, or in a shop; that random feeling of thinking you know someone, when of course you don't – the eternal hope of finding family; like love.

The theatre she loved, studied and taught, portrayed dysfunctional families and relationships: the monstrous Macbeths, childish Lear, everything by Pinter and Orton – modern English sadism. Even Ayckbourn – her guilty pleasure: no one in academia mentioned him. His plays weren't about kings or eccentrics, but ordinary people, and though the plays masqueraded as comedies, they were really tragedies, tragedies about ordinary but unhappy families. Theatre couldn't be about happy families or relationships – without conflict, there was no drama; who wrote that? Oh god, was that going to keep her awake now too?

It was late, all calm and quiet. She closed her eyes; perhaps she'd sleep well here, nearer the tranquillity of the countryside. There was nothing to worry about. Jazz had a great job in a lovely school, with kids who adored her, and – if her oh-so-active mind would let her sleep – she herself was about to start a new job tomorrow morning.

It was quiet, all morning she'd rarely heard even footsteps in the corridor outside her office. It was great, she'd get so much more writing done here. Time had gone quickly, she had made a good start on her work. Now she felt hot. She went to open the window wider, but there was some kind of lock. So peaceful, the soft green smudges of fields in the distance. Below, people were smoking, or wandering along texting or speaking into their phones. She should text Jazz, tell her she was fine, how she'd love to plan a ramble soon, before the days got too short. Everything was going to be just fine –

'Hello?'

She jumped, startled – a voice so close to her ear, male – she couldn't help her strangled shriek as she swivelled –

'I'm so sorry. You didn't hear the door?'

He was so close, standing next to her desk – how hadn't she heard him? It was such a small office, especially now with the two of them. She wasn't sure what to say; she leaned a hand against the wall, stepping back nearer the open window.

He smiled. 'So sorry.'

She relaxed; he sounded polite – the English middle-class accent, the familiar voice of the university. He looked familiar too, he wasn't on her interview panel though, perhaps a conference – such a small world, academia. She'd looked at the department website before the interview, checking out the staff specialities; that must be it. He looked like a Beckett specialist, black polo neck, jacket and jeans – inwardly she smiled at her pigeonholing of him. The sort of thing she'd say to Jazz, home after an intense conference – so important and absorbing at the time, but afterwards, well, it wasn't Paris or Berlin in the thirties but England in the twenty-first century.

He was looking at her, an eyebrow raised, as if concerned.

She should say something. 'Sorry, I'm fine. I was just in a world of my own. Um … you are?'

'Phil,' he said. 'The department secretary sent round an email to say you were starting today, to come and introduce ourselves.'

'Thanks, that's good to know.' She wasn't sure what else to say. She moved, putting a hand on the back of her desk chair, then picked up her notebook from the desk.

He took a step towards the door. 'I must be getting on, all the beginning of term prep. Do let me know if you need anything – the induction has never been very useful here, I'm sad to say.'

'Oh, you've reminded me, I should be on my way –'

'So lovely to meet you again, Tesya.'

And then he was gone, although now he'd made it clear they'd met before, he was on her mind. Where had she met him? She picked up her bag and went to the door – then remembered she needed the letter with the induction room number on it. It wasn't on her desk. Perhaps she'd folded it away when unpacking her files – so many papers. She'd be late; she'd have to ask reception where to go.

Finally she was outside her office, then, while struggling to check she had her new office door key in her overstuffed bag, the door slammed and locked itself anyway. In the silence, as though she had flicked a switch, the corridor lights came on automatically. The windows in the row of office doors either side of the corridor were dark; term hadn't begun though, only newcomers like her would be in – and people like Phil, whatever he was like. Probably really conscientious, given what he said about the department email. It was nice of him to introduce himself; that had never happened to her before – but then this was only her second job, after all the years of studying and research-assisting. Perhaps most workplaces were like this, friendly and welcoming. On the heading of the induction letter she'd managed to lose, the university's logo was an open book, emblazoned with the slogan 'Welcoming Diversity'. It was living up to it. She set off down the corridor, relaxed and ready for the induction programme – wherever it was.

LESSON TWO

'Nice people give bad people the benefit of the doubt. Or, to put it more graphically, as in this session we're dealing with first impressions: nice people believe the best, even when the worst is staring them in the face.

'Looking back over your life, there will have been times when you had doubtful thoughts about someone the first time you met. You would have pushed these thoughts to the back of your mind, not wanting to be negative about someone so soon just because of minuscule suspicions. Think about the first time you met a neighbour or work colleague: that first impression, over the garden wall or in the staffroom? Something small, perhaps the neighbour parked fractionally over into your parking space, a centimetre closer and they'd have grazed your car? Or what about your body: someone new brushing past you and touching you "by accident"? Proximity and touch are powerful, they're related to sex, but mostly they're about power.

'Think of those tiny actions that feel odd. A look held for slightly too long. Or an apparently platonic embrace that lingers, or lurches a little higher, or lower, than expected. Actions that our bodies respond to with flushed skin and raised temperature: the physicality of uncertainty. You will have experienced it, on the receiving end, but also, as you're here now, you will have experienced being the giver of uncertainty, I'm sure. It is the easiest first step, that first impression, and you will work on that initial uncertainty at the profitable later stages.

'What is true of uncertainty in social or domestic spaces is even more ambiguous in the workplace, where roles are more fixed and where boundaries can be played with more easily. We also spend more time at work than at home, work colleagues have plenty of time, even on day one, to make complex first impressions.

'So, take the advantage by making a good first impression yourself. Your physical appearance and behaviour will count in the wider context, especially if things get analysed in the future. You will need people to say you were an exemplary member of the community, so the suspicion of paranoia will be thrown on the accuser, the person apparently playing the victim.

'The key is this: somewhere within your first-impression performance you must subtly leave an ambiguous sign, perceivable only by the victim. Their unique first impression of you should anchor their weakness within the specific context. Something that only the victim will notice, but so ambiguous that they won't understand what it was exactly, not until it is too late, when they will remember. They won't mention it at the time, because they'll be uncertain. Uncertainty is the mother of paranoia, and the paranoid victim is easy and interesting prey.

'Although the ambiguities of close proximity and actual physical contact are possible within seconds of meeting, the first impression may be psychological, and that may be more powerful in self-fertilizing in the victim's mind. Ambiguous signs breed ambiguous thoughts, working well on those who are already vulnerable: self-conscious females, those who are insecure, and those of a different race to you, who are inevitably going to be lower in status in any professional setting.

'The ambiguity of encroaching on personal space, coming just a little too close for comfort while not quite touching, remains a simple but powerful first-impression tool. The overarching aim is to plant a seed so that in the future when the victim looks back, they will think, if only. However intelligent the victim is, during the first impression they won't be able to tell the difference between a nice person and the worst person that will ever happen to them: you.'

3

TIME'S WINGÈD CHARIOT

AUTHOR'S NOTE

What happened to my antagonist, in childhood, and later as an adult? What might make a person racist?

Even as a child I knew the racism I experienced wasn't about me but about something else – like bullies venting on those more vulnerable, easy scapegoats at school rather than the powerful adults bullying them at home. It doesn't make it easier to face, but if we could understand more about how racism works, it might be easier to combat – is what I think when I'm optimistic. Now, with this character, I'm not sure; I feel more pessimistic. Perhaps it's this era, the resurgence of the politics of white supremacy, of the British Empire, now in the twenty-first century.

A few days after the 7 July 2005 suicide bombings in London I was walking across Trafalgar Square when a woman shouted at me, 'Go back to where you come from,' in a middle-class accent.

For a moment I stared back: white, middle-aged and in a well-cut pastel-coloured summer dress, she could have been anyone. She looked away, and started chatting to someone.

I walked on slowly – the square was filling with a crowd for the Mayor of London's event, bringing people together after the first coordinated suicide bombings on the capital city's transport network. There was the metallic reverb of a microphone being tested, and then that weird, almost non-verbal sound of a crowd corralled by the police – it was only a few days after the attack, anything could happen because it already had – a feeling of edginess.

I felt edgy too. The power of terror is how it poisons the mind, fear follows you afterwards: as you walk, you're aware of being aware, of your surroundings, other people. Because it will happen again. Terror always does.

Racism is a form of terror – not that I've ever heard it called that, but it is. I was terrified that day in the crowd, terrified of a seemingly innocuous woman shouting, 'Go back to where you come from,' in the midst of an event celebrating London's diversity. It's good cover for racism, being at a noisy event. No one tried to stop her – or support me. Perhaps nobody heard – or they looked away, pretending not to hear. It's easier not to listen, when it's not happening to you.

There was terror in my breathing, that battling for breath and dry mouth I get when I'm scared. Turning back through the crowd, I crossed over the river to south London, back home – over the river, not over the oceans; I was born here. Truth, like time, is immaterial to racists: our home is the colour on our face, not a word on a birth certificate. I think of Obama; I think of so many of us. I think of the word home, and how politically charged home has become, in a country obsessed with home ownership.

There are different types of racists. My antagonist wouldn't shout racist abuse in the street – too easy, too short-lived for someone comfortable biding his time. If you get away with something and it makes you feel good, you'll continue; racist crime works.

Have I mixed up my real-life invisible antagonist with my fictional character? Does it matter? It's funny how I don't know the real person, but am starting to know my fictional character. Thinking of home and where we come from makes me wonder where he'd feel at home. I'm not sure he is recording in his office, and I don't picture him in a home with others around. No, he's alone, somewhere that's just his, and for some reason he's unanchored from a home and others. That's why he can anchor himself to the Lessons, to what he's trying to –

What if he's literally anchored, even temporarily – offshore, on a boat? But why is he at sea? What has time done to him?

LESSON THREE

'Never underestimate the power of technology, nor the weakness of human underestimation of its power in the moment and over time.

'Think about it: have you ever felt you've found your soulmate, someone who seemed to know you intuitively, like you were made for each other?

'Now think about e-safety: using different passwords, not revealing personal details, working hours or holiday dates. Yes, we're used to guarding against anonymous people online, when we're sober. But after long working days we end up in the pub drinking. Relaxed, under the influence, we text, and take photos, especially selfies. In a few clicks our images are uploaded onto Twitter, Facebook or Instagram for the whole world: where we are, who we're with, what we're up to. That record of changing relationship status is a gift for tracking the vulnerable over time. Look at the details. Two smiling people in a selfie, arms round each other, but are they looking in different directions? And who is holding whom, and how? Are the smiles softly real, or frozen in the rigid lines of contrived "happy"? What about extra person-to-person touching outside of the central pair, at the edges of the frame, a hand or a knee, a third person? What's out of sync? There's always something. No one's perfect. You aren't, so why would anyone else be?

'Which leads me to time's wingèd chariot; how I like that phrase. No one is here forever. Life is a series of incidental meetings between people, some more significant than others, though not always to both participants. Someone gets hurt. Time heals; we move on. At the time of an emotionally difficult event, particularly relationship upsets and endings, we feel we'll never survive or ever get over it. Give it a year or so, and most people do move on. The blame game helps: they weren't the person you thought they were. And there's the tried-and-tested: a new lover. The examples I've given are connected with intimate relationships – I'll continue this; it's why many of you are here. Something's happened to you: someone you can't forget.

'Some of us never forget. We are meticulous in remembering details that other people don't. Most people are too wrapped up in themselves to remember anything much about other people. We're different, that's what people like about us early on. We remember favourite colours, perfumes, places; whatever matters to someone. It's a great resource for surprises, and surprises are a delicious way of reminding someone you haven't forgotten them, especially people who'd rather forget us. It's all about time: birthdays, anniversaries of key dates like the first kiss, the wedding proposal, even the first betrayal.

'Everything is connected to time, and its passing. So the date, and whatever you choose as a reminder. Even if the recipient is the sort that doesn't remember dates, their memories can be reawakened and time past will flood back, like a frozen joint of meat once defrosted looks freshly slaughtered.

'To conclude: nothing is lost to time, and all loss incorporates a feeling of nothingness, the time before we began and the time after we end: a reminder of the limits of our significance. When we remind people of the past, we give them a premonition of their ultimate insignificance, the inevitability of their finite lives: death.'

Outside the wind is whipping up. The tide tugs the boat; it thuds against the quayside then ricochets back. Pulled to its limit by the mooring rope, the helm points out towards the black vastness of the sea. A perfect image.

Now time to switch off, and get on with the day.

Cabin door locked. One stride, then land again. The darkness of England in the autumn, even in the day, shadows slant and slice, reshaping buildings, vanishing people in the murky air between earth and cloud.

It's the perfect time.

· NOW

It's Thursday. She's swept away the dust drifting along the floorboards since yesterday, when they moved the boxes. Jazz had thankfully pre-booked movie tickets at the Odeon – an overhyped blockbuster, but at least it took her mind off it. She'll work from home for the rest of the week, and put off unpacking the boxes until she's next in. Now all that's left is to change the bedding and make a coffee before starting work – until it's time for a shower before Holly arrives. She smooths the covers, then checks the time on the alarm clock; soon fresh coffee wafts around the studio as she moves towards her desk.

The whole day it's been dark. From time to time she's looked up from her screen to the window above, the rectangle of darkening clouds. Difficult to know whether it's night or day – not that she can escape time: it's always there, at the corner of her eye, her waking life lived through a series of time-based screens.

She glances at her handwritten notes on Jacobean revenge tragedy, and back to the screen, typing up next week's lecture. Her eyes flicker to the time again. Must concentrate, but it's difficult on days like this, when in the back of her mind she's counting down to when –

Across the room her mobile vibrates a text alert.

She saves the document and walks over, slowly though, putting off the moment. She's a feeling of who and what – and she's right: Holly's 'Really sorry, can't make tonight, something's come up. I'll call you later.' No X: like she was in a rush to press send, to cancel their date.

Should she reply, check Holly's OK? Still standing in the middle of the room, she rereads the text. That phrase, 'I'll call you later' – she puts the mobile down on the coffee table, it flashes the time back at her and then goes back to sleep. Those white against black numerals linger: wasn't it about the time Holly would have been setting off?

Across the tidy room, the shining floorboards lead through the open doorway to her freshly made bed.

So last-minute: 'something's come up' – a poorly kid, the child-minder's car broken down en route? Even so …

She snaps to, annoyed at herself: she's being mean. Poor Holly. How awful to be widowed and looking after kids alone, stuck in the middle of nowhere.

Back at her desk, the blank screen hides what she was working on before the arrival of Holly's text; her mind is blank too: where was she? She hovers between carrying on working or having a shower now as planned, even if Holly isn't coming. She presses a key, the document returns. She stares for a moment, prompted by a word here, a phrase there, but can't focus – why can't Holly come, what's happened? She powers down, and tidies the papers on her desk ready for tomorrow – her eyes flicker over the calendar on the wall: there's plenty of time.

Under the spray of the shower, she cries, and when the water washes away her tears, she cries some more, remembering last week, missing Holly. Nothing else matters when they're together. Even their inconsequential talk matters – Holly remembering a wine she'd love to share with her in the future, or her liking the design of what she's wearing at that moment. Then carrying their glasses into the bedroom, spilling the wine on their fingers, laughing as they set their glasses down either side of the bed – knowing which side, like they've been together years, and have all the time in the world. Just like in the dark, how she's never in a rush – it's only when Holly holds her close that she can hear her fast-beating heart, echoing her own.

Holly's a feeling she wants all over again, how her lips say softly, 'Tesya …' like she's the most important person in her world. How she makes her feel – the opposite of now, as her dream shifts and swirls away, like the water circling beneath her, down the plughole.

Yesterday after the movie, in the car with Jazz, they'd discussed the movie's female superheroes – superheroines? Their weird mixture of hyper-feminine bodies and hyper-masculine clichéd attributes, killing to save a nation. Then what was it? Oh yes, they'd jumped to politics – *Question Time* the other week, and that obnoxious politician who's made a living from making incendiary, factually inaccurate statements about immigrants.

What would it be like with Holly, doing something cultural and then talking afterwards? Holly recently sent her – via Amazon – a few books published by independent presses, so it was obvious they both liked similar non-mainstream contemporary fiction. Not that they had ever so far had time to discuss what they were reading –

She faces the steamed-up cubicle wall. Holly's everything she wants – she's also a series of question marks punctuating the time they're apart. Turning her back to the hot spray, eyes closed, gradually her shoulders relax in the heat. Soothed, she reaches for a towel. There's always another time.

Dried and dressed, she checks her mobile: nothing, but now she's back to normal she texts Holly: 'Hope things OK, nothing too serious? Speak soon.' She adds an X, and presses send. Before she's put her mobile down there's a text alert – it's just Jazz, almost as though she's guessed she'd be free: 'Fancy Sadler's Wells tonight? My colleague can't make it now, let me know?' She replies, 'Love to,' glad to be getting out, not spending the evening unexpectedly alone.

Soon, in transit, she has a surge of excitement: that feeling before curtains up. She only goes to the ballet with Jazz. And with Jazz she knows where she stands, she never cancels or lets her down: there's something about friendship.

There's no time to talk when she meets Jazz in the foyer, just time to find their seats as the house lights go down.

A drum beats, like a heart, as a pink blush of light spreads across the stage, and single dancers drift on, intermingling, like at a party. Bodies merge, tender like the sweet bells' trickling twisting sounds –

*

A clash of cymbals, then two bodies entwine in a pool of red light, like love at first sight – no, their limbs intersect fast like blades, until one withdraws into the shadows. The discarded body contorts, limbs askew, clothes torn to shreds – she falls in continuous movement, until wracked in disarray, exposing her nipples and the darkness between her thighs, she lies down, the broken shell of a woman – the human debris of a human storm.

There's a pause – it's over? No, the light dims, more bodies couple up – or fight; it's difficult to know. Camouflaged in shadows, others watch equidistant, echoing their movements – then drumbeats: one, two, three – they hurtle towards the woman spent like a corpse, prodding her limbs, pulling –

Drumbeat like a pulse – lightning flashes across the stage, she can't watch –

Suddenly she remembers Holly's text, and then the nothingness. Should have called; what if it's serious, she's never cancelled at such short notice before –

Jazz leans forward on the balcony rail, focused, her neck rigid. There's a red glow from the stage. It's terribly hot. That urgent drum-pulse, then someone screams. Jazz's hands clench the rail.

Now it's Sunday night. She's tried Holly once again since her text on Thursday, but she's not replied, which is weird. It's the longest she's not heard from her. Whatever it was that stopped her coming on Thursday had got her caught up over the weekend too. Surely she could have texted at some point?

The washing-machine spin cycle builds to a crescendo then stops abruptly. She yanks out the damp clothes and hangs them on the clothes horse, her jeans and t-shirts smelling of fabric conditioner rather than the sweaty club of Saturday night – it had been such a strange mixed week: from that unsettling avant-garde dance performance at Sadler's Wells, to clubbing in Dalston on Saturday night. Now she can't remember why clubbing seemed such a good idea –

It had been last orders at the crammed pub opposite the theatre. City suits with loosened ties downed pints, while ballet aficionados, wilting scarves discarded, sipped champagne fast. They bought a couple of glasses of red and found space by a window. Outside teenagers careered past on bikes, weaving between taxis queuing for the lights to change. Jazz propped her dance programme on the window ledge, reminding Tesya to click a photo of it to tweet like she does for all performances she goes to – not that she was sure what she'd say. The body left lying alone at the end stood up for the curtain call: the dancer curtsied to the applause, caught a bouquet and threw a smile back in that bizarre eruption of reality – whatever it is that makes lived reality different to what happens on the stage.

She said something to Jazz about it – perhaps about the violence, the woman lying like a mutilated corpse? Whatever she'd said, their conversation was stopped by the loud club music blaring from the windows of a snazzy car going past, and Jazz changed the subject: 'God, I haven't been clubbing for ages. Remember how we used to, every weekend?'

'Couldn't do that now, those all-nighters –'

'Shall we, Saturday night?'

'A club? Haven't most places in Soho closed down?'

Jazz must have been going out on the scene more than she mentioned; she answered, 'There are a few Soho places still – but what about one of the new ones in Dalston? Quicker to get to? I'll drive?'

'Won't they all be twenty-somethings?'

'No, Dalston's the new Hoxton; everyone goes there now. And what if they are? We can enjoy the music. You haven't got anything else planned, I guess?'

So to shut down any potential questions about Holly, besides her own feelings since Thursday, she said yes.

She'd got into the idea by Saturday evening, getting dressed up and then dressing down, eventually going with being comfortable in Levi's and her old much-worn leather jacket, and underneath an expensive t-shirt she'd bought ages ago, kept for a special occasion but not worn yet. Jazz beeped her horn downstairs. Tesya picked up her still-silent phone, relieved to be going out on a Saturday night.

It wasn't far, but once there, time disappeared. Queuing to get into the club in a line disappearing down a dimly lit alley. Then, inside the huge warehouse, more time queuing in a throng to get to the bar, and then eventually on the heaving dance floor, they quickly lost sight of each other.

In that moment of realizing she couldn't see Jazz, she drifted, carried along by strangers' movements to the pounding sounds, between people's backs, and faces momentarily close then gone – when suddenly she glimpsed the glitter of red hair –

It wasn't Holly – she'd be at home, doing whatever people with kids do on a Saturday night. And Holly had only recently discovered she liked women – she'd whispered it to her under the covers. She couldn't imagine Holly clubbing anyway, especially not on the scene. The redhead turned, and the woman's eyes – electric blue, and pinned – locked onto hers, and for a moment they danced together – until the track changed, and those eyes hooked onto someone else and she vanished into the crowd.

She headed for the bar, thirsty – and there was Jazz. She'd seen her dancing with the woman –

'Thought you'd pulled –'

'Just enjoying dancing – where were you?'

'Bumped into some of the old crowd – though they've left already, lightweights now they're partnered up.'

It was impossible to talk over the heavy beat, their conversation absorbed into all the other sounds echoing against the shiny steel and glass – she'd forgotten how clubs absorb talk and time. They went back to the dance floor, and then the sound too loud to think of anything else, she was lost in the music, the tempo changes – the adrenaline rush of the dance floor – and the crazy fun of clubbing with Jazz, her eyebrows signalling over-the-top dancers around them, or ones she fancied.

*

Funny how some faces we forget minutes after meeting, while others are clear years later. There's something else though: faces we don't immediately recall in a new context, but when they speak, the past sidles back into our minds.

Weird, if she hadn't been waiting outside for Jazz at that particular time? But Jazz had left her to queue at the coat check, then eventually outside, past the bouncers frisking early-morning clubbers still arriving, she'd waited near the kerb for Jazz's car.

She had been checking her phone, but looked up at the spark of a flash of light close by: a woman lighting a cigarette. She was wearing jeans and a black leather jacket, like her; like lots of people on the scene. She took a drag of her cigarette, and as the white smoke faded into the darkness she glanced down at her phone in her hand, like she was checking the time – probably waiting for someone too. She looked slightly familiar, but then people do on the scene, even if you've not been out for a while. There was something about her face though –

She caught her stare, and smiled. 'Hi, Tesya.'

'Sorry, I –'

'People who've met me in uniform never recognize me without it. I'm PC … or rather, Jo. We met in –'

'Oh, of course, Jo.' She walked closer to her.

'I'm really sorry we never got to the bottom of it. The case is still open, of course. I haven't heard from you for a while?'

'No, I've been meaning to ring you. I've left, and started a job here in London.'

A beeping sounded nearby and Jazz drew up to the kerb, with vehicles queuing up behind her.

She turned to Jo. 'Sorry, I have to go.'

'Whenever you're ready, it would be good if you came in. We can go over the file together. A case review is due soon.' She added, 'Often with a gap of time people remember things that didn't seem important but might be in retrospect.'

*

Now it's Sunday night and everything else has gone out of focus, but what Jo said is in sharp focus, like the illuminated red numerals on the alarm clock ticking over, reminding her she should be getting an early night. 'The case is still open, of course' – that 'of course'. Jo was always so thoughtful, calming her down, even though every conversation they had had started with her all het up from whatever had just happened. Jo reassured her, saying, 'We'll get to the bottom of it, eventually,' and that 'it just takes time.'

Funny bumping into her outside a club, she'd never thought Jo might be gay – but then sexuality was the last thing on her mind, meeting her in a police station, in the middle of everything. Though perhaps that's why she felt safe with her, instinctively – she was the only person she trusted there, when things got bad.

She doesn't want to, but now she has to go back. What's happened isn't going to go away, even though she can't see how they'll ever find out who's behind it, or was behind it. Now she's moved, nothing more has happened – not since that last awful day – but –

What was it Jo said, something about time?

She always asked the right questions, getting her to notice things she wasn't aware she had noticed in the panic of the moment. Things her conscious mind didn't remember, until prompted.

Like Holly in a way; she didn't realize she felt so alone, until she met her. In Holly's company she forgets time, it's when she leaves she feels loneliness draping itself around her; like those nights in the children's home, hearing car engines and people chatting outside on their way home.

She craves something sweet and makes a hot chocolate, then procrastinates: go to bed, or stay up and watch some TV? She presses the remote; the news comes on, the image of a traffic pile-up, somewhere on a B road outside London. She thinks of Holly driving around, dropping her kids off at play dates, or picking up shopping. Too late to call, but not to text – she does: 'Hope things are OK, a good weekend? X'.

When she switches off the TV, after the weather, there's silence, then she notices the flashing light of a text notification.

Holly's reply: 'Busy weekend, an old acquaintance came at the last minute, nightmare weekend tbh. Call you in the week X'.

As she switches off the light she wonders who the old acquaintance is, and why the weekend was a 'nightmare'.

There's that dense silence of Sunday nights, her neighbours already asleep, work clothes ironed for the morning and packed lunches waiting in the fridge for the day ahead, to be eaten in the staffroom next to colleagues.

In the dark, about to go through to the bedroom, she stops by the window and glances outside. Down, across the deserted street, under the light in the apartment-block doorway opposite, a woman stands smoking. Like Jo on Saturday night, or rather Sunday morning – what people do nowadays: smoke outside clubs, offices and downstairs outside their rented no-smoking apartments.

She starts to roll down the blind as a police car sirens past fast. Afterwards, across the empty street, the doorway is deserted, the smoker's gone inside – then, no, she's there, walking along the pavement away from the building. How quickly she assumed her to live there, because she was there. The woman wasn't doing anything wrong, just sheltering, smoking there for a moment, but the thought spooks her for some reason.

The blind down, now it's totally dark. She feels for her diary on the desk, and brings it with her into the bedroom. When could she go and see Jo? When will she be able to bear it? She switches on the bedside light, and drops her diary next to it, and puts her mobile on top of the diary. What's normal now, moving around with a phone, not that it means people communicate more; it just means we're available. She's available; Holly isn't – although she must have been for her surprise visitor: did she literally mean whoever it was just turned up out of the blue, at her front door? What had she said – here it is – 'an old acquaintance came at the last minute, nightmare weekend tbh'.

Did she mean the acquaintance was a nightmare – but surely not, why would she stay friends with someone she found a nightmare?

Nightmare's just an expression; she probably means it's been a packed weekend, what with her friend around too. She's probably exhausted.

She switches off the light. She hears the silence more clearly now she's in the dark. That expression, exactly how she feels about then, how she feels about now too: in the dark. As a kid she always felt when she was an adult everything would be easier, but actually as time goes on things feel more complicated. Time felt slower then, and faster now – except when she's lying in the dark, trying to sleep. The red light of the alarm clock is too near, too bright. She turns over, closing her eyes, though the red fizz of the time lingers, like the silt of the day flickers then fades: the twisted remains of a car crash on the news; the black and white of a text message she's not sure about.

She should buy an old-fashioned alarm clock that wouldn't glow red in the dark –

Oh to be the kind of person who's out like a light, not struggling, worried about the time, worried about then and now.

4

COFFEE AND
OTHER DRINKS

LESSON FOUR

It was the right day; of course she remembered.

Simple, ringing the bell, saying, 'Just passing.'

She didn't want to open the door, and struggled, putting on a rigid smile and robotically polite voice, 'Oh, what a surprise.'

'A quick cuppa?'

She couldn't say no, not when she wasn't alone.

A quick cuppa sounds innocent, but it's always ambiguous with someone you're familiar with who doesn't want to see you, especially when they're inevitably thinking of you: anniversaries unite people even when they're inextricably divided.

Once inside, it's never just a cuppa. Easy to look around while the kettle's boiling, note changes: clothes, nails done; clues to what's going on. Then stay just long enough to upset plans.

'You've ruined the weekend,' she shouted from the front door, slamming it, revealing herself – revealing a successful operation.

Now on the water again, the kettle's boiling next to a couple of cups and the coffee and tea canisters. Looks good. Time to switch on, but tea or coffee?

Coffee, oh yes: 'Would you like to come in for a coffee – or – do you wanna fuck?'

'You've guessed it: an alternative title for this Lesson would be text and subtext, or the art of getting what you want. Think about that suggestion, of coming in for a coffee, continuing a date, inside someone's home. No one wants to drink coffee, not at that time, but the suggestion signals – well, you know the subtext for coffee.

'But now think about the different permutations of drinks, depending on context. Tea sounds cosy, but not if it's a forced cosiness: a manager having a cuppa with an employee in the staff canteen, to tell them they are surplus to requirements; or a partner bringing up the morning cuppa, with, "I have something to tell you."

'The most innocent-sounding of drinks, tea and coffee are ingredients for complex lessons of nuance depending on the target. Think back to Lesson One, on multiculturalism, and combine with Lesson Two on the minutiae of time. You may be able to see where we're heading today: the simple operation of playing games with people's minds, using everyday substances people normally wouldn't think twice about.'

THEN

'Thank you all for attending, and welcome again.'

The induction session had been what she'd call 'interesting' if she ever told Jazz about it, not that she would. After all, it was just how these things are. It was only interesting in that it proved Jazz correct: if training changed anything, it would be banned. To be fair it was only an induction session, but there was something about how organizations explain their policies with a scattering of stock phrases about equality and diversity – their own institutional stock phrases, like the one on the university letterhead – which sound great, but …

What was it? She wasn't sure, but perhaps ... the more something gets repeated, the more mechanical and meaningless it sounds.

At least this induction had been slickly run – but even so, she'd already read the policies in the staff handbook when it was emailed to her.

'Coffee will be served in the foyer area, through the doors behind you.'

Coffee was what she needed; she'd almost nodded off. Hope no one noticed – or that she'd been late to the session. She'd found the room eventually, sneaking in at the back, just as Angela, the smart-suited black Human Resources woman from her interview, had been enthusing about the infrastructure supporting students, 'Particularly those from a widening participation background' – she meant people like Tesya herself: ethnic minority, working-class origins, and a survivor of the care system. 'Widening participation': how she hated that phrase.

'Milk please, just a little, thanks.'

Widening participation was usually diluting what the elite had; giving people something, but less. You could see it in the hierarchical architecture in higher education – from the Golden Spires, to the Red Bricks, then the New Builds – unattainable heights, for the upper echelons; the solid respectability of walls with doors, built after the Industrial Revolution, for the growing professional classes; then the newer concrete tower blocks, like council estates, to house the lower classes and even –

It felt different here though – despite, as usual, the catering staff all being ethnic minority, but that was everywhere – yes, at this New Build university the new staff were a more multicultural bunch. Though she was the only one from Arts – the other ethnic minority staff were all destined for Engineering or Science. Everyone was looking interview-suit-style corporate – apart from her. She'd have to stick to her first-day smart casual at least, to fit in – and get some new clothes.

The coffee was good. Perhaps she'd have a second cup, chat to a few more people, before heading upstairs –

'I'm so glad you've joined us, Tesya.' It was the Human Resources woman, Angela.

'Thank you, I'm delighted to be here.'

'Here's my card in case you ever need me. Now, let me introduce you to –'

A few minutes saying hello to people whose names she'd try to remember, although as they were in other faculties or non-academic areas of the institution she'd probably rarely meet them again, but she should try – everyone was so friendly.

As people started to disperse, she went to the canteen and bought a sandwich to take back to her office for lunch. Upstairs, as she walked along the corridor she searched for her office key in the depths of her bag – then remembered the door slamming shut earlier, when she was leaving. It was probably under the files on her desk – and now she was at the end of the corridor, right outside –

She stared.

As though someone had thrown a cup of coffee at her door, aiming high, just above the perspex holder, brown liquid was soaking through her name card and dripping down to the floor. Milky coffee: there was that slightly going-off smell of milk that's sat in coffee for too long.

Down the corridor: silence, no lights on in the other offices, no one around.

Her hand felt sticky – she must have clenched it – mayonnaise oozed out of the folds of her now-squashed plastic-wrapped sandwich. She wiped her hands with a tissue from her bag, and then screwed it up and put it in the side pocket – she felt a card: Angela's. Her friendly face, above her corporate suit, saying, 'Just in case you ever need me.'

Or should she go through Admin? She got out her phone and rang reception, but she was held listening to a complicated numerical menu of options. She didn't know the extension number of the person she required – she didn't know who she required, and the staff directory was in her office.

Through the small square window in her office door, through the congealing coffee stain, she couldn't see the key on her desk – it was covered with her files and papers. She'd have to go down.

She set off, her shirt clinging to her suddenly rather sweaty underarms in the warm synthetic air along the carpeted corridor. At the end, by the lift, the window was the type that didn't open. It was a high floor; presumably it was a health and safety thing. Even so, there could have been a slither of air coming in – it was stifling.

The lift arrived. Inside it, as the doors closed, in their mirrored surface in front of her she saw the dark patches of sweat spreading under her shirt arms – like the coffee stain spreading and dripping down her office door. In her bag, she had a rolled-up linen jacket, in case it got colder. She took it out and put it on, then checked in the mirror – OK, for now. Then she looked up at her face. Under the fluorescent light, her skin was the colour of milky coffee.

Oh god. Her heart thumped, even though it was a ridiculous thought –

And yet also it wasn't. Could it be that …?

The lift doors slid open, her reflection divided in two, and then disappeared. She faced a blank wall in the middle of a long corridor, with its row of silent office doors and their typed name cards, spotless – not like hers.

Try not to think about it.

Which way: left or right?

Feel like going straight home, and it's only lunchtime.

NOW

Thankfully she's on another corridor, at another job, in the solidity of the Red Brick Victorian building in central London, and not far from home.

Almost the end of the day now, the team meeting over, she's halfway along the corridor, when Ben, the Head of Faculty, catches up.

'Tesya, I've been meaning to say, we have a Thanksgiving party each year, and it's coming up again soon. Love to have you over; I always invite the whole team. I'll send you the invitation tonight. We're not far, Hampstead?'

'Sounds lovely. What should I bring?'

'Just a bottle and yourself: Phil – he's the American in our "special relationship", why we do Thanksgiving – does all the cooking. There's a theme each year. Don't ask me what, we'll find out on the day.'

'Thanks, Ben, I'll look forward to it.'

'It'll be lovely to get to know you more, outside of all this –' He waves his handful of papers, and then carries on up the corridor.

In her office, she picks up her bag, and then sets off down the corridor. En route a few people smile and call out, 'Bye, Tesya,' as they leave too.

It would be good to hang out with the faculty, get to know them, particularly Ben and Phil. The problem with all the moving around to new jobs – especially now she's on her third job in three years – it's difficult to make like-minded friends, or even just friends.

That 'our special relationship' was a nice touch – he knew she was gay, like she had guessed he was; now Phil proves it. Wonder whether he's an academic too – or, that cooking, perhaps he's a stay-at-home husband and they have kids. Phil. There was a Phil before – a guy at the New Build, or the Golden Spires – was that his name, or was it something else? She vaguely remembers a face on the staff web page, someone never around, probably on sabbatical that year. Lucky guy. Everywhere she's worked, you have to have been there for ages before applying for a sabbatical. Hopefully here she'll be able to stay put that long.

Down the grand Victorian staircase – such a beautifully well-kept building – and across the polished black-and-white tiled foyer, then she's outside in a dark wintry evening.

Cutting between rush-hour taxis and red buses she crosses the road and walks alongside the iron railings around the garden in the centre of Russell Square, through the tangled shadows of branches overhanging the locked gates.

She's about to cross to the Tube station when a police car sirens past urgently and other vehicles back up to let it through. She must call Jo, set up when to go over. She's busy, though: weeks into this new job and she's already been asked to sit on a number of committees, so much paperwork. Plus there's a potential research project she's been invited to collaborate on; things are looking up.

On the Tube, it's packed. She holds onto the rail near the door; only a few stops.

Perhaps meeting Jo won't take long, a few hours one afternoon. She could suggest meeting up with Holly for a coffee afterwards, if it's early. Can't be that far from where she –

What's she thinking? She'd have to tell her why she's nearby at the police station – that would involve telling her what happened. All Holly knows is she worked there then, and now she works here. She'd said something about having a change, and career progression – which it isn't; it's a sideways move. That didn't feel good, but she can't talk about there; Holly thinks she's so together, and she is now, but even so, she can imagine getting upset talking about it; her eyes are welling up even thinking about it now –

Somewhere in this bag, surely there's a packet of tissues.

She scrunches up the used tissue in her fist, and with the other hand she picks up the free newspaper someone's left behind. Zehra would say 'Why read that drivel?' whenever she'd picked one up on the way home from sixth form.

Zehra. She wishes she could manage to call her mum.

She hasn't seen her for ages; that's what she needs – she'll stay on the Piccadilly Line, she's always home at teatime.

Walking down Green Lanes, past the Turkish shops with boxes of vegetables displayed outside on the pavement, she's already reminded of Zehra's kitchen. It's the ripe tomatoes, generously sized and misshapen, rather than the uniform cellophane-wrapped ones of supermarkets. Great sprawling bunches of coriander and mint smell savoury like the wholesome cooking of a homely kitchen, rather than what she'd been used to before Zehra: the spag bol, overcooked greens and the bland whiteness of mash; a diet of institutional meals in echoing canteens, eaten at plastic-covered trestle tables – or more often left to be scraped away into aluminium waste trays.

That first night Zehra asked her, 'Tell me what you love to eat.'

She didn't know until that moment you could love food. Or what love might feel like.

When she was first told by her social worker that someone called Zehra was offering to foster her, she imagined a traditional veiled Muslim woman, who would insist on her wearing shalwar kameez. How could she have thought anything else? She'd been brought up by a series of mostly well-meaning white social workers, all trained to treat ethnicity with respect but who in a weird kind of way reinforced all the stereotypes, like making a thing about Eid and Diwali but forgetting different cultures the rest of the time.

It had been the same in school when they were taught about black history, but it seemed to be all about slavery; or Religious Education, where it had been about how religions other than Christianity were backwards about women; it was all so negative about other cultures. Diversity seemed to be about difference, backward beliefs and the atrocities of other cultures, and how the British Empire was good because it became the Commonwealth. Whereas of course now she knew that the British Empire had committed atrocities, divided people and lands, and that other cultures had had female leaders and enlightened policies like banning slavery long before Britain – besides having spicy curries and herb-scented couscous, yes, those foods she learned that she loves.

She loves Zehra, and she turned out to be the opposite of what she'd imagined. When she opened the door to the social worker's office, there she was, waiting for her. She fell for her immediately: Zehra was wearing a rose-coloured linen jacket over skintight blue jeans; she wore dark-red lipstick and her long straight hair was hennaed – and she smiled as she came forward to meet her. She told her about her work: she owned a couple of restaurants – she'd worked her way up cooking and managing in the food business until she set up on her own to focus on the things that mattered to her: organic and ethically produced products. Once she'd moved in she learned more about Zehra's politics, from the books around the house and the phrases scattered in her conversation, like herbs and spices in her tasty cooking: reacting to the news on the radio as she cooked, it might be that 'It's a woman's choice' – on abortion – or an exclamation that 'Black lives matter too' when another death in police custody was announced and skated over.

The most wonderful thing, what she'd never experienced before, was that Zehra always had time to talk, to listen, and she also knew when to just give her a hug. Zehra turned out to be the perfect person to take her on at age fifteen. In her dreams she had wanted to be part of a family, to have brothers and sisters, but if she'd been placed somewhere with other kids she would have struggled – she knew now – whereas she had Zehra all to herself, for a while. Zehra was exactly what she needed, even though she couldn't have imagined her before she came along. What had Zehra imagined? Being single at the age she was then, she'd faced up to the fact she would never have kids, so she'd decided to foster, and she was too old for babies. School hours suited her work life and so Tesya was the first teenager she took on.

Almost there, past a few more privet hedges, recycling bins and garden walls, protecting toy-scattered tiny pockets of lawn. Who'll be there? Zehra's often got one of her kids over – after Tesya, there was one after the other. Now they're all grown up, they wend their way back, just like people must do with mums and dads.

Past the front gate, there's a newish mountain bike propped up against the hedge shared with next door. One of the boys must have popped in, or perhaps Zehra has a new kid now – she's not spoken to her for a few weeks. There's Zehra's herb garden, a series of pots of different sizes, overgrown with fronds trailing down onto the path. She bends down and rubs a sage leaf between her fingers, then, standing up, smells a reminder of Zehra's Sunday roast. She rings the bell.

Zehra's always in round about five, the PM programme playing on Radio 4, a black coffee going cold on the kitchen table as she chops vegetables for dinner, diced onions sizzling for a sauce.

Through the opaque glass door, there she is, coming towards her along the hallway, and now the door's opening –

'Darling, come in. What a lovely surprise.'

Zehra hugs her; she's wearing her citrus-scented perfume.

They move apart and she follows Zehra into the hall. There's jazz music coming from the kitchen.

'You've come straight from work? You are settling in OK this time?'

'Yes. Feels like it's going to be a really friendly place to work.' She takes off her coat and hangs it up. There's a biker jacket flung over the next hook. She drops her work-bag on the floor and eases off her shoes, leaving them next to the overflowing shoe rack – Zehra's shoe habit mingled with various teenagers' trainers she'll not throw out until the owner reclaims them.

Their bare feet are next to each other; Zehra's not rushing back to stir something on the stove – not that she can smell cooking.

She stands up.

Zehra smiles. 'I'm so glad it's working out. And it means I'll see more of you now? Come on.'

She follows her towards the kitchen, and the music. There's the sound of a cork popping. She's interrupting something – 'Sorry, you've got someone here, I should have called –'

Zehra stops, facing her. 'It's fine. I've got a new friend here and that means it's a good time for you to meet him.'

She opens the door.

A slim man, dressed in sleek black jeans and a pristine white t-shirt – as though they're on a date – stands next to the kitchen table, an open bottle of red in his hands.

'Tesya, meet Hamid.'

'I've heard much about you, Tesya, so pleased to meet you' – he speaks softly, and with a slight Middle Eastern accent, like some of Zehra's other friends – 'I'll get you a glass.'

He puts the bottle down on the table next to two glasses and takes another glass from the cabinet behind him – he knows where they're kept – and hands it to her.

'Thanks.'

There's a moment of silence. Zehra gestures for her to sit, and then sits down next to her.

Hamid pours the wine then sits opposite – though it's obvious they were sitting side by side earlier as Zehra reaches across the table for her open iPad.

Things start to feel more normal as Zehra updates her on the business: she's opened another branch of the restaurant, appointed some new staff, including an 'inspiring' chef. 'And' – Zehra turns the iPad towards her, so she can see too – 'look, our new revamped website.'

The screen shows her website's menu page: the usual Middle Eastern fusion items, but the design has changed. What used to be bazaar-like, jam-packed with colourful photos of dishes, is now minimalist with sparse text, listing just a few signature dishes and drinks, with some lovely, almost abstract images: pools of glimmering liquid, scattered herbs and powdered spices on the restaurant's beautiful jewel-coloured glassware. She scrolls: it's a work of art.

'It's the best you've had, gorgeous design.'

She smiles. 'Yes, it is, isn't it?'

Hamid nods and smiles too, but doesn't say anything. Zehra looks at him. Tesya looks away, outside. It's dark; in the reflection three people sit at a table lit by the overhead light. How did they meet? The reflection blurs: Hamid reaching behind him, picking something up from the kitchen counter. He places a terracotta dish of olives between them. A mobile buzzes the other side of the room, where there's a soft leather man bag on the floor.

Hamid checks his phone, then looks up. 'Work. Might be an emergency job.' He goes out to the hall.

Zehra changes the subject to Tesya. 'So, tell me about your new job?' – but Tesya asks, 'Emergency?'

'Don't worry, he's got a dry sense of humour. He's not a doctor but a graphic designer.'

She can't stop herself. 'Is that how you met – the new design?'

Zehra smiles. 'Sort of – I met him at a friend's birthday do a few months ago. We hit it off, and we've been spending time, dinner at our mutual friend's place, drinks, theatre, a jazz club.' She gestures to the radio playing in the background. 'And, yes, that's Hamid's work.' She nods towards the iPad, then looks at her. 'Tesya, I was going to tell you when you were next –'

The door opens, Hamid comes in. 'Just next week's schedule.'

Zehra gets up and says to him, 'Oh good. Shall we make dinner?'

Shall we … like they're living together? She's suddenly terribly hot and needs fresh air. She puts her empty glass down and then pushes it away from the edge of the table – not wanting to accidentally break it as she stands up.

Zehra turns to her. 'You are staying, aren't you?'

'Thanks, but I have so much work.' Then, to Hamid, 'Great to meet you.'

He answers, 'Likewise,' as Zehra cuts in, 'Are you sure? It'll be something quick, darling – save you from cooking?'

She wants to go, and at the same time wants to be with Zehra, but not like this, not with the two of them – not yet. 'Next time.'

Behind her Hamid moves around the kitchen counter, like he'll make a start on the cooking, but Zehra's still looking at her. 'Come then, I'll see you out.'

In the corridor she puts on her outer layers and picks up her bag, while Zehra's leaned against the wall, quiet – then in the doorway, she hugs her, whispering, 'Don't worry, this doesn't change anything. I love you, darling. I'll call you tomorrow.'

'I love you too.'

She stays in the doorway waving, and from the other side of the garden gate Tesya waves too, then she's walking fast and within minutes she's on the Tube home.

*

She rarely drinks coffee in the evening, and she knows she won't sleep, but she's fuzzy from the wine, Hamid refilling their glasses before they'd finished the first. She should have asked him about himself. Now she feels mean at leaving so soon. Especially as in the little time she was there she'd picked up that he seemed such a sensitive artistic new man – perfect for Zehra.

Zehra: the only constant adult in her life, since her teenage years. She deserves to be with someone – but will they want to live together, he move in with her, or she with him, or they might get somewhere together? Would she, her feminist mother figure, marry? All the conjugations of relationships –

Though sadly not hers …

She gets out her phone: nothing. She remembers a photo of Holly's happy family life, her twins playing on swings at the end of a long idyllic garden. She swipes to her gallery and scrolls down through recent photos, then remembers Holly showing it to her on her phone. She hasn't got a photo of her, only the profile one – one time she was about to snap her picture, Holly said, 'Don't,' putting her hands over her face. 'I hate how I look in photos.'

She has so many photos of Zehra, and Jazz, and other friends, besides selfies, and lots of cultural images – images to upload to Twitter, for work social media. Here's a weird one from the other week in the pub after Sadler's Wells. She'd meant to photograph the ballet programme, but someone must have knocked her arm so the programme is almost out of frame, it's mostly the road, car tyres and a blur of bike wheels cycling away. She scrolls until she finds the last one of Zehra. On her birthday, in the restaurant, blowing out the candles on her birthday cake. What did she wish for? She wants Zehra to be happy, with someone –

But she doesn't want to lose her – she knows she's being ridiculous, and if Jazz could hear her thoughts she'd tell her to grow up, that Zehra deserves a life and a lover, after the past couple of decades looking after kids on her own. Perhaps Jazz would understand though in a way: that reflex reaction to different types of loss, even potential withdrawing from friendship. When she'd told her about meeting Aisha – prematurely, as it turned out, given what happened – Jazz went quiet, and changed the subject. That evening she drank too much, they both had: by the end of the evening there was a collection of empty glasses on the table between them. Just like when Aisha left and Jazz picked up the pieces, and they'd had drink after drink sitting side by side, leaving a line of empties on that Brighton bar. The relief of friendship, unconditional love, like Zehra's.

She pours the rest of the coffee into her cup.

Zehra had taught her to make coffee the Turkish way. After they'd drunk the sweet darkness, they would examine what was left – Zehra would tell fortunes from the strange shapes in the sediment at the bottom of the little cups. Never clichés, no tall dark handsome man, but sweet things: a stray cat will appear in the garden wanting milk, or a rainbow will appear after it's been raining; things that would happen naturally at some point. Was Hamid the man she fantasized about in the future, when she'd stare into the cup and momentarily forget Tesya was there?

She stretches for her phone and texts her. 'Lovely to meet Hamid. See you soon X'.

Zehra texts straight back. 'How's Sunday lunch in a few weeks, some of the others should be coming? XXX'.

She imagines them all sitting around the extended dining table, her waifs and strays and friends, like at Christmas – except with Hamid sitting at the head of the table. She gets up and puts the cup in the sink then pours a glass of red, even though it won't help, not later when she needs to sleep, and not in the morning when she has to go to work – but at least after a few minutes she's texting back 'Yes' to Zehra, when there's an incoming call: Holly. By the time she answers it's engaged, it's gone to voicemail – though there's no message, just the sound of her hanging up. She calls back, but it goes straight to Holly's voicemail – she's calling someone else, or switched off for the night. It's late; she might be in bed. There's the unfinished reply to Zehra; to the 'Yes' she adds 'I'd love that X' and presses send.

Then there's silence. She picks up her wine glass then thinks again and puts it down; it's not helping. Her stomach rumbles; ages since lunch, far too late for dinner. She faces the too-bright lights of the kitchen and turns on the tap, pouring away the wine – there's a flush of blood-like red circling the drain, then it becomes transparent, just water. That red swirling image stays in her mind, the way the colour red does, how it flows and clots, like blood. She picks up the coffee cup and scrubs at the stained inside until it's clean again. Like after the coffee stain on her office door was cleaned away, that first day at the New Build; like nothing had happened. Just a splash, wiped clean away – that word: just. How it cropped up in people's comments:

'It was obviously just an accident. You know academics, clumsy bunch.'

Accidents, and other excuses –

She puts the bottle of wine back in the cupboard, and then there's a sticky reddish stain on her fingers, red for emergency.

Hamid's calm tone, 'Work. Might be an emergency' – and Zehra saying something about 'Hamid's sense of humour'. How is emergency funny? And how has Zehra got to know Hamid so quickly?

Suddenly her heart beats faster.

She goes back to her phone, types a brief email to Jo, then presses send. Next week – that's it, she has to go. Can't go on like this.

She makes toast, then slathers it with butter and Marmite: calcium, vitamin B, iron. Zehra explaining the nervous system, how what we eat and drink affects our moods, our health; what she remembers when it's too late in the day, but still, she's trying.

No one teaches you how to deal with difficult unimaginable things. People want you to brush those aside, wash them away down a drain hole and then cover it with a plug, pretending it's not happened – but horrible things have a habit of gurgling back up again.

Once you've come close to evil, it's always there and you can't escape it. It lurks in your mind, and, like an infection, it spreads. It's worse after drinking: for a while you forget, but when the wine wears off it returns; it's been there all the time. Like a red wine stain on a white shirt, even if you've doused it with salt immediately, there's always a shadow, the darkness omnipresent even in the light of day.

AUTHOR'S NOTE

Funny how I've created this character Zehra, inspired by women who've supported me over the years, people I've trusted. Besides a perfect role model and mother figure in Zehra, my imagination has given Tesya a supportive friend in Jazz – countering other characters.

It's classic story theory too: the protagonist meeting friends and enemies in the ups and downs of a narrative arc, building suspense so the audience worry about what might befall the character they care about but at the same time leaving the chance of hope for a positive ending. That's so not my experience. In real life, friends and enemies don't crop up at regular intervals, fitting into the ninety minutes of a Hollywood screenplay or the couple of hundred pages of a genre novel. At difficult times life's more like a depressing modernist novel: the trauma goes on and on, getting worse, like it's never going to be over. My absolute fear has always been that the ending may be even worse than the present.

5

SHADOWS

AUTHOR'S NOTE

Although I try to be optimistic, I should be pessimistic – my life experience has shown me many people have a shadow side, not always something bad, or criminal, but a characteristic that might be difficult for others. Mine is I don't deal well with conflict; I shy away from it. Friends notice it when they see me avoiding facing the shadow side of people I like, not wanting to argue – particularly white acquaintances, when I can tell they're about to reveal their racism but they don't know that's what it is. Like recently I've often been with someone chatting about the news when they start to say something about Diane Abbott, the long-standing black female London MP:

'It's how she talks, strident and angry, her voice grates –'

I'll say, 'I really like Diane. Actually I volunteered on her leadership campaign a few years back.'

There's always a pause. The other person looks away, then remembers something on an unrelated matter. Moving safely on to another topic, we avoid the conflict of me naming what it's really about, misogynoir: their inability to see a woman of colour in that position.

Sometimes the other person doesn't listen to what I said, and replies, 'But can't you hear it too?'

Then I say, 'No. Can we change the subject, perhaps we need to agree to disagree?' I can't face a friend not backing down, and refusing to see how racist their view is. Afterwards I feel the unsatisfactory nature of the exchange – keeping the friend or acquaintance's views in the shadows to keep the peace, while hoping the brief disagreement might help change their opinions.

The problem is, once you've seen movement in the shadows, you can't stop seeing it. But white people don't like having their racism pointed out.

Even though it's uncomfortable, I try to confront racism, not shy away from it, even if it means losing a friend. But that's it: what I'm avoiding is facing even the smallest possible common ground between those I like and someone who hated me, hiding in the shadows.

LESSON FIVE

'When you want to surprise someone, do it when they're least likely to be thinking of you. That's going to be when they're busy doing something everyday, so surveillance of the target is important to prepare for when to make your move. Late afternoon is good at this time of year, when dusk turns to night. Hide in the shadows of buildings, or trees, but be aware of your own shadow, don't give yourself away. Once you have an idea of where they'll be, it's time to reveal yourself when they're on auto, doing routine activities, and least aware of others around them.'

Time to stop. The backdrop works: the shelf above the dashboard, box of tissues, tin of boiled sweets, an old road map; could be anyone's car.

Time to go. Key in the ignition; ease out into the traffic. Cruise. Don't want to be too early, and get spotted.

NOW

On the train she reads over next week's lecture, almost forgetting where she's going, until she looks up. There's the greenish-brown blur of fields and isolated buildings.

She's such a classic ethnic minority Londoner, hardly ever visiting anywhere in the UK, except for work – or Brighton: London-by-Sea. Only with Zehra has she visited other places, where her friends have moved once they've had kids and needed space: Totnes or Hebden Bridge; friendly alternative places with vegetarian cafés, gastro-pubs – and gay culture. If she ever has kids perhaps she might move, somewhere safe to be who you are – not that there are many places like that. No wonder Holly's so closeted, wherever she is; somewhere in all these miles of fields and so few houses. In such isolation, how would you know who's out to get you for who you are? You'd have to stay in the closet, until you felt sure it would be safe to come out.

You can't do that with race; you can't hide race in a closet.

So much of being an adult is guarding against other people's preju-dices. Not just race or sexuality – class too. Britain is a minefield. When you're a teenager, before you learn not to reveal yourself is the most delicious time. She remembers the stickiness of melting ice cream, and the rippling summer dresses of girls in the sun: one weekend in Totnes, her first holiday with Zehra staying with out-of-London friends.

Eating ice creams, walking uphill towards the Saturday market, a march went past carrying the words Gay Pride aloft on a banner at the front, while people waving rainbow flags spread across the road onto the pavement. Just ahead, two girls holding hands, their pastel-coloured sundresses mingling in the breeze, stopped and kissed each other on the lips.

Zehra called to get her attention – her ice cream was melting all over her hand. She licked the ice cream from her fingers – and as they walked on, she couldn't help glancing back: the girls' arms were around each other as they danced along in the rainbow-waving march.

What was wonderful was at the top of the hill, where they were to meet with her friends, Zehra said, 'If you want to go look around, you can catch up with us here at the café later' – her way of saying it was all right, whatever it was that drew her to stare at two girls kissing.

Over the tannoy, an announcement warns, 'We will shortly be arriving –' as the train slows entering the commuter town, past executive-style apartment blocks and rows of parked cars.

Outside on the platform, in the place she never wanted to return to, she checks her watch: she's planned it with just enough time to walk to the police station, see Jo and get home before dark. There's something about being outside London when it's evening that feels darker than the city: the unleashed sounds of young men at pub closing, when you're walking home alone; being aware of her skin colour and being a woman in a way she rarely feels in London. Perhaps it's just here, where she was unlucky – she walks fast along the dual carriageway, then up the road to the bulky outline of the police station ahead.

Surely now's her time for luck – yes, the miracle of meeting Holly, and the new Red Brick job. Everything's better since she left – but now she's back, pushing open the heavy door to the police station. Almost at the high counter, someone barges past, hands bloodied, needing more urgent attention. She steps back. There's a trail of blood on the floor. Oh god. That takes her back.

THEN

Once her name card was reprinted and replaced, and the door cleaned, Angela from Human Resources had been the first to brush off the coffee incident with, 'Accidents happen. Carrying books and a flimsy takeout coffee – none of us have enough hands.'

Tesya tried to push it to the back of her mind. Most of the time she was at her desk, head down, preparing for the semester, but when she logged off and headed out of her office, closing the door, she'd remember. Then she'd walk back to her digs, tired before she'd even started the trudge uphill in the growing darkness.

Soon it was the first day of the autumn semester, with student inductions and tutorial sessions – and when the day was almost over, the faculty welcome drinks.

The lift doors opened onto the foyer that reminded her of an airport waiting area, with its corporate reception counter, glass walls and plastic seating. The reception was in full flow, the conversation amplified by the glass surfaces. The staff mingled, drinking wine from plastic cups.

There was no one she recognized, but by the drinks table she got talking to someone who poured her a drink, and then forgot how nervous she'd felt on her way down.

When the wine was running out and people were trickling away, Alice came over. She'd met her earlier, when she'd seemed rather standoffish over a mix-up – they had both been put down for the same induction-day tutorial room. Tesya had ended up sorting it, taking her students off with her to find another room. Now Alice chatted to Tesya as if she'd known her for ages.

Alice's hair was clearly dyed black, like her long-sleeved midi dress, contrasting with her pale petite face – a rather Goth look. As she spoke it was obvious her full make up had taken time and was carefully and freshly applied – whereas most of the other women she'd spoken to looked like they'd come straight from their desks with the remnants of anything they'd put on earlier, a stain of lipstick, a smudge of eyeliner. Like a delicate china doll, Alice had graduated coloured shadow on her eyelids, and even her lipstick was framed with lip liner. It was difficult to concentrate on what she was saying; she spoke fast and quietly. There was no one near, but Alice lowered her voice so Tesya leaned closer to hear.

Alice was saying, 'That guy in the corner, teaches the contemporary literature module. Wears a wedding ring, often works late in his office – with the door locked – he's so very helpful to female students who get incredibly high marks …'

He was in the shadows. All she could make out was the top of a white balding head above a dark suit. He was talking to a young white woman wearing a short skirt and high heels, and what looked like bare legs – which made her feel cold.

It was getting late to walk home. Alice was further up the table, checking bottles for more wine.

She glanced back to the corner. The guy was leaving, a hand in the small of the back of the young woman, ushering her into the lift. Alice was right. She'd heard similar stories elsewhere; there were always seedy older male lecturers taking advantage of female students, and students who might end up with higher marks. That was horrible, but nothing new. Difficult to prove too: both sides had too much to lose – wives or marks.

One of the cleaners pushed his trolley past her. Time to go. 'I'm heading off, Alice, see you around.'

'You live in town, right? I can give you a lift, meet you by the main door in five minutes?'

Upstairs she picked up her bag and then went downstairs again to the ground floor. Alice wasn't around yet, and everyone else had vanished.

She wandered over to the display area, where a series of large photos were mounted on free-standing boards. The photos had been taken that morning during induction: informal shots of staff chatting with students, more formal ones of students listening to the Head of Faculty doing the welcome talk, and other staff introducing their modules in seminar rooms.

Behind her, down the corridor, a door slammed. Turning, she glimpsed a photo further down the display boards – taken when she was talking to students. Like right now, there she was wearing her purple top and black skirt, the matching jacket thrown over a chair behind her – but there were what looked like knife marks stabbed across her face, her hands and her legs.

She stared –

'Tesya,' Alice, behind her. 'I know, it's awful. Sorry, I should have stayed to warn you, but as soon as I saw it I went to get Rob.'

'Rob?'

'Head of Faculty.'

Behind Alice, Rob walked towards them into the foyer.

'It's dreadful, Tesya. I'll take this down myself now.' He was unpinning the photo from the display. 'Let's chat tomorrow? Have to dash now, pick my wife up from the station.' He wedged the photo between some papers and snapped his briefcase shut. He looked at her. 'It'll be some silly student thing, too much freshers' fair cheap alcohol.' Putting a hand on her shoulder, he said, 'Go home and put your feet up. It's been a long day.' Then he walked away; the main exit door clicked shut behind him.

There were holes on the board where the drawing pins had been. The next photo was of the guy Alice had talked about earlier, talking to a group of young women.

Alice was saying, 'Let's go, Tesya. I'll take you home.'

'I'm coming.' She almost tripped over her bag – she must have dropped it with the shock of the photo – she picked it up, then, stepping away, she slipped on something. She moved her foot. There was a reddish smear. She bent down. Blood?

Alice was calling from the door, 'Tesya, what is it?'

There was something at the corner of her eye, something else red, beneath the display board. She peered closer. Just a sachet of ketchup, oozing the red stuff – someone must have walked on it, spread it around. Not blood.

She stood, her heart beating fast; she needed to get out, get home. Thank goodness Alice was waiting for her, she wasn't alone.

'Coming, Alice, thank you.'

NOW

Jo's back in uniform, facing the computer in the interview room, with one hand on the case file, the other on the mouse. The room is bare apart from a box of tissues, like a therapy room – fitting, as today feels like therapy, going over what's brought her here.

Jo's been through the initial notes, checking again why she'd not reported it to the police immediately, which was tangled up with when she finally had reported it: Rob's 'Chat tomorrow' hadn't happened. When she'd emailed his secretary to find out what time to go to his office, she'd snapped back an Outlook Calendar request for a week later.

And a week later she'd asked him, 'What are you going to do about it?'

He replied, 'Actually, Tesya, there isn't anything we can do –'

'But it's racist or sexist –'

'No, I wouldn't call it that. We can't possibly guess the intention, if indeed there was one. It was probably quite random.'

His fingers rested on the photo. He moved it aside, revealing two more photos underneath. He pushed them towards her.

Less obvious than the first photo, in these she was one among other lecturers and students. But in these too there were slashes and holes in the photographic paper, like her face and parts of her body had been stabbed with a knife – mutilated.

She pushed the photos back towards him. 'Why did no one tell me about these?'

'The cleaner found them, on the other side of the display boards.' He stacked the photos and slipped them inside a desk drawer. 'Tesya, I know this probably doesn't help, but these silly things happen to everyone –'

'Everyone?'

'Happened to my staff photo, early in my career at another university. We were all put on display – so to speak – in the entrance, next to the porter's office. One day, someone blacked out my eyes with felt-tip pen. I was most surprised when I first spotted it: all the students came from public school. Though in those days anyone could walk into universities before CCTV, it could have been a tourist or vagrant. I forgot about it, until now. The point is, there are some things we'll never know, and the world is full of funny people, so silly to waste time wondering, isn't it?'

He didn't mean funny ha-ha, and it was a rhetorical question; she stayed silent.

His eyes flicked sideways at an A4 desk diary as his hands tightened his navy tie. He said, 'You must put this aside; rise above it.' Standing, he ushered her out of his office and closed the door – though not before she heard him telling his secretary to 'File this away' – shoving her out of sight, like the photos in his desk drawer.

Jo was saying, 'So you retrospectively reported the coffee incident when you came in to report what we have logged as the first incident, what you called the "mutilated photo".'

'Photos.'

'Yes, photos.' Jo checks the text, then turns to face her again. 'Sorry, but I have to ask you again: why did you say the photos were "mutilated"?'

Does mutilate mean blood? 'It was the first word that came to me.'

'I know this is difficult, but –'

'My face, eyes, mouth, hands, legs – every part of me that wasn't clothed was stabbed at with a knife. Like whoever did it wants to do that to me, mutilate me. I know there was no blood, it was just the stabbing of photographs, but –' and then she's crying.

'Tesya, sorry – here.' Jo passes her the tissues. 'I shouldn't have –'

'No, sorry, I haven't talked about it for ages.' She dries her eyes.

Jo goes out and brings in a cup of tea.

'Thanks, Jo.'

'Take your time, no rush.'

They continue.

'The next item on the log is a call with the university's Human Resources. Angela promised to send over the CCTV footage – even though she said it wasn't worth it, unfortunately. It turned out the cameras didn't cover the area of the foyer where the display was hung. And there hadn't been any movement triggering CCTV recording of the rest of the foyer area once the reception emptied out – nothing until your colleague, and then you, appeared on it later.'

She remembers that. At lunchtime, inside the tiny office of the Facilities guy – what was his name, Alan or – Andy? In the semi-darkness, Angela perched on the windowsill behind her, blocking the light. A bank of blank computer screens faced them across the desk. Andy's tattooed white arms were the only movement, leaning forward, pressing buttons on his keyboard, until on the largest monitor a split screen appeared. He sat back and opened his lunch box, and the smelliness of egg and tuna sandwiches filled the room – she wanted to open a window, get some fresh air, but she couldn't take her eyes off the screen.

One camera shot showed the black-and-white static image of the internal area around the main entrance door. The other one showed the opposite side of the foyer, where the long reception desk counter was placed in front of the glass windows through to Admin, with the lift doors to one side.

Andy took his time, taking a bite out of his sandwich, but then he pressed a button – and on the screen Alice walked out of the lift, past the reception desk and went out of frame. After a short time, she came back, walking swiftly off the way she came – when she went to get Rob.

Jo continues, 'Both the display area and the corridor entrance aren't covered by the cameras; someone could get into the foyer to access the display, and get out too, without being recorded.' She looks up. 'That's when you contacted us, right after you'd seen the CCTV footage?'

'Yes, I asked Angela what they were going to do.'

Walking back from Facilities, to the Arts building, Angela had said, 'There's nothing we can do. No CCTV, nothing to link it to anyone.'

She couldn't get it out of her mind: those images. 'But –'

'It's horrible, I know, but we'll never find out who damaged the –'

She stopped Angela. 'Damaged? It's like the photos are mutilated. It's not accidental. Someone meant to do it.'

'I'm on your side, you know? Some advice, Tesya: drop it. There's no way we'll ever get to the bottom of it. Get on with your job – you've just started here. Forget it – unless anything else has happened you've not told me about?'

After the coffee incident the week before, Angela had said, 'An accident, pure and simple.'

She wondered what Angela would have said if it had happened to her. They had things in common: both ethnic minority women – although Angela in her chic grey suit and high heels looked more corporate, and part of the machinery of the university. Perhaps horrible things don't happen to people like Angela?

Angela placed a hand on her arm. 'Next time you and I meet up, I hope it will be about a promotion. You're talented, Tesya. We were really happy to appoint you, you know?' Then she was swiping her card to open the door, and before she'd moved to follow her, Angela disappeared and the door clicked shut. Through the opaque glass Angela's shadow merged with all the other shadows, mobile and static, the humans and the inhuman – all the mechanics and masonry upholding the institution.

Angela meant well. She would try to focus on her work. Upstairs though, when she opened her office door, the computer screen stared blankly back, like the absent footage of whoever did it. She couldn't get it out of her mind that afternoon. Difficult to get any work done, eventually she gave up trying. She left early, avoiding eye contact with other staff in the corridor, between lecture rooms and their offices, carrying on with their work.

Outside the sun glared down, and students were sunning themselves on the well-kept lawns between buildings. She walked briskly past, feeling their stares. At the edge of campus, where the security guards manned the car park and the perimeter fence, she stopped. She couldn't face walking uphill. Or standing in line at the bus stop. She called a cab.

Finally, in the tiny white box of her digs, she collapsed on the sofa with a cup of tea. After a while in the quiet, she could think clearly again. She called Jazz.

Jazz said simply, 'Oh Tesya, it's a hate crime. Call the police.'

An hour or so later, Jo's finished tracking through all the incidents that happened over the year before she eventually quit her job – after the last one, the worst one, the one she never wants to go over again.

Drained, she looks outside. Through the frosted windows, in the dimming light, a street light switches on.

Jo swivels from the screen to face her. 'We've recorded the series of incidents as serious racially aggravated harassment. The question remains: is there anything you can remember now, anything odd perhaps that you haven't mentioned before, however small?'

'Nothing I haven't already told you.'

'Have a think.' She rests her hand on the file. 'Any odd emails, messages, or difficult relationships with staff or students?'

She wishes there was something she could remember. Through the frosted windows, the shadows of people on the pavement move in and out of frame, like her former colleagues and herself on the CCTV screens in the Facilities guy's office. Alice walking one way, then back the other way – off-screen.

She turns to Jo. 'It's not really odd, but ... there was Alice – the lecturer who reported the photo incident to our Head of Faculty?'

'Alice?' Jo types a few letters, and a highlight appears on the screen. 'Oh yes?'

'She was really nice that evening. Gave me a lift home. And afterwards she'd call round to my office, checking I was OK, suggesting coffee or lunch. We often did that, the first semester ... but it was odd, it quickly became almost too often.'

Alice, poking her head around the door, would say, 'Coffee?' in her forlorn voice. If she didn't get up, Alice would step into the room, her long black skirts wafting around her – although petite, her presence dominated the office, like her words. If she didn't stop what she was doing, Alice would add, 'Come on, Tesya,' as though she was annoyed with her.

So she'd lock her computer in the middle of a sentence, guilty about abandoning her work, guilty about not wanting to stop and smile, but she would, and say, 'Coffee would be lovely.'

She must have gone silent; Jo prompts with, 'Are you saying she was over-friendly that first semester?'

It was delicate. 'It's probably nothing, but one moment she was being supportive because of what had happened, and suggesting drinks after work, or the cinema. I always said no; a new job, I was busy. It was like she was desperately trying to be my friend, or perhaps more – I mean, it was obvious from the Faculty website, my area of performance research, that I'm gay –'

'Is she?'

'No, she's got a live-in boyfriend.'

'Did you ever meet them? Go to her home?'

'No.'

'OK. You were saying something about her being odd?'

'That first semester, in the evening at home, I'd be chilling out, switching off from work – and she'd often ring. It was irritating – it wasn't like it was a potential new friendship, or even a relationship ... if she was attracted to me, I mean. My friend Jazz teased me about it one weekend, when she was over from London – Alice had been ridiculous that day. Jazz said something about her being obsessed with me, or –'

'Jazz, who you were with at the club?'

'Yes.'

'Go on.'

'Apart from our workplace, we had nothing in common. Basically Alice was time-consuming, and I was trying to settle in.' Alice at the end of the line was like she was inside her flat. 'Whatever inane thing she was talking about, I'd zone out – then it would all come back in an instant: the coffee incident, the mutilated photos, everything –'

'Because –'

'I associated her with work, and what had happened – not because I think it was her.' Hot, clothes sticking to her in the stuffy interview room, she takes off her sweatshirt and sits back exhausted. 'But she changed anyway, after I said something to her. It was a Friday, when most of us worked from home on our research. I'd tried to ignore her ringing, and missed calls, so I switched my phone off – I had a deadline for a conference paper or something. When I turned my phone on, there were so many message notifications from her I was worried something awful had happened. I called her back. She said she'd called so often because I hadn't answered. It was ridiculous.' Panicky, hoping not to get sucked into a long phone conversation, irritated by Alice's quiet whine; she felt trapped. That was it – 'I felt trapped. It's ridiculous, just a phone call, another woman – but I hardly knew her.'

'It sounds awful. How did you handle her?'

'I tried to be caring, but I was really annoyed. Because of turning my phone off, I'd missed a message from Jazz – she was coming for the weekend, and had caught the earlier train. Jazz called again, and I went out to meet her halfway – but what I mean is, Alice was interrupting my social life. Sorry, it sounds like I'm exaggerating, but what with the incidents, I really needed time away from work and everything about it – to relax with my real friends.'

'Don't worry; I get that. What did you say to her?'

'Just to ease off a bit, and I'd see her at work the following week. She tried to stop me from hanging up, arguing how she was just trying to help. I said, "Alice, I have to put the phone down now and go and meet a friend," and so I did.'

Did she slam the phone down? No. Might it have felt like that to Alice?

'You look puzzled?'

'Yes, because the following Monday she walked straight past me in the corridor, no eye contact, nothing. She stopped calling, which was great. Then it was Christmas, and when the next semester came, she was the same – the silent treatment – then that semester went so quickly, and it was the Final Examination Board.'

She remembers finding where she was supposed to sit at the long table, papers lined up for each member of staff – then seated, facing the other end of the table, where Alice sat, still in black despite the heat. Her eyes stared back with almost no recognition – just a flicker, like she saw her but was trying not to – then her black-lacquered white fingers wrote a few words on a notepad, tore off the page and slipped it towards someone next to her.

'That whole year she was the closest I got to anyone. When she was gone I was alone, dealing with the stress, week after week of – well, you know.'

'Yes, it was almost every week, mostly Mondays – Sunday nights must have been stressful for you, when you had no one to turn to at work.'

'I'd hardly sleep, wondering what I might face the next day.'

That movement – the folded white note. What had she written, something nasty – about her? It doesn't matter now. It was soon afterwards she wrote her own note of resignation, after that last awful –

Jo prompts, 'It's odd, isn't it, she was the first to "see" the photo incident, but no one else was around?'

The day of the photo incident, Alice drove her home afterwards, her carefully manicured hands on the wheel; she'd been so caring – 'No, I'm sure it wasn't her.'

Alice's office was filled with books in alphabetical and politically correct order, from Affect and Critical Race Theorists, to Feminism and the Post-structuralists – from Ahmed to Žižek. Academics are voracious readers – including readers of people. The Humanities are all about appearance and reality: how people and societies behave. It's also how academia works: who you know counts for far more than what you know. She wasn't useful for Alice, being too new.

'No.' She pauses, trying to make sense of it. 'Academics are like that, especially if they're ambitious, interested in you one moment, then they're on to someone more useful. Alice and I taught on different days: that's why we hardly saw each other that second semester.'

'That first semester, her temporary befriending of you could have been good cover –' Jo pauses, then more slowly, 'You don't think she was stalking you?'

'Stalking?'

'Someone being like that, making you feel uncomfortable, it's stalking; it's a criminal offence.'

'No, but …'

When she had met Jazz halfway, the Friday of that awful phone call, she'd told her what had happened with Alice that day. They had been wandering around the one and only department store; she still needed to get more smart casual clothes for work. She was searching for her size along a rail of separates, when Jazz reminded her, 'Remember how we had our name labels sewn into the necks and waistbands of all our clothes?'

'Oh yes. And what about waiting for our key workers on a Friday, for those measly clothing-allowance vouchers that never covered anything we actually wanted?' Finding her size, she held the shirt against her, for Jazz's approval – 'What do you think?' – when she spotted Alice across the floor. She whispered, 'God, that's her,' and ducked behind a display cabinet, Jazz whispering, 'Who on earth are you hiding from?'

'The Goth.'

'Where?'

When the coast was clear, she went to pay, and then in front of her in the queue she found the Goth-haired woman she'd glimpsed – and she wasn't Alice.

As they were going down the escalator, she turned to Jazz. 'It wasn't her at all. Am I getting paranoid?'

Jazz said, 'Definitely time to talk about whatever's going on, and for a drink. Although I'm guessing there are no gay bars round here.'

The first place they came across, a chain bar, could have been anywhere, which was comforting in a way. With a bottle between them, Jazz spelled out exactly what she thought about Alice. 'Look, she's odd: she's got a boyfriend, and calls you all the time. You're the new single woman, captive at work, and obviously lesbian? Stop being so nice about her, feeling guilty, because let's face it, she might be behind all these horrible "incidents".'

Jazz was right about her own anxious guilty feelings, but she was wrong about Alice.

To Jo now – 'No, Alice had nothing to do with it, and anyway, she backed off after that phone call.'

'People can take a plea to stop as encouragement: they see any communication with them as showing an interest: what they want. So they change tack –'

'You mean giving me the cold shoulder – if that was what she was doing?'

'Yes.'

'I think she was just lonely, and perhaps I upset her. Now I feel sorry for her.' And perhaps – like Alice's dyed hair wasn't really black – having a boyfriend didn't mean she was totally straight; Jazz might have been right about that.

Jo makes a note then looks up. 'OK, let's move on. What about where you're teaching now? Anything difficult happened there?'

'It's really friendly. I feel at home in my new job.'

'Good to hear.' There's the alert sound of an Outlook Calendar reminder. 'I know it's awful, not knowing, but unfortunately these cases take time. You have people looking out for you, don't you?'

'Yes, don't worry.' She stands up.

Jo gets up too. 'Ring me if anything comes back to you?'

'Yes, will do. And thank you.'

'I know it's difficult, going back over things, but sometimes that's what triggers memories?'

'Yes –'

The phone on her desk rings.

'That'll be reception wanting to buzz in my next meeting.'

Outside through the gloomy darkness, she walks towards the station in and out of pools of light from lamp posts and the brightly lit entrances of buildings along the pavement. She's exhausted, going back over the past. Oh to be home.

Round the corner, on the main road the other side there are the entrance gates to a school, and nearby the glow of a chip shop, and a newsagent's shopfront with the day's papers bundled up in a rack outside. A couple of kids dash along the pavement into the shop.

Hungry, she craves something sweet or savoury, crisps or chocolate, familiar tastes. She checks her watch – there's time. She waits on the kerb, the traffic is noisily head-to-tail – she pulls her scarf up over her nose and mouth against the fumes.

Across the road, the kids come out of the shop, opening bags of sweets – then suddenly they're screaming with excitement, sweets scattering all over the pavement, as they run towards a man walking towards them. Now they're all hugging. A dad and his kids; a cute family scene –

A car draws up, parks awkwardly, leaving a line of beeping cars – a woman dashes out –

Gosh, she lunges into the man, pushing him away from the kids and bundling them into the car. Over her shoulder she shouts back at him – with the beeping cars it's impossible to hear. It happens so fast; now she's in the car, slamming the door and driving off –

And what's funny is how she reminded her of Holly, from the back, all she saw: Holly's red hair. Holly's got two kids too, twins; but they don't have a father.

She can't see the father, not with all the rush-hour vehicles now moving both sides of the dual carriageway. He must have been waiting for the kids to come out of school. They were so pleased to see him – unlike the woman.

There's a gap in the traffic; she crosses. On the other side the pavement is empty, apart from a teenage couple sitting on the bench outside the chippy, an Asian girl and a white boy sharing a bag of chips, their arms around each other, and at their feet the pastel-coloured cellophane-wrapped sweets strewn like confetti at a wedding.

Inside the shop she picks up a bag of crisps and a can of Coke for the journey. At the till there are bags of sweets on special offer, the ones the kids bought and lost – toffees. She prefers soft centres; she picks up a bag and adds them to her purchases.

Outside the young couple have disappeared, but on the pavement the pastel-coloured sweets twinkle under the street light, reminding her of Holly; smudges of her powder or lipstick left on the pillowcases long after she's gone. She looks back the way the car went; it wasn't her, of course. How she wishes she was going to see Holly, and could forget everything for a while in her arms.

She hovers at the side of the road for a chance to cross back to the other side, but there's no gap in the stop-start of traffic. She walks on. Lights go out in office buildings, and shadows merge with other shadows. Someone walks up fast behind her and then overtakes – a man who disappears into the darkness ahead.

Everything's dark now; colour is an optical illusion of light, and darkness its absence. Colours are like feelings, complicated, never straightforward. Black on Jazz always looks smart and modern, but on Alice it felt oppressive and performative; she wasn't a Goth, she just dressed that way to the tips of her nails. Holly's pale shades, from beige to cream, are calming, and her red hair feels soft like silk when it brushes her skin. Whereas red hair on that woman driving away felt angry and manic –

All the things married people must know inside out about each other, after make up is removed, or stubble has grown back by the end of the day. What people really look like, and what they like – like toffees or soft centres – how people are, once you've tasted them, whether they're soft or hard inside. She saw the kids' faces as they ran screeching happily towards their dad – in contrast to their sombre maroon uniforms and the dark blur of the dad's clothing. The woman's bulky coat looked pulled on quickly for the school run – not the sort of classic elegance of Holly's clothes. Why did she remind her of Holly? Her red hair – and because she hardly sees her, the world taunts her in Holly's absence.

That poor man, obviously the estranged father; he must miss his kids, perhaps even the woman – but what was he expecting? How happy the kids were to see him – and how the woman was so the opposite. It's funny how she can't remember much about the man. She's remembered what she liked: the happy kids, she'd have wanted to have been like that at their age; and the red hair of the woman she misses – we see what we desire.

She crosses the road. There are more people this side of the street, all white – like that family. Whiteness is something she's surrounded by, she notices because she's in the minority; it must be different being white, being in the majority – not thinking about skin colour in the same way. Skin colour's only mentioned on the news when a crime suspect is black or Asian, and victims are assumed white, unless mentioned otherwise. Not that that was a crime she witnessed today; there were no victims, just the tabloid cliché of a tug of love over kids – in a white family.

She opens the bag of sweets and swallows one as she walks the last few steps to the station. Under the fluorescent lights, the London platform is packed, a good sign – and now here's the train. Everyone crowds to the edge; she's some way back, but she gets on and others sneak on behind her, then the door slams. The train moves off. Held between sweaty-suited post-work bodies, at least she's out of the clutches of suburban shadows, and the past. Oh for London soon, and the safety and space of the city.

6

BLEMISHES

AUTHOR'S NOTE

Those mutilated photos? That's not fiction.

It was about my body. A mutilated photo is a premonition of what is intended, and the knowledge of that became a fear, rocking me with anxiety. That must have showed, like a blemish or a scar that people don't mention – but you know they see it, like skin colour. Perhaps that's why white people don't know how to respond, instinctively seeing skin colour other than white as a blemish, so they don't talk about it, as they can't reveal that – unless they're making a living out of being racist, like far-right politicians.

My fictional antagonist won't be seen as racist. Racism is something they do, that they get away with, hidden in a supposedly liberal workplace. People there would rarely reveal their racism directly anyway, at least to those of us who are ethnic minority – they would be racist in covert ways, so they don't get caught out.

People slip up though, when they're tired, then they show what they're capable of. Over my many career changes and jobs down the years, white male and female colleagues have shouted at me, or been patronizing or insulting. It's always when we're alone that aggression or condescension erupts in someone's voice, and they slip out of their normally courteous professional façade into a whole other persona. Never when another white person is there, someone they would consider an equal witness, unlike someone like me. Sometimes glimpses of those hidden personas are revealed, from disparaging remarks about diversity initiatives, or Islamophobic or homophobic comments, to inappropriate touching in the workplace. Beneath the multicultural veneer of management speak most workplaces are blemished by classist racist homophobic misogynists, camouflaged by their powerful positions of authority, their beautifully cultured-sounding accents masking ugly views of others.

Someone who sustained a campaign of racial harassment wouldn't let their mask slip at work, but within friendships or relationships – wouldn't they slip up sometimes? It's difficult thinking one step ahead of someone all the time – what criminals and victims do too; we think about each other. Like a writer thinking in the voice of her antagonist, while keeping in mind her protagonist – trying to guard her from harm.

LESSON SIX

'So, to blemishes: not the angry red spots of teenage years, but the psychological equivalent: when people's behaviour reveals what's bubbling under the surface, ready to burst when their guard is down and their perfect image fractures. Today we're going to get closer, more intimate with our prey. Because when people let go, that's when you take your chance.'

That was the thing, shouldn't have let my emotions run wild, but seeing the kids after so long, and her reacting the way she did: what a scene. Why I dashed into the shop to escape the embarrassment. Funny though – if I hadn't, I wouldn't have caught sight of that woman. As I was opening the shop door, its security bell jangling above my head, I'd glanced back to see if the car had gone. The woman was directly across the road, staring at the same car – still manoeuvring out into the traffic – why?

'Can I help you, sir?' The shopkeeper behind the counter was inevitably Asian.

'Just a packet of cigarettes, and, oh yes, there are some other things I should pick up –' I checked through the window again; she wasn't there, or I couldn't see her through the traffic now moving both sides of the dual carriageway.

Those small twenty-four-hour shops, so many curious things besides staple sales of sweets, tea and sliced white. I found the torch and batteries I needed, bizarrely next to the cake colouring and hundreds and thousands, and even jars of curry paste. That took me back.

Round the corner in the side street, I packed my purchases into the boot then walked round to open the car door, when I saw that same woman again. At the end of the street, she looked both ways and then crossed, making her way along the main road, the red of a can of Coke in her hand.

She was about to go out of my frame of vision, it was dusk, and she was wrapped in winter clothes, but even so, she reminded me. Was it her?

Then I thought, what the hell, why not?

Though now on the train, in the smelly atmosphere of commuter sweat and fatty fast food, I'm beginning to wish myself back in my galley having sardines on toast with my feet up and a glass of Merlot. God knows how people put up with this on a daily basis, the crush, the standing and the snorers. No wonder there are so many knocking back cans of alcohol, and some discreet hand-holding too; the perks of the commute.

Where's she got to? She can't have disappeared on a packed train.

NOW

Like thinking of the spelling of a word until it starts to look strange, the problem with thinking too much about anyone is how strange people seem –

She should get some work out of her bag, but she's tired. At least she's found a seat at the far end of the train.

She never saw Alice as a culprit, even though others had. Not just Jazz, but the cleaner who dealt with her office door after yet another incident later that first semester.

It was one of the incidents that shook her the most; it made her angry, not just upset. It was so targeted, angled so precisely on being racist against someone who looks Asian, someone like her. When she remembers that day, she remembers how weird that felt. Unexpected. Even though, when she thought about it, it was the most simple but precise racism against Asians she had ever experienced. That's what racist incidents are: generalized attacks against a whole group, a scattergun approach that will hurt anyone, any individual, yet it still took her by surprise. She hadn't grown up in an Asian household, and, like other people she's sure, it's not like she's walking around thinking about herself as Asian, she's just herself, a human being. But that's how racism, why racism works – racism shows us how we're seen: we're just one of a whole hated group, we're not individuals, or equal humans.

It was still a continuation of the pattern: a Monday morning, and her office door, but –

In the middle of her fear thumping, heart racing, pulse pumping, dry-mouthed breathlessness, she stared at the brown-coloured stuff on the door handle. Was it …?

She withdrew her hand, and clutching her keys, she looked over her shoulder: no one around. Whoever it was had gone, or –

That isolating force of fear, not knowing who or where or when, and what might happen – and why, what did they want, what would they ultimately do? Kill her? Stop –

She switched to automatic, as she'd learned to do, contacted Sebastian, her line manager. A rather suave white man, Seb was by then in charge of logging the incidents that were happening on a weekly basis. She dropped her keys into her bag, and pulled her mobile out to call him.

Soon, in one of his signature well-cut charcoal suits, with a white shirt showing, he appeared at the end of the corridor, walking calmly towards her.

When he was standing next to her, and saw what she was looking at, he tackled it – as he had each time – in an understated way, like she imagines he'd speak to a child.

'Oh, what's that?'

Like he was looking at an insect, or something that he wasn't particularly interested in. Or, to be fair, perhaps he was trying to keep it low-key, to counter how she was –

Her body shaking, her mouth dry – she couldn't answer his question. If she opened her mouth she'd break down. And wasn't it obvious what the dark brown messy smear was, wiped over her name card, across her office door, right down to the door handle she'd almost touched?

Seb took a biro out of his jacket pocket and used it to touch the stuff, then brought it close to his nose and smelled it. 'Oh, curry paste.'

She didn't say anything.

He looked at her. 'Are you OK?'

Obviously she wasn't – how could she be? – but the answer to 'Are you OK?' is some kind of 'Yes', so she nodded reflexively, just wanting it to be over.

He turned away, concentrating on his phone, photographing the door for the Incident Report Form.

She stepped back, and leaned against the wall opposite.

Times she'd experienced curry-related racism as a kid, those easy things people call out and forget in a moment – curry mouth, paki this and that – in the playground, it was always after a high, a good mark in class, praise from a teacher. It was always later when teachers weren't around, or friends. They do it when you're alone.

Like in a workplace when you have a private office along a usually deserted corridor.

Could there be something she'd done – but what, other than just getting on with her job? It wasn't a playground – and yet here she was, an adult lecturing and working with other adults, and it was still happening. Her face burned, like it had when she was a kid; just like her skin colour hasn't changed –

A flash of white light blinded her for a moment, then Seb was putting his phone away, and he glanced at her. He would ask her the same thing he did week after week on a Monday morning, when she'd be on the edge of tears and almost on the verge of walking out.

'Do you want me to delay your lecture; want to sit in your office for a while, get back to normal?'

She stared at the stuff covering her office door, in the angry heat of backed-against-the-wall emotion.

'Tesya, you OK?' He glanced at his watch, then back at her.

He had a lecture starting in a few minutes, like she had, but even so, time is different when you've had a shock – from when you're wondering whether you can fit in a flat white before a lecture on modernism.

She felt like screaming but knew he was trying to be caring, so managed to say, 'Sorry, Seb, thanks, but …'

Down the corridor there was the swish of the lift coming up. They both looked towards the empty space where someone would inevitably appear soon.

'I'd like to try and get on with the day,' she finally answered, not wanting to admit that a few students had complained about her Monday lectures not starting on time last week. She wasn't sure what Seb had said to the students when he'd gone down to delay her lecture the week before, or the week before that, but it was obvious they had no idea what had been happening to her. She hadn't told them either: she couldn't talk about it to students straight afterwards, and later it wasn't appropriate in the midst of lecturing about whatever aspect of performance they were exploring that week – and anyway she was always relieved to be attempting to get on with the day. But if Seb hadn't told them, why hadn't he?

Was it possible Rob had warned him not to worry the students? Of course it would be absolutely nothing to do with the Race Mark Charter the university was aiming for –

She was getting cynical, the longer this stupid time-wasting energy-sapping stuff was going on – perhaps.

Seb said, 'If you're sure?'

She wasn't sure of anything other than that it was going to be difficult to get her mind in gear to give a lecture in a few minutes, but she had to – 'Yes, I'd like to just get on with the day.'

The cleaner appeared, pushing his trolley along the corridor. Sebastian nodded at him, and said to her, 'Have a good day,' then he walked briskly towards the lift.

The cleaner's skin shade was like hers, rather than Seb's, and what sounded like a Brazilian Portuguese accent when he said 'Hello' reminded her of visiting friends near Elephant and Castle in London's Latin American village, hanging out together in one of the tapas bars between there and Stockwell.

He quickly sprayed disinfectant and cleaned the handle first, then started on the door, wiping it in circles. For a moment, the dark paste was smeared even more and it looked worse – just as Alice turned up.

'Oh, Tesya, whatever's happened?'

'Alice, sorry, but I don't have much time, I've got my morning lecture –'

The cleaner said, 'Your key, please, to check inside the lock?'

She handed it to him, and once he opened the door she squeezed past him into her office as he started to dry the wet smear from the door.

'Oh, how awful. How can I help you, Tesya? Tell me.'

Alice. Everything about her suddenly felt really annoying, from her cloying perfume, to the black cloud of her feminine dress lurking beside the cleaner, in his way as he tried to clean the door – and blocking her escape route, to getting on with the day.

'Tesya, whatever you want me to do, let me know?' Alice's voice quivered like she was the wounded one.

She focused on her desk: what did she need?

Hot skin prickling, out of breath, out of words, out of feeling, she grabbed the lecture notes she'd left ready the week before. She breathed in – it wasn't Alice's fault that another sunny morning had been broken as she walked in, key in hand, and found – her eyes welled up, but she had to keep it together, and get rid of Alice –

'Thank you, Alice, I'm fine and I want to get to my lecture on time. Might just make it.'

Someone at the other end of the corridor called out for Alice, 'Do you have a minute?' So she was diverted, reluctantly. She set off, but called back, 'I'll come check on you later. Don't worry, I won't forget you.'

Alone with the cleaner, her shoulders relaxed. He was putting away his cleaning products but stopped with the soiled cloth in his hand and looked down the corridor as Alice walked away.

'If you're finished, I'll lock the door?'

'Yes.' He spoke softly. He looked at her briefly, then back at Alice as she disappeared round the corner, into someone's office.

What was he thinking? What kind of racism had he experienced? It must be worse being in a job like his, compared to hers. She's heard how management and academic staff talk to the cleaners and catering staff. Could there be at least solidarity in numbers, as there were more ethnic minority people in the service jobs than in the academic and administrative ones?

But they all faced racism, in different ways, regardless of class and status; it was just one of those facts of life – or, rather, a fact of ethnic minority citizens' lives.

She didn't even know his name, and yet she instinctively felt closer to him than to Seb, who had always been appropriate, talking of his 'duty of care' – but who had no idea how she was really feeling. How could he? He'd never experience racism, not unless the UK suddenly changed its balance of racial power, and that was not going to happen, especially not in the current anti-immigration anti-multiculturalism climate.

He turned back to her and said, 'Take care of yourself,' like he really meant it, not in that way people do as a matey sign-off. Then he gestured subtly with his hand, holding the dirty cloth, and nodding towards where Alice had disappeared, whispered, 'I've got your back.'

'Thank you,' she replied. She stared where he'd gestured, somewhere beyond that wall where Alice must be; he suspected Alice – but did she?

After that she discovered he had really meant it. Popping his head around the door when he was vacuuming the corridor, Enrico – she discovered his name – would say hello and check on her, and definitely not in the way that Alice did, which felt claustrophobic and made her want to hide away.

Of course because of the lack of CCTV at her end of the corridor – at that time – there was never any evidence of a culprit; whoever was behind each incident was never caught. And when there was extra CCTV installed –

But she doesn't want to think about that. She doesn't want to feel weirded out all over again.

There's a flurry of people standing, pulling down briefcases from the overhead racks, queuing to get quickly off the train when the doors open, to make their connections in the crush of London's rush hour.

On the concourse, she struggles between people staring up at the departure screens and others grappling with luggage or supermarket carrier bags. That reminds her; she turns back towards the M&S, picking up milk and salad, adding a bottle of white as she makes her way to the till; she's earned it today.

Outside the station there's the happy sight of a flower stall. She buys a bunch of flowers, reduced at the end of the day but still in bloom, smelling sweetly of the countryside she'd imagined when she'd taken that job, before it went wrong. She's got to try to look forward – to what though, what is she looking forward to tonight, tomorrow, next week?

At the crossing, she waits between couples holding hands and others bickering. It's that time of evening, post-work dates and domesticity. The lights change, and she crosses the road. Waiting for her bus, smelling the delicate flowers in her arms, she wonders what Holly's garden is like: despite the winter, would there be budding evergreens and the green shoots of spring-flowering bulbs?

The bus arrives. There's the usual scrum to get on, with people pushing their way on behind her, just in time. She feels like she remembers something, someone pushing behind her – but she's just come off a commuter train, and it's London: there are always people pushing to get on, pushing to go; it's not a memory, it's what happens.

On the top deck she cradles the flowers as the bus lurches into the slow-moving traffic. The pavements are packed. You can lose yourself in London, there's such safety in numbers, all the people getting on with their lives, doing their thing.

When her alarm wakes her in the morning she's slept without waking once, as though there's nothing to keep her awake any longer. Once she's made her coffee, the meeting with Jo the day before comes back to her, but it's in the past, not here in London. Now when she feels OK, it's almost like it's something that's happened to someone else: a character in a play, or those TV crime series that people binge-watch. Except crime drama is never really about racism – even if it involves a dead ethnic minority body, the person isn't there to talk about the racism they experienced, the drama is about the aftermath dealt with by the usually white detectives. The crime might be racist, but racism isn't examined in the scientific minutiae of forensics – just like a corpse changes colour as the blood drains away and all the heat of human emotion disappears, leaving only the physical body.

Even when you're alive, people make it difficult to talk about racism.

After she had filled in one of the many Incident Report Forms she'd been asked to fill in, she would email it to Seb and usually hear nothing back apart from a 'Received, thanks' – but once he phoned up to her, and called her down to his office.

'Look, you've put here under "description of incident" that it was racist.' He gestured to the document on his screen. 'You're supposed to only write what happens. All we know is you seem to be the one being attacked –'

'Seem? I'm the only person it's happening to – unless something's happened to someone else?'

He made her feel like a stroppy teenager with his response.

'Look, Tesya, I'm just trying to help. We are all trying to help, actually. The simple point I am making is that you must only put the facts down on these forms, not conjecture about why – after all, we don't know, do we?'

He sounded so reasonable, so well-meaning, and academic with his cautious use of language she couldn't argue with him. He quickly changed the subject anyway, his way of bringing their meetings to a close, by enthusiastically mentioning something cultural – that day it had been about a new UK garage music artist he thought she'd like. She wasn't sure why, she'd never initiated a conversation about music with him – she wasn't into garage anyway – and music wasn't his area of specialism. He taught on the Critical Studies in the Arts, and specialized in the architecture of the Bauhaus.

As she headed back to her office, she supposed he was just being sociable, although she also wondered whether he thought she'd be interested in this new music artist as he had an Asian-sounding name, like her. It was funny how right-on people never recommended opera or classical music to her, as though they imagined a kind of apartheid in arts interests.

When she got back to her office that day and unlocked the door, the fact remained that all the incidents were aimed at her: her name, her skin colour, and thus her body. Wasn't that enough to label the incidents as racist on the Incident Report Forms?

When Seb first emailed her the official Incident Report Form pro forma to fill in, it made her feel like it was being taken seriously. Though as the forms mounted up in her sent tray, and then got saved presumably in a folder on Seb's computer and wherever he forwarded it onwards to management, she never heard anything about the forms again, apart from Seb's courteous 'thanks' emails in reply.

Frustrated with how long it had been going on for, and how nothing seemed to be developing in terms of stopping it happening or finding out who was behind it, one day she went down to see him.

His door was closed, so she knocked.

He called out, 'Come in.'

She pushed open the door.

He looked irritated, but quickly put on a smile and said, 'Tesya?'

She stayed in the doorway and asked quickly, 'What happens to all those Incident Report Forms?'

'I forward them on to management.'

'Yes, but … what do they do with them?'

'There's nothing they can do, not until there's a suspect; they file them. Sorry, Tesya, I know it's tough, but now unless there's anything else –'

Later on in the next semester, Diane, her union representative, got involved. She was also ethnic minority – mixed-race Turkish-English, with a strong London accent – so she felt at home with her.

Diane asked Seb exactly what the police had made clear to her: 'How will there ever be a suspect unless there's a CCTV camera up near Tesya's office door?'

Seb explained, 'I've put that down as essential on the Incident Action Plan Form. They're just waiting for the funding to be sorted, signatures on the paperwork, then they'll contact the security company to come and install it.'

Diane said, 'When? Hasn't Tesya put up with this long enough?'

'Soon.' Seb always sounded so reasonable, just like the working-through of procedures and the thought of CCTV technology sounded so reliable, so trustworthy.

She thinks of TV crime drama again. Unless crime drama includes CCTV scenes these days, it isn't believable; there's CCTV all over the UK, everyone knows that. But crime drama, like CCTV, is always after the event, it's never about the victim alive. The last moments of a princess walking down the chandelier-lit corridor of an exclusive Paris hotel, her lover beside her – the lover she's destined to die next to, minutes later. Then there's that little boy holding hands with two slightly older kids, walking away from a crowded shopping centre and a mother whose eyes were diverted, just for a moment, but that's all it takes as minutes later the hands the boy trusted leave him for dead, alone where there's no CCTV.

A moment – watched at a distance, or unwatched – is all it takes.

She's no longer sure why CCTV reassures people; it's not actually everywhere, and it's rarely monitored live. It's just a record of what's happened – but it doesn't stop things happening.

'The university has to install CCTV outside your office,' was what Jo had told her, the first time she went in to see her, 'but the thing you need to be aware of is that CCTV might warn off and stop any potential further incidents, which means we might never find out who was behind it.'

'How do you mean?'

'CCTV cameras aren't invisible, it's expensive to install the really discreet ones – so what I mean is the culprit will probably see it and think again. In that sense CCTV can be a useful deterrent.'

So the awful incidents would stop, but if she never knew who was behind them there would be that constant state of anxiety still: who was it, and what about if that person tried doing something else to get at her, away from the CCTV-monitored areas?

Sometime later, when she was reporting another incident at the police station, she mentioned the ongoing lack of CCTV to Jo again.

'Well, yes, CCTV would help, but – I'm sure you've thought of this – although more CCTV on your corridor would stop someone from tampering again with your office door, given the photo incidents in the foyer, and the recent one –'

One Monday morning before she had even got to her office, in the staffroom checking her pigeonhole, between the envelopes from academic publishers and her journal subscriptions, her hand had felt something oily: a scrunched-up paper packet containing the crumbs and bits of potato and onion left from a samosa.

Seb, examining it a few minutes later, flattened the packet out. There was the logo of the nearest supermarket, and an eat-by date. He said, 'So they bought it last night or this morning.' The receipt was in the bag: a receipt for the single item, paid with cash. Someone had chosen to buy and eat the snack, and then had left the rubbish in her pigeonhole. They had chosen to eat Asian food – but then tikka masala was the UK's favourite dish, so it didn't narrow down who did it. It could have been anyone.

'Yes, the pigeonhole staffroom incident shows that one extra CCTV camera, by your office, isn't going to stop someone who has managed this long not to be discovered. Especially when they have the confidence to act in other places – not just your quiet corridor, but the foyer and staffroom – public places where someone could interrupt them at any moment.'

She didn't need to say more; it was obvious that it would continue, whoever the person was would keep getting away with it.

Although CCTV hadn't yet been installed, Jo's other deterrent suggestion had happened: an email was sent to all staff about the incidents, reminding everyone of the university's Equality and Diversity Policy. The email had said there 'had been a few incidents against one member of staff and their property' – she'd received it too. It was brief and it hadn't been clear whether they were asking for help in finding the perpetrator; it was more of a reminder of their policy, 'embracing equality and diversity', like they were telling whoever was doing it that it wasn't on, and to stop, for the sake of the university.

It hadn't worked, of course. No one came forward with a possible suspect, or to give themselves up. What it did do was bring out all the amateur sleuths from among colleagues she'd hardly met, and people who had never shown any interest in her before – the word diversity gave away that it was her – she was the only ethnic minority staff member within the Faculty of Arts, where the email had been circulated, as the cc list showed it wasn't distributed to the whole university. She wasn't sure how the university swipe cards worked, whether a student or staff member from the rest of the university could access Arts or not. She asked the Facilities guy about that. He said all student and staff swipe cards could access the public university areas, like the faculty foyers, but only staff cards could access staff-only areas, like the staffrooms across each faculty of the university – but of course sometimes doors were left open by accident, or wedged ajar temporarily for cleaning.

It could be anyone.

For her colleagues, that's what made it like a TV crime drama.

People who haven't had anything happen to them seem to find it exciting to discuss, or rather gossip about, crime. All the CCTV of crimes, after the event, played repeatedly on news media – all that public access to what used to be available only to the police makes people play at being detectives.

Perhaps with all the conspiracy and evil on TV, in dramas and on the news, it's easy to talk about aggression and evil, it feels normal – like talking about the weather. So when something unexplained and potentially criminal started cropping up in emails circulating around work, then it obviously became water-cooler gossip, behind her back – and in front of her too, digging for more information, in the guise of concern, of course. It always felt like gossip when people asked about what had happened to her, like they were chatting about the latest Scandi-noir TV drama: wondering who did it, their motives, how they got away with it. They'd ask her questions, one after the other in quick succession, and she'd find herself answering even though she didn't want to, but gradually the questions would build up and she'd feel they were cross-questioning her – although not how the police do, slowly and methodically. Especially not like Jo, who took time, noticing when she got upset and when she needed a break. Colleagues just wanted to know how it ends, like when you binge-watch TV box sets to find out what happened, so you can finally go to bed, sleep – and forget it. Except when crime is happening to you, you can never really switch off. When people are curious, they don't think about it from the perspective of the victim – what it's like when you don't know what's going to happen next, and who to be afraid of. It was like they forgot it was something actually happening to her in real life –

No one ever asked how she felt, or even said something like how sorry they were to hear this was happening to her, but they did express shock that anything like this was 'happening' in a university – people shied away from naming it as racism.

Yes, when people did use the word sorry, it would only be a general 'Sorry to hear what's been happening', and fishing for specifics if they didn't have an office nearby and so hadn't seen the latest incident before it was cleaned up. It would be people who'd ended up sitting next to her early at a meeting; people who'd heard about it from someone else: it was gossip. Perhaps they'd ask her about it to make conversation, to pass the time – or they might even have thought they were showing concern. Whatever it was, once they'd started, they couldn't stop. It definitely wasn't sociable, and rather than pass the time, for her it made time go even more excruciatingly slowly. She would will the meeting to start – anything to stop their questions.

She would feel her eyes dampen, but maybe that wasn't noticeable to others, just her being conscious of trying to keep her feelings under control, not to cry. Once she started crying it was hard to stop. She only did that with Jazz, who she felt safe enough with to cry – and Jazz would take her mind off it with a drink, and Netflix, and a laugh – so she could carry on. Which she had to do.

When she felt it was becoming one of those cross-questioning situations, and she couldn't take it any more, she'd say with as much courtesy as she could muster, 'Sorry, I don't want to talk about it any longer.'

Puzzled – like she'd hurt their feelings by spelling it out – they would say something like, 'I was really only trying to help,' their lips slowly performing the apparent generosity of their words, elongating their vowel sounds, but their mean hard-edged consonants constricting those vowels betrayed how indignant they felt: she was ungrateful and should be thanking them for showing an interest.

That cross-questioning was another never-ending incident, poisonous darts piercing her in the same place all the other incidents aimed at – and hit her: she was a target. The strange thing was how she felt guilty, even though she'd think, why – why am I feeling guilty just because someone says they're helping? It made her feel worse.

How could a barrage of questions help, when their inquisitorial white spotlight on her bleached out what she knew: this is about race – and the spotlight on her, the victim, sheltered the aggressor hidden somewhere in the shadows.

Those conversations would bug her, going round and round in her head, buzzing like a fly furiously stuck in a room with the windows shut tight.

When she thinks about it now, the cross-questioners were never gay or disabled or working in the lower-paid support areas at work, people who would have also experienced diversity incidents too; instead, they were all people who would never have experienced anything like what had happened to her – and they were all white. They would have no idea what racism feels like, how it makes you feel bad about yourself, how it scars. It was never the cleaners or canteen workers who cross-questioned her – she thinks of Enrico, who looked out for her.

She's doing her make up in the hall mirror – she only uses lipstick in the day, for work. Alice always had an immaculate full make up on; she never saw her without it. Not like friends, under the bright lights of the gym, or late in the evening on the bus home, when make up has worn off in the heat of a bar – when flawless skin or scars and blemishes get revealed. Was Alice just one of those women who feel naked without their 'face' on – or was she hiding the acne scars of her youth? What had she got to hide – the condition of her skin, or anything else?

She pulls on yesterday's coat then glances at herself in the mirror – there's a yellowish-brown smudge on the front, from clutching the flowers on her way home. She tries to brush the powdery stuff off, but it doesn't work: the colour spreads further. She takes it off and rolls it up into her bag to take to the dry-cleaners' later. She puts on another coat, an old charity-shop tweed one that's well worn but comfortable and which she can't bear to throw away, then leaves quickly – she's running late.

Along the street, then finally she's standing on the Tube, in the stifling crush of rush hour. Between passengers' heads, in the glass of the window opposite, next to other people's reflected faces, there's her own shiny reflection against the darkness of the tunnel the other side of the glass.

It's funny how some people don't sweat much, if at all. She's never got in the habit of wearing all-over make up, foundation; she's often in a rush, and she sweats when she rushes – when she's anxious she sweats too. Foundation would never last on her skin, not how it did on Alice. If Alice were the culprit, she wouldn't sweat; but that doesn't mean Alice is the culprit. Some faces show everything: like hers, the sweat of running or her eyes welling up when her heart beats fast. Just like it must have shown on her face when she felt frightened in front of Alice, next to the mutilated photos – and when she reported the incidents week by week to Seb, her face heating up and her eyes moistening. Later in the quiet of the staff toilets she'd face herself in the mirror, her shiny reddened face staring back at her against a wall of pristine white tiles.

As she is leaving the Tube, coming up the escalator, there's a text alert. It's Holly, about meeting tonight, so she's smiling as she leaves the station – it's been ages, and tonight's almost here. Soon, at work, she's still smiling, she can't help it – but she's about to start her lecture.

She looks down, focusing on her notes, trying to get into a frame of mind more suited to talking about 'The Revenge Tragedies of the Elizabethan Era' – but she can't hide what she feels. It's always there, stress and tears, heat and happiness. So as she starts the PowerPoint, she faces the auditorium and smiles anyway. 'Good morning, everyone.' She clicks for the first slide, glances behind her at the screen, and then continues. 'Tragedy is a form of crime drama, and these plays of another, long-gone era, are of the same sorts of crimes of our time, crimes of passion or ambition, like jealousy.'

She clicks for the next slide. Behind her, the production photo appears. The graphic sex and violence of the play are foretold by a shaft of blood-red light falling across the stage and over a bed draped with white silky sheets.

'We start with the symbolism of blood and a bed, but is it the blood of birth or death, and is the whiteness of the sheets connected with the innocence of virginity – or prophesying the winding of death sheets to come?'

The students smile back; they're already hooked, they lean forward or relax back in their seats, ready to get stuck into discussing all the sex and gore of the long-gone characters.

What's great about education is being in a safe space to explore the worst of human behaviour – she'll get properly into that later in the lecture, the slide quoting Freud on 'Psychopathic Characters on the Stage' that she alludes to indirectly now: 'Watching a character murder another on a stage, we explore our secret desires against others that we wouldn't act on, but in the darkness of the theatre, when all eyes are on the stage …'

It's the same thrill people get in real life, discussing crimes committed against others. The masks of humanity people wear – like the masks of the amphitheatres in the ancient world, those exaggerated facial expressions of fear, the open-mouthed cries of horror and awe – just like those vowel-emphasized cries of 'oh how awful, how dreadfully unbearable for you'. Like masked actors with their shining pinprick eyes visible from the furthest seat, the glistening of eyes reveals their salivating pleasure too: eyes reveal an inner world of criminal desires. What we can do to other people, if we so desire.

7

WHAT IS CRIME?

AUTHOR'S NOTE

What I feel strongly about now is that racism is a crime. It isn't generally seen as crime, even though it's there in UK law; so few people get prosecuted, and anyway we have prime ministers and other politicians who are racist and get away with it. So we're supposed to brush racism off: that English playground chant, 'sticks and stones may break my bones but words will never hurt me' – whoever made up that rhyme was white. For those who grew up with words about our skin colour hurled at us by children, and adults, the hurt lingers. Racism is bullying, and both are a fundamental part of British life, like its empire, and the ongoing myth of so-called British values of tolerance. Tolerance …

All of the evil in the world is contained within the human frame.

LESSON SEVEN

'What is crime?

'Crime is defined by the rules of any given society. When laws and law enforcers deal with actions against the rules, individuals will wait for the authorities to deal with crimes committed against them rather than committing other crimes in pursuit of their own justice. Retribution is deferred, but ensured: rules on crime are a society's promise to its law-abiding citizens. That promise of retribution produces faith in the workings of the state apparatus, even though rules on crime are formulated through imagining the worst of humanity and how that might affect the status quo rather than the individual. And all states are patriarchal; although laws exist to protect women, they generally protect men.

'Take rape: it's extremely hard to charge cases as the physical evidence may be similar whether sex is consensual or not. Even though men are generally stronger than women, and thus most rape accusations are likely to be true, women aren't given a higher believability factor at trial, so the likelihood of conviction is minuscule. The status quo and its apparent liberal credentials over gendered crime are protected, while crime can be committed easily given the minimal probability of being found guilty.

'That was an extreme example, of course, but what I'm basically saying is this: intelligent people can get away with anything; you just have to think laterally, or hierarchically. Look for people who don't have much power – women, minorities, or a combination of both – then you can do whatever you want. However, the most powerful crimes are the smallest. Things that appear insignificant the police dismiss as not worth their time investigating, offering the opportunity to committing to a series of crimes over a longer period. Note my word choice: committing. Successful crime takes the commitment of time and thought, and crime against an intelligent person is the most rewarding of your effort. Intelligent people think they believe in humanity, and a belief in humanity takes a long time to crack open, but it's the only way you force them to see you, to see who's in control.'

White tiled walls in a toilet cubicle, and the chain hanging down, waiting to be pulled. Could be anywhere.

What a buzz to continue where I left off; worth the wait.

Better hide here in the alcove outside the Gents, wait to hear the results of my endeavours.

NOW

At the end of the lecture, her eyes flicker back to the last PowerPoint slide – 'What is crime?' – the question filling the screen: the thinking point for their next session on Lorca's tragedies.

She leaves it up, as a few students are still finishing their notes, while the rest are moving towards the exit.

She's been thinking about that question about crime on and off for so long. As a child, she wondered why some things are called crimes but other things aren't. There would be theft and murder on TV, in the soaps and thrillers of evening entertainment they watched in the common room at the children's home, before the workers would catch them and switch it off. Snatches of scenes would linger: the cracked outlines of broken windows; fear, with its intake of breath, and then the thwack of a strong arm, hitting someone weaker; the dull sound of death's submission, sliding into silence, leaving the aftermath of blood dripping, drop by drop. The unforgettable nasty violence on TV was definitely crime – but what about other nasty things that happened at school, and sometimes in the children's home too?

Home then wasn't a place but a feeling she sometimes felt at school drama club losing herself in rehearsals, or in books at the school library, reading until the librarian would come and find her at closing time. She would borrow a library book and carry it with her, those pages a temporary home for a while. It would take her a few moments to come to in the outside world – and walking back to the children's home, the nasty things would return. They were there all along: what might have happened the evening before at the children's home, or that day at school – like someone pinching the skin of her arm as they ran past, whispering racist or sexist words in her ear and then running away. The bully's giggles would echo down the corridor while her skin would be reddening at the point of contact and her ears would inflame with the pounding pulse of fear.

What did she do? What do you do when you're a kid? School would be closing, and there were never any teachers around.

TV crime drama often flashes from the opening glimpsed scene of a crime to the siren on a police vehicle zooming in. With what are seen as small, psychological things, like racist bullying, there aren't any given sequences from the crime scene to a police siren. In schools they don't call the police, or really deal with racism; kids don't speak about it – she didn't. There's just what's happened, and how you feel afterwards.

It was mostly before she met Jazz – before she had a friend. She met her in the worst of places, the children's home, but she immediately made everything better, school included. Jazz would bolster her up with words, and physically too; she'd push the bullies away, and then with a hand on her shoulder, the pep talk would begin. Jazz was a brilliant debater at school – like she's good at encouraging her to tackle things from a different perspective now. Jazz is always on her side.

God, the time. Must drop today's papers back in the office, grab lunch and then do a few more hours' prep for next week, before heading home early, Holly coming over tonight.

She's turning the key in the lock, but it's weird – when she pushes her office door, it's stuck, like there's something wedged the other side.

Not here, please – she stands for a moment, trying to keep calm.

Steps and, 'Are you OK?'

She turns. 'Ben – I can't open the door?'

'Let me try.' He takes her place and tries to turn the key and push the door – it doesn't move. 'There's something blocking it.' He lets go of the key – the door's obviously unlocked. He stands back then gives the door a good push with his shoulder. It opens enough for him to peer through the gap. 'Just a pile of papers.' He glances back.

'Perhaps you left the window open and they fell from your desk?' He kneels down. 'I'll shove them aside, so we can open the door.'

When they get inside, there is a whole pile of leaflets and posters crumpled up on the floor. Ben picks up a handful. She does too. The first one, when she opens it out, is a poster advertising an anti-racism demonstration, with the black on white and primary colours of activist groups. She picks up another: a flyer for an arts event, a fundraiser in aid of refugees. On the ground there are multiple copies of different posters and flyers, the sort posted up all around the university campus. Photocopied on cheap paper, produced by student-union societies, they're what made her happy when she first got the job here: there were so many displayed along corridors, in seminar rooms, in the toilets – anywhere with wall space. It's weird to see them on the floor, pushed under the door, all scrunched up. Under her door.

'The window isn't open.'

Ben's looking at it – but it's the other side of the room from the desk. No, the papers were pushed under the door, and, given what they look like – a pile of rubbish – they were already screwed up before that.

She sits down on her office chair, looking at the floor, trying not to feel a sense of déjà vu – surely it must be some kind of mistake?

Ben picks up the rest of the papers, piling them in the bin. 'OK, I guess students leafleting pushed some under the door, and then got muddled up as to where they'd leafleted, and accidentally pushed more under this door – why they look like this. All the corridors look the same, after all.'

It's what students do, push their essays under staff doors, and flyers too; none of the doors have mailboxes, and students can't access the staffroom pigeonholes. So it could be – just rather a lot of flyers and posters in one go, and –

Ben's mobile buzzes an alert; he checks it. 'Better go, I was on my way to the board meeting.'

The posters are all positive ones, about immigrants and refugees – or rather, they were positive ones, but now they look like rubbish in the bin.

'You OK?'

Should she tell him – even though this isn't like before, it can't be, can it? 'I'm fine … it's just … oh, nothing. You've got a meeting to go to.'

'You sure?'

'Yes, thanks, Ben.'

He's almost out the door, and turns back. 'Oh, and see you this weekend – you're still free?'

'Yes, I'm looking forward to it.'

'I forgot to ask, have you a plus one? You're welcome to bring someone.'

'Oh thanks, yes – I mean, yes, I do have a plus one – but it'll just be me this time.'

'Great. OK, better dash.'

Yes, she has a plus one, but whether Holly would ever come along to anything is a mystery – it's not become that kind of relationship.

And no, she doesn't feel OK, even though Ben must be right: it's some silly student mix-up.

Ben's left the door open.

She gets up and peers down the corridor: silence, no one around. She's closing the door when there's the sudden slamming of a door at the end of the corridor, where the staff toilets are, the entrance obscured by a grand Victorian marble pillar. Just one of the lecturers. She closes her door.

She needs to get lunch, and some work done, then go home early for Holly's arrival. Then she'll relax.

Holly arrives in a cloud of perfume, and her heels clatter across the kitchen floor where she opens the bottle she's carried in. It fizzes and starts to bubble over – Tesya hurries with the glasses, just in time.

As they chink glasses though, there's something –

Holly smiles and says, 'Ah, just what I needed,' then takes a sip from her glass, but her smile fades quickly. She looks serious.

'Are you OK?'

Holly answers, 'Yes, of course,' and then puts her phone on top of her bag, on the arm of the sofa, like she's waiting for a call, but she turns to Tesya saying, 'OK, I'm all yours for a few hours,' and leans forward to kiss her.

So everything's fine. Holly's easing off her heels, they lounge on the sofa, sipping their drinks, then Holly cradles her, and they kiss. She forgets everything else, when love is holding her in her arms – but this evening that feeling's too brief: Holly moves away and gets up. For a moment she feels like she's done something wrong – then she watches Holly's back: opening the fridge, retrieving the bottle and returning; she tops up their glasses. As they sip, she shifts in her seat – wanting to reach out – but there's an uncomfortable silence, then she thinks to ask, 'How was your day?'

Holly starts to reply, 'OK –' but there's something different about her. She looks off into the distance, like her mind's somewhere else while she talks about her dreadful commute, then her worries over the kids' school fees.

'Have the fees gone up?'

Holly looks startled: she tacks back, 'No, that's not what I said. No, it's fine, I just worry that perhaps it's a waste of money – they might be better at the local comprehensive.'

Her double negative is confusing – surely she has the same income to cover costs now, with life insurance or pensions – and her own work? How she dresses, she's obviously got a good income to afford designer labels. It's nothing really – they live in such different worlds. Her concerns are her kids; Holly rarely talks about her work in IT, and anyway she'd probably not understand if she did.

Although perhaps there's something, her make up seems more perfect today, like film make up: coverage for up-close photography. Not just foundation in her creamy skin tone with a rose blusher. She looks paler than usual; she's wearing powder too – for some reason she remembers an actress in a Hitchcock film, opening an old-fashioned compact and puff. Which film? The woman's gesture, powdering her face, is a ploy to use the mirror to see behind her without turning round. Why did she think of that? She looks away for a moment, towards the DVD pile – that's when Holly asks, 'How was your day?'

Now, moments later, she wishes she hadn't answered Holly's question but kissed her, stopping their pointless chatter, and they would have moved into the bedroom – but until she answered Holly's question she would never have imagined how she'd react – and, anyway, it's what happened:

'Today? Today was a weird day, really,' she'd answered truthfully – though how she wishes she'd answered, 'Today was fine,' keeping them in the moment.

'Weird, why?'

That put her on the spot. She hadn't told her what happened last year; she wanted to keep it in the past – so how to explain how she felt about the papers stuffed under her door?

'Oh, it was nothing really; just some mix-up –'

'Over what?'

'A silly mix-up over some papers.' She took her glass from the coffee table and stood up, making a 'Shall we …?' gesture with her glass towards the bedroom.

But Holly didn't get up; she said, 'So why did you say weird then?'

She tried to think of a reason, to backtrack, but couldn't, until looking towards her desk, seeing her diary there, she remembered what Ben asked. 'Ben, the Head of Faculty, has invited me to his Thanksgiving do; it's this weekend. He asked about my plus one –'

'You didn't mention me?'

'No – I mean he asked if I was seeing someone. I said yes, but that it would just be me.'

'You didn't say anything about me?'

'No, like I said –'

'I wouldn't like you to – I mean, not yet.' She closed her eyes and tilted her head back. Her neck looked whiter than her face, whiter than her foundation, suddenly drained of blood, like a ghost. 'I should have stayed at home –'

She sat down again next to Holly. 'Why, are you feeling ill?'

She opened her eyes, then said, 'I don't think I can do this any more, Tesya, I'm sorry.'

'What do you mean?' Her heart thumped; she put a hand on Holly's knee.

Holly sat still, until she lifted a hand and gestured around the room, from the open doorway to the bedroom, to the champagne glasses on the coffee table, and then her hand dropped down onto Tesya's hand. 'I mean this, all of this.' She sat back, and closed her eyes and went still again like a doll.

'Holly, what's wrong?'

She didn't answer.

'You're worrying me. What is it?'

She opened her eyes slowly. They looked reddish, like she was about to cry.

She reached out to put an arm around her –

But Holly stood up. 'I can feel a migraine coming on.'

'I'll get you some water. Would you like a painkiller?'

'Just water, thanks.'

When she returned with the water, Holly was in the hallway, by the mirror, powdering her face, even though she still looked immaculate. She took the glass and drank the water in one go.

Was she avoiding eye contact? Why?

Then it all happened fast:

Holly said, 'I'm not feeling at all well. I better head home while I can still bear the light.'

So it was just about the pending migraine. She helped Holly on with her coat.

'Shall I call a cab, and come with you to the station?'

'It's quicker during the rush hour to walk. Don't worry, I'll be fine.'

So then Tesya must have been the one red-eyed in the doorway –

'Don't worry, darling, all I meant was this has all happened so fast. Hasn't it?'

She wasn't sure what to reply. It was true; they hardly knew each other.

'I'll call you; give me a few days.' And then Holly was gone. No kiss, just the breath of her perfume in the air, mixed with the smell of alcohol from their glasses.

At the window now she leans on the sill, watching Holly walking away below, against the murky street, her light-coloured shoes on the dark pavement, the whiteness of her coat and hands as she passes briskly under the street light.

She turns back to the room, hovering by the desk. There's the pile of DVDs for the film-theory course, ready for the first session: 'Hitchcock's Women'. Then she remembers; wasn't the woman with the compact the accomplice – wasn't there a nasty ending?

She moves away to clear up, even though it's just the two glasses and the bottle. She gets that déjà-vu feeling – she's been here before, which of course she has: she clears up after Holly's gone. Except there's something more this time than wishing she'd stayed longer: something dispiriting about what's just happened. Rather than a romantic evening, an edgy, incomplete, frustrating time. She checks her watch; Holly arrived less than an hour ago. It wasn't just the migraine – Holly was fine, initially. What did she do wrong? She must have done something, said something – but what? Her mind circles; there was just whatever she said, or rather salvaged about having an odd day, by mentioning Ben's party invite. No, Holly was weird tonight, but why? So random – the thing about not knowing each other long was true, but still … It was all so sudden, like she'd hit a nerve – she became someone else. Perhaps she's overthinking. Migraines obviously come on suddenly – and Holly said she'd be in touch, not to worry, didn't she?

She looks at her watch again: the whole evening stretching ahead for hours. She wants to call Jazz; they haven't spoken for a while, but she doesn't want Jazz deconstructing Holly – and she'd guess something had happened. Not that her mind isn't doing what Jazz does. She picks up her phone – then puts it down. No, she doesn't want to tell Jazz what's just happened.

She puts the kettle on, makes a mug of coffee, then coming back into the studio room sees the pile of DVDs again. She might as well rewatch one tonight and do some work. She puts a DVD in the player, and presses play.

Later, when the DVD is ejected and back in its box on her desk, she thinks a while and picks up her notepad and scrawls, 'Discuss white as the colour of innocence?' Strange how some film characters stay in her mind; like some real people.

She turns off the lights in the studio room and glances into the kitchen area. Upside down on the draining board the two glasses glint in the darkness, reflecting the lights from the street.

Holly's heels swiftly speeding away, and her white coat-tails swinging behind her.

She worries again; what did she do wrong? She goes into the bedroom and closes the door.

She tries to get to sleep, but there's still the silly – or something more sinister – thing: the immigration and refugee posters. And there's Holly, and there's what's missing: someone she can discuss what's going on with, and relax with too.

In the dark she turns, burying her face in the dip between the pillows – but still seeing Holly in the doorway, leaving without kissing her. Retreating? But her eyes were almost closed as she left – she obviously wasn't well; she's not an actress.

She sits up against the pillows. She switches the light on.

She thinks about Holly, like she's a protagonist in a Hitchcock film she's preparing a lecture on; the questions she might put on the PowerPoint, to expand on, to discuss:

Is it a crime to take love, without giving emotionally back to the lover in return? Is it a crime to want more than sexual love, to want emotional time together?

Is there such a thing as an emotional crime? How would you define it? Or is that even the right question? Look at it the other way: like, why, when she could be in a normal relationship – the kind where the couple meet all the time, perhaps even live together – why is it she always meets people like Holly and gets hooked, even though her relationships always go nowhere, if she's honest? Her relationships are about her missing the other person, when probably her lovers only think about her when they're together, making love, or rather having sex – what it feels like when it's ended. Has she ever really felt love, reciprocal love?

Funny how being busy is a thing; everyone says how busy they are with work and other responsibilities – though sometimes it feels like people are exaggerating, because we're all supposed to be busy. Not that the word busy couldn't be covering up when people aren't sure what they feel, so they put someone in a holding bay until they're sure – prior to more major covering-up, working late, when really it's infidelity that's keeping them busy.

Why's she even thinking about infidelity and game-playing, when it's Holly, who she trusts – doesn't she? She has to trust her; she loves her. No, this is not an emotional crime, and Holly's not an emotional criminal.

It's her though, she is a victim of something even if it's just the context she and Holly are in right now: so little time together, the absence and silence of being busy. But then how can she be a victim, if emotion is not a crime?

8

EQUIVOCATION

AUTHOR'S NOTE

There are things we don't talk about, but we show – old friends can tell.

If we're going out nearby, my friends come to pick me up, and after I've locked the front door – my hand checking again that it's locked – I've seen their faces. Alone I don't notice what I do, how my body and mind work together, like an army protecting me.

Anxiety is its own battleground. Being on the defensive, focusing on the object of fear, imprisoned in uncertainty, you don't act. You blame yourself; that's how it works: negativity gets embedded, and someone else's thoughts and actions control you. When you're in the middle of it, you can't see how crime makes you passive –

Back to that crime on emotion: I've mixed up love and crime again, but diverse emotional scars make you vulnerable to fresh wounds, stopping you acting – unless you drink, when you shouldn't act but know you will. Then your emotions show like an actor on a stage. You can't see the audience in the dark, but they can always see you.

LESSON EIGHT

A close shave; followed by a detour in a rather leafy part of London. Funny how I wasn't sure at first it was her, but it is. Worth going on gut instinct.

Nostalgic being in a university again: the quiet working environment. How lecturers, so used to projecting their voices in lecture halls, are unaware how far their voices carry; who might be listening.

Boat-ward bound, need a good night's sleep. Now, where did I leave the car? OK, here.

Turn on the camera; angle it away. That's it, perfect: the road ahead.

Now, think aloud while I'm driving. Especially as I'll be busy, back again tomorrow. Things are coming together incredibly well all of a sudden.

'Today in the middle of my latest case, we're on the road. And this afternoon is about working with what you find, going with the flow, and being wary of equivocation. There's a reason in the play *Hamlet* that the so-called hero makes a balls-up of answering his father's plea for revenge. It's that famous Hamletian equivocation: balancing thought upon thought, weighing up what to do; his indecision gives others time to act and get ahead. So when he acts he's destined to fail, ending up as a corpse along with everyone else.

'So, strike a balance between acting and not acting, biding your time until the moment is right. It's all about surveillance. People's fingertips are constantly typing out what they're feeling, where they're going, giving everything away. You can be physically miles away and yet simultaneously in the palm of someone's hand, but watching as that person types, you're the one with ultimate control.'

NOW

She'd WhatsApped Holly earlier to see how she was doing, but she hasn't read it yet, there's no tick by the message. She hates that tick system, knowing someone hasn't read your message is almost as bad as not getting a reply. She puts her phone down and switches on the radio. A group of professionals is discussing domestic violence: it's *Woman's Hour*. She's about to swivel the dial to a music station, when she's stopped by –

'In the surgery we don't just look at the injury, we look for other changes: clothes, cosmetics –'

'Make up?'

'Yes. Often women come in with bruises, and a supposedly rational explanation, like walking into cupboard doors in the chaos of home. But one of the clues to hiding domestic violence is wearing a scarf, or a lot of make up –'

'Heavy layer of foundation?'

'Exactly.'

She turns it off. Holly lives with her kids, not with anyone who might hurt her. Sometimes women wear more make up than usual. She does, if she gets a blemish –

A text alert: Ben, reminding her she can bring a friend on Saturday. She texts back, 'Thanks, I'll let you know.' Her finger hovers over Jazz's name in contacts. Perhaps she should go on her own though, they'll all be new to her – or would she feel better to have Jazz with her, it'll probably be mostly couples?

She texts Jazz, 'Free tomorrow night? Be my plus one at a Thanksgiving party, nice gay guy from work? X'.

Ben announces the fireworks will start soon. There's a flurry of coming and going, people picking up their coats from the hall. She and Jazz do the same. It's an elegant Edwardian house with parquet floors, child-battered mostly IKEA furniture, and on the walls the bright colours of countercultural prints – Keith Haring's happy cartoon activism and one of Warhol's Marilyns.

Now they're outside, overlooking the garden: under their feet, reclaimed railway sleepers are laid as decking, and beneath the wintry shrubs nearby there's a large spherical stone water feature trickling silvery droplets over a minimalist rock garden. It's tranquil – though now everyone is outside, the sound of overlapping conversations fills the night air.

Phil is going round with a tray of hot chocolate and marshmallows. He comes over. 'Here, Tesya, and, it's Jazz, isn't it?'

'Thanks, Phil.'

'Thank you, yes, I'm Jazz.'

'Glad you could make it too.' He moves on. There's the giggling of kids' voices, and then he's saying, 'OK, I'll hand the rest of these out. You can give out the sparklers now, guys.'

She was right about Phil being a stay-at-home dad. Their three kids seem well behaved, or at least for the adult occasion. They set off, excitedly handing out the sparklers. The terrace is packed, but they're tall teenagers, two girls and a boy. They look mixed-race, perhaps they're adopted, but then Phil and Ben are both white, she's not sure that's allowed now. There hasn't been a mother figure mentioned, not that it means there isn't one.

Ben follows the kids' trail through the crowd – going round with a lighter, by the bursts of fire, the sparklers lighting up the terrace. Phil is by the kitchen door, chatting to someone, but his gaze is on the kids, keeping an eye out. How amazing to have two fathers – to actually have a father.

She's about to say something about it to Jazz, when one of the kids, the son, hands them their sparklers, so she thanks him. 'How exciting, I haven't had one of these for years.'

He smiles. Walking away, he looks like a shorter version of Phil, slim and athletic; of course these are his biological children.

Jazz says, 'Tesya?'

It's Ben, lighter at the ready. There's something magical about the fast fiery fizzing of light. They copy others, circling their sparklers in the air, watching the trails of delayed light against the darkness. Jazz signs her name in the air, and she does too, then others join in with much laughter and trying not to splash their drinks. It's something like being kids again –

She has a vague memory of sparklers, long ago at the children's home; a joyful moment in the darkness. Like the flickering of the sparkler in her hand now, its light burning out too quickly – as good things do. She catches her pessimistic thought – she just wants things to last.

Jazz, by her side, says, 'This is fun –'

'Yes,' she smiles. 'Glad you're here with me –'

There's a massive boom, a spray of stars lights the sky, flashing pink, and purple, and red. Then another boom, and another, and the play of light and fire explodes above their heads.

When it's over, there's the smell of explosives in the cold still air, and it's darker, only the slither of a moon and the stars above. It's quieter now, people are moving inside.

She looks at her phone. She'd taken a photo of the fireworks at some point, now she sees it's a blur.

'Do you remember that Halloween party when we were teenagers?' Jazz is sitting on the parapet overlooking the garden.

'Yes, I was trying to remember when that was. We had sparklers then, didn't we? That was my first time.'

'Mine too. It felt dangerous. I thought my fingers would burn – I'd hardly even lit an oven by then, only in Food Technology, with the teacher hovering near.'

There's a rustling of dry leaves from the darkness at the back of the garden, the trees and shrubs mingling with the growth over the wall, the expanse of Hampstead Heath. Perhaps a fox –

She looks back at Jazz. 'Isn't it ridiculous how little the care system prepared us for: from cooking to fireworks? I hope it's better for kids nowadays.'

'Probably not, the way the kids at school are –'

'So how long have you two been together?'

They both jump – it had been so quiet, everyone else inside, or so they thought. It's Phil with a tray in his hand, picking up the last few empties from the table.

'Jazz is my best friend –'

He looks mortified. 'Oh gosh, I'm sorry – I meant how long have you known each other,' he says, backtracking – signalling quote marks in the air. 'OK, too much to drink. Talking of drinking, I'm about to open the bubbles. Coming in?'

They both say yes, and laugh it off, and Phil heads inside.

The moment's passed, or she thinks it has, but when Jazz picks up their hot chocolate mugs from the wall next to her and stands up, in the light from the kitchen window her eyes look shiny, like she's upset about something.

'You OK?'

Jazz shakes it off. 'Yeah, of course, why wouldn't I be?'

Jazz leads the way, and she follows her cool leather-jacketed back – then she gets it: it was what they were talking about before Phil interrupted. Jazz is still angry about then, in the children's home; she was there much longer than her. There's then, and then there's also whatever happened when she was in Iraq. She can't think of what to say. She wishes Jazz was happier than she is; like she wishes she was happier too. She puts a hand on her shoulder momentarily, as they walk through the open doorway –

Jazz glances back, and says, 'Tesya, no wonder people think we're together,' but she's smiling. She puts their mugs on the crowded kitchen counter, and quickly exchanges them – Phil is handing out flutes of champagne.

She thinks of Holly arriving with a bottle, what they do together. She leans back against the kitchen counter, feeling for her phone in her coat pocket, wanting to text –

Jazz seems to guess what she's thinking. 'So what's up with the girlfriend?'

'Jazz, give me a break. I don't want to think about anything apart from having another glass of this –'

'Good idea, me too.'

And of course they drink far too much, rather quickly.

Later, in the lounge, they're with the diehards, lingering on comfortably worn-in leather sofas, Ben and Phil's eighties record collection playing on a real record player. There are a few people dancing rather slowly in the darker L-shaped part of the room, while the rest of them are having the kind of conversations they won't remember in the morning – or given it's the early hours, after they've slept. She finds her head slipping drowsily down onto Jazz's shoulder; Jazz shifts, accommodating her while continuing talking with Ben about her teaching, then asking him about their kids' school.

She sits up: why on earth can't Holly involve her in her life? It's the twenty-first century, there's gay marriage and adoption, and gay families like lovely Ben and Phil and their kids. She could have been here.

'Tesya, are you OK?'

'Yes, why?' She stands slowly. Her head hurts, she's acutely aware she's a bit drunk, and she's angry – with the world, and with –

'Oh, just – nothing.' Jazz looks at her, but she looks away. She can't look Jazz in the eye and tell her what she's feeling right now, she'd probably say I told you so.

There are fewer people now: just a couple on the sofa opposite, and another couple slow dancing to the smoochy music.

Phil brings in a steaming pot of coffee. It's time to go, but after a coffee she and Ben get talking about theatre, while hearing snippets of Jazz and Phil discussing American politics and Trump, then the military, British politics and inevitably Brexit – she overhears his, 'It's all a load of rubbish,' and relaxes; they're with friends.

It's only when Ben goes upstairs to tell the kids to switch off their devices and sleep, and downstairs the music is stopped, that finally it really is time to leave.

She looks for her coat among those hung up in the hall, but she can't find it.

Jazz is by the open front door, chatting with Phil. Behind them the last remaining couple make their way together, rather unsteadily, down the front garden path.

She checks again – it's not there.

Phil asks, 'You still looking for your coat?'

Jazz turns. 'You could have left it in the kitchen, when we came back after the fireworks?'

'Oh yes, of course.'

The kitchen's dark. She flicks the light switch and glances around. All the surfaces are covered with party debris, glasses and plates, and on the floor next to the bin is a black bag overflowing with bottles and cans – and next to the open garden door, hung over a high kitchen stool, is her old tweed coat. She puts it on, feeling the cold air from the doorway. What they talked about, or was it what she thought about – sparklers, and homes, and fathers. How she touched Jazz's shoulder when they came in – they don't touch often, not like she does with other friends, a hand on the arm during conversation. Jazz is different in the heat of the playing field; she's seen her grappling other players for the ball –

It's weird what we remember and what we don't; she can't remember leaving her coat here, but then she's drunk too much. She fills a glass with water and drinks it quickly, then puts it in the sink. There's a whiff of cigarette smoke wafting in from outside – they're not the last to leave after all.

In the hall, they say their goodbyes. Phil says, 'Come again, you're both welcome anytime, friends or whatever –'

They're laughing, and then he's hugging them both, like old friends, and he adds, 'God, sorry, I've drunk so much, I feel all sentimental, but I mean it, anytime, I mean –' peals of laughter again, and, 'Gosh, I should shut up and go to bed, shouldn't I?'

Laughing, they walk down the garden path. She feels in her pocket for her phone, but it's not there.

Had it slipped into the lining? She feels around the pocket. 'Wait, I can't find my phone.'

Jazz stops ahead of her.

She tries the other pocket – and then relaxes. 'OK, it's here.'

They start walking again. And she's fine really, panic over, she's got her phone. It's just it's something she's never thought about before, how she always puts things in her right-hand pocket, or she thinks she does. She's right-handed. It doesn't matter though; she's got it now.

They walk downhill to the minicab place on the corner. Her shoes slip on the sludge of fallen leaves, and she steadies herself against Jazz. Phil was funny; what was it, how long they'd known each other – no, how long they'd been together, what couples get asked.

Soon they're in a cab, and the driver calls over his shoulder, 'No smoking, girls.'

Strapping herself in, she gives Jazz a look like: what's he on about, neither of them are smoking.

'I was wondering where it was coming from – it's your coat. Tesya, you haven't had an illicit fag tonight?'

She looks down and sniffs her coat collar; Jazz is right. 'No –' But there was the open back door, and her coat on the stool with smoke wafting in from outside – 'People were smoking in the back garden.'

They drive back uphill, past the house. The lights are still on in the front room and upstairs. Ben with the kids; Phil dealing with the stragglers, whichever guest was smoking in the back garden, or whichever couple – how parties are, as you get older, people are either paired off or perpetually single, with a few serial daters in between. That silence at the back door: the smokers could only have been a couple who've been together years and don't talk much any longer – or a single who couldn't face going home. Or someone like her: in a relationship, but alone.

Jazz is texting. They've passed the Archway junction, now they're stuck in traffic on the Holloway Road, as busy at night as it is in the day, all the late-night fast-food places and clubs. They pass the turning for Green Lanes; she thinks of Zehra and Hamid, Christmas soon. Jazz is in a messaging dialogue to and fro. She's about to ask who with, who's up so late, then she doesn't; she plunges her hand into her pocket and takes out her own phone instead.

In the palm of her hand, the screen is dark, no flashing green light. She turns on the screen anyway, just in case, even though the technology is what it is: green light means new notifications – no light means none. Normally. Except what's weird is when she opens her messages the first name that comes up is Holly's, whereas the last one she remembers reading was Jazz about tonight. It looks like a read message, but when she opens it she hasn't read it before – she couldn't have done, it was sent a few hours ago when the phone was in her coat pocket in the kitchen. She must have accidentally swiped the notifications when she found the phone deep in her other pocket just now. The message is nothing much: Holly's feeling better, and she's thinking of her – she'll 'call soon'. She closes her eyes. If Holly was here, and they were heading home together –

But they never have, that's the frustrating thing – they never have gone anywhere together. Not the theatre, or the cinema, or even a restaurant or bar – other than that first time when they met. Holly arrives at hers, and then later she leaves. They've never had a night together, sleeping and waking up together. Like a Swiss clock: a woman in a dirndl skirt coming out of a little doorway, or a man in breeches from the opposite one – never both together; usually they're hidden behind their closed doors, only appearing every now and then.

She opens her eyes, her phone's rectangular blank screen stares back. Like Holly's mysterious front door hidden away, wherever she is in the darkness of the countryside. She has to see her at her home; she can't go on like this – home alone again to her empty bed.

The cab driver calls out, 'Where we going first?'

Jazz snaps back Tesya's address without looking up, and adds, 'Can you drop there first, please?' then she smiles down, swiftly reading another message.

She looks outside. The pavements are heaving, people queuing to get into clubs, going to places or going home, hanging out – together. Who's Jazz messaging in the middle of the night – has she started dating someone and not told her?

Looking down, she scrolls past Holly's name to the next read message: Jazz replying to her about meeting up to go to the party together, with a 'Yes great, see you later' and signing off with her usual 'J X'. What she loves about Jazz, now she thinks about it: she always says yes, if it's possible, never says no. Holly always said no whenever she's suggested theatre or the movies, or pushed her to stay over; she's stopped asking. Though how she's feeling now –

The car stops. She glances at the meter, then hands Jazz cash. On the pavement, through the open window, she calls back, 'See you soon?' But Jazz is leaning forward, telling the cab driver where to go; she doesn't hear, and then the car's pulled out and doing a three-point turn.

Closing the front door, she catches the tail-lights of the cab disappear – in the opposite direction to normal: Jazz isn't going home.

Soon she's in bed. Tiny thoughts buzz around and expand their wings, like shadows, how thoughts do at night, trailing and enveloping her. Tail-lights going in the wrong direction, or rather a different direction – now her mind travels there too: Jazz's quick hardly-there goodbye, directing the cab driver to somewhere she's been before and goes often – but hasn't mentioned. Does it matter? She should be happy for her; she is, sort of – or is she jealous?

Cold, she curls up, pulling the covers up around her neck, in her double bed, single on a Saturday night. When did she last actually sleep in a bed with another person?

No, she's not jealous of Jazz, she's happy for her, and, more importantly, perhaps now she won't bug her about her situation with Holly.

Who was the last person Jazz was with – or rather dated more than once? It must have been ages ago, last year. She never met them, it's when she was living out in –

She gets up rather than allowing her brain to go in its vicious downward spiral, circling uncomfortable thoughts – that's it, uncomfortable; how she feels.

In the kitchen she turns on the tap and runs the water until it's cold. She drinks standing in the studio room in the darkness. She switches on her phone, even though it's the early hours when no one calls, or texts –

And she starts texting, what you're supposed to not do when you've drunk loads, but the letting-it-all-go happy feeling of being drunk has worn off, and she's tired, emotional and not thinking straight –

She texts, 'Holly, we have to have a night together, soon. I know it's difficult, but … T XX' and presses send, before she can change her mind.

She looks down at the sofa – then remembers how Holly was, when she was last here. What did Holly say? 'Too fast'?

What if her text is too much, pushes her away?

She looks at Holly's last text again. Her usual: she'll 'call soon'. Her phone goes to sleep, to its black screen. That momentary panic earlier – when all the time she was getting more and more relaxed on fizz with Phil and Ben, it was next door in her pocket, or rather, her other pocket.

Their friends seemed nice, like the few of their work colleagues who turned up too. Nice, yes, but – isn't that what she first thought of her colleagues in the last place, nice and friendly … before the photos and her name and everything else –

Can't go there – but she does, momentarily – those shadowy figures on a screen, like a TV drama, though it's real life, her life –

Stop. She holds her breath, like she holds the fear so it doesn't get out and take over, and then she slowly breathes out. She has to let it go – nothing has happened for ages. The flyers under her door were just a silly mistake, couldn't have been anything else. Now she's safe.

Switching her phone off, she drops it on the sofa, among the cushions. For a moment she lets herself conjure up Holly, her red hair, her pale white hands and her beautifully kept clothes – like how she makes her feel, cherished, when she's here. She's what she wants, and she has her –

Or does she? What if she's …?

Get a grip –

Get back to bed.

Walking towards the bedroom, past her desk, the glow from the street light outside falls on her noticeboard – among photos pinned up next to theatre tickets and old postcards, there's the one of her and Jazz in Brighton; their last weekend away together. They're leaning against a bar, and she's leaning on Jazz's shoulder. What she does, Jazz is such a rock. She should encourage Jazz to lean on her too.

Outside a car engine hums. A door slams, and the engine hums away: a cab dropping one of the neighbours off on a Saturday night.

Those tail-lights.

The city's slippery almost silence, cars' motors petering off into the distance, slithering off elsewhere, the dull repetitive sound of something hard knocking against a wall downstairs, a washing machine set to come on in the early hours – or a couple in the throes of sex, rocking their headboard against the adjoining wall, oblivious to others' sleeping.

She doesn't want to spend every night alone for the rest of her life, every weekend hanging out with friends, when she'd rather be with her soulmate, the love of her life – but is Holly?

She's still holding the photo of Jazz and her. She puts it back.

So tired. To sleep, to dream – perhaps it'll be good for her to see how Holly responds, now she's texted what she dreams of, a night together, nothing much; what other people have. Like taxi tail-lights for a late-night flit to a lover.

Telling her is better than holding it in any longer. She thinks so; she equivocates, yo-yoing, restless at what she's not sure of, what she might have misunderstood, and what she sort of thinks she knows but can't face. Like she's left the bedroom blinds up, and it will be dawn soon. Too tired to get out of bed, she turns over, facing the other way, her eyes open, watching the darkness – just when a car's headlights spray a fan of white light across the bed, and then the wall she's facing: the projection of a U-turn in the darkness.

9

SYNCHRONICITY AND NAMING

LESSON NINE

Such a high over the synchronicity, going all the way to London, and even the leafy suburbs, until I was thrown, hearing someone call, 'Phil?'

Hidden in the trees at the end of the garden, I took a quick look. Just the guy I followed here the other day, calling out to a tall guy surrounded by a gaggle of kids. Tall Phil called back, 'Coming,' but continued chatting to the woman, Tesya, and the black athletic-looking woman she arrived with.

How our minds play games with us: Phil is a common name. I'm Phil for short, so part of me was thinking what amazing synchronicity, but there are plenty of people with the same names. Repetition feels meaningful, but it's not. Not if it's not in a poem or literary text. Real life is random and seldom has much meaning, unless we make it mean something – what I'm working on now. I wished I could record my thoughts for the next Lesson right then, but the fireworks were about to start, and I was in the firing line. I walked to a place of safety, among the partygoers gathering on the terrace.

No one notices balding middle-aged white men, especially when we're in the majority, so it was easy to hide in plain view at a party like that; it's non-white people like Tesya and her friend who stand out. Looking up, all eyes on the fireworks, no one noticed someone in the shadows, wandering into the deserted house.

A bite or two of the food, a glass of wine from an open bottle, fortified, I bided my time. Then what always happens when I relax – I almost, but not quite, got caught:

Phil came and dumped a tray on the kitchen counter. I opened the nearest door, the downstairs loo off the kitchen. He'd only have seen the back of a middle-aged man, unexcited by fireworks. There would be other toilets upstairs; I could hide without people queuing up outside. The perfect place for eavesdropping on one-to-ones in the kitchen, and the ultimate goal: accessing the right phone. After a few glasses, people let go of the things they usually hold close. Not just objects, as it turned out. Drinking loosens the body and the mind, revealing desires people may not even be aware of.

A successful evening: her phone accessed, and tracked ever since. Need to be careful though, it's a whole different terrain this time.

Now I'm in the quiet, the next Lesson. On synchronicity, definitely: this chance meeting has been a turning point, though it involves working on two projects simultaneously. Something on naming: naming what you're trying to do, and not losing the initial plot when other opportunities turn up.

Record now, while I'm driving in the dark. Angle the camera towards the clock on the dashboard. It's about time too, not letting time trip you up while the clock is ticking:

'The opportunities of synchronicity, and the importance of naming.'

Hope this won't be a lesson I'll learn to my cost later on.

NOW

Massive hangover. Pot after pot of coffee, scrambled eggs on buttery toast, and then she's almost OK. She clears the table and wonders whether to go out for some fresh air. Whether to text Jazz if she's around, though probably she won't be after last night – then, amazing synchronicity: she calls.

'Hey, how are you this morning?'

'Hung-over; aren't you? Had a massive breakfast to soak it up. I was thinking of going for a walk. You around?'

Before Jazz answers: kids screeching and metallic squeaking, swings or roundabouts – she's walking home through the park?

Jazz answers the unspoken question. 'A walk sounds good. Just going home for a shower. I'll buzz you when I'm setting off. Meet you by the canal?'

Sorted, she heads for a shower too, and as she's drying herself her mobile buzzes – she checks: Jazz. She holds her phone for a moment – but Holly would be cooking a Sunday roast or whatever she does – she wouldn't have had time to text back yet. She dresses, choosing leggings and a sweatshirt, and then a windcheater and trainers. She picks up her mobile; on automatic, she goes to put it in her pocket, the right one – and remembers walking down the garden path and yesterday's panic. Now she brushes it off, and pockets her phone with her keys once she's outside.

Across the park she's squinting into the sun. She should have worn her sunglasses, but she won't go back, it's good to be in the fresh air. Avoiding the glare, she looks down at the grass, though her mind is walking down last night's garden path again, on the edge of a thought, hunting a phrase, trying to pin it down. Walking, no, leading someone down a garden path: her mind had led her down a garden path, wanting nothing else awful to happen, convincing her for a while that it was an accident – but it couldn't have been, technology doesn't lie: she hadn't read that message.

At the gate to the canal path, she looks up and is blinded again by the sunlight; she turns away, her hand on the gate – it creaks.

A door wide open, with smoke wafting in over her coat – and her phone in the wrong pocket: of course there was someone there, but who would sneak a look at her phone at Ben and Phil's party? It had been mostly white middle-aged middle-class men, like she works with, though it was mostly gay men, their friends. Not that class, age, gender, sexuality or race have much to do with committing right or wrong. So many people she knows have admitted snooping on their partners – and not just the obvious, stalking them on Facebook, surveillance by another name. People lower their voices when admitting hacking a partner's email, with the excuse the password was easy to guess. It's always the name of the lover, ironically, the person they trust, who obviously doesn't trust them – otherwise why hack a lover's phone? Now smartphones are with us 24/7, only left momentarily – but that's all it takes to snoop. The stupidest thing about smartphones is everything's there: your whole life.

'Hey' – Jazz is right in front of her, smelling of a sporty fragranced shower gel and wearing shades. 'You OK?'

'Gosh, I didn't see you coming – the sun's in my eyes. Yes –'

She's about to tell her about her worry, but once they're walking away from the sunlight she can see her better: she's wearing a new rather chic fitted woollen coat, and like a model in the weekend fashion pages it looks like she's had a really good night, despite lack of sleep. And there's something else: is she going to tell her about last night, after the party? She lets go of her mobile, and asks, 'How about you?'

They're walking side by side along the canal path and, without discussing it, east towards Hackney. Jazz doesn't reply, so she prompts her with a 'So?' and a smile, and just at that moment a woman jogging towards the light almost crashes into them. They move apart to let her through, and when they're back walking side by side, Jazz says, 'Yes?'

She tries, 'So, you rushed off somewhere last night?'

Jazz is walking faster than her; she steps up her pace to keep up.

'Yes.' Monosyllabic; what she does when she doesn't want to talk about something. 'I was tired, I rushed off to bed – I had hockey this morning. That party was fun. Ben and Phil are great.'

Confused: her texting – and the direction of the cab; how has she misinterpreted it?

'Took ages to get home, the cab had to detour – horrific accident near yours, must have happened just before we dropped you off, we just missed it.'

'How awful.'

'Yes, lucky escape – could have been us.'

Her shoulders relax – she thinks how weird, she didn't know she was all tensed up until her shoulders did that. Then she's so relaxed, she does what she'd never normally do, and pushes Jazz further – 'So who were you texting last night. Someone nice?'

'When?' Jazz stops, and faces her.

Aware of a man walking a dog, about to cut between them, she moves closer to Jazz to let him pass by the wall – so now they're on the narrower section of the path, under a bridge, close to the water.

Jazz is staring at her, like she's no idea what she's talking about, so she prompts her, 'In the cab, coming home?'

'In the cab? No one really, just a woman from hockey.'

'Late to text?'

'She was up, like us. It was Saturday night?'

Jazz starts walking again, like the conversation is over. Perhaps she's got it wrong – after all, she and Jazz often text late into the night too.

She catches up, and they're side by side when a family – kids and two women – pass by, so they're close together again by the water. Jazz takes off her coat – it's warm now – there's that sporty fragrance again. She's usually such a no-fragrance person – there must be someone even if Jazz doesn't want to tell her, her body has: she's seeing someone, stayed over, showered with someone else's gel – and went home to change her clothes. She just doesn't want to tell Tesya.

Does she want to know? Don't friends talk about their lovers, one-night stands – whatever it might be? Like Jazz obviously thinks hers is a failing relationship, and she lets her know – and she finds that difficult. OK, fair enough, she'll drop it until she wants to tell.

Another family group cycles towards them in single file, the parents having a loud discussion or perhaps an argument – they're speaking a language she doesn't recognize. Their kids whizz past, way ahead fast on their bikes – she moves nearer the water's edge, but through the blur of fluorescent cagoules between them, Jazz moves the other way.

Sometimes Jazz feels so far away, it makes her want to reach out and touch her, tell her she loves her – and not in that 'love you' way of phone sign-offs. However she said it, Jazz would laugh about her being all emotional, so she'd add, 'I mean as a friend,' like people do, which is stupid. Why categorize love, why is friendship seen as less about love than romance?

As they walk off the canal path towards the café, her mobile buzzes. It's Zehra texting a reminder of dinner tonight: 'Do you want to bring a friend?' She hasn't told Zehra about Holly – even though she was thinking of it, the evening she met Hamid. Because she rarely sees Holly, she doesn't naturally come up in conversation when people ask what she's been up to. She's not told many people, now she thinks about it.

At the café serving hatch they get mugs of builder's tea and then go and sit perched on the wall overlooking the still water.

She could ask Jazz to come to Zehra's tonight – but Jazz's phone rings, and she gets up and answers, walking a few steps away – so she doesn't ask her; she's probably busy. Jazz hangs up near the serving counter, and the woman behind the counter must have said something to her as she's smiling back, saying something. When she returns she's carrying a sachet of sugar; she tears it open and pours it in her tea.

Someone goes past, laden with grocery shopping. That reminds her. 'I need to get a bottle and flowers for Zehra – dinner tonight at hers.'

'Oh, say hi from me. I'll walk back with you that way then, past the shops.'

So everything feels normal again, even though she hasn't asked Jazz to come too, which she normally would, so it's an abnormal kind of normal.

At Zehra's she has such a lovely evening. They eat roast chicken and there's nut roast too – Erwin is here, and he's become vegetarian. He's talking with Hamid about websites; they have their online design businesses in common. She listens, not understanding what they're talking about. It's good seeing Erwin again; she should see him more often, but as he came after her in Zehra's fostering years, they didn't overlap. They've only spent a few Christmases and Sunday dinners together at Zehra's. He's fun, and quick-witted, always winning at

Scrabble and other games they play together in the evenings, after eating too much and sharing the washing-up, then vegging out on the sofas in the lounge.

She hasn't got many photos of Erwin, and none of Hamid. She gets her phone out and focuses on the two of them, clicking the photo just as Zehra comes into view carrying a dish of apple crumble.

She says, 'Oh, send it to me.'

'Me too, please.' Erwin returns to what he was saying to Hamid.

She forwards the photo to both of them. A phone buzzes on the sideboard, and Zehra goes and picks it up. Erwin's phone must be on silent, he's such a millennial – he picks it up and smiles. 'Nice photo.'

'Thanks.' She looks at the photo: Zehra is placing the crumble on the table and Erwin and Hamid are both smiling up at her. Her family. She suddenly wants a photo of herself with all of them.

'Erwin, how do I set the camera to take a photo of us all?'

He takes her phone and sets up the self-timer, then they arrange themselves at one end of the table, close together, laughing – they have a few failed tries, Erwin checking and finding one of them slightly out of frame or eyes closed. Then he's counting to ten again, and it flashes.

She checks. 'Perfect. I love it.'

Hamid looks over her shoulder. 'Great photo.'

She passes the phone to Zehra, who smiles. 'Oh yes.'

Then her phone is in Erwin's hand – 'Can I forward it to me?'

She answers, 'Sure.' And then, 'Yes please,' to Zehra's passing of the jug of cream to go with the apple crumble.

Erwin says, 'That's an interesting photo.'

She looks up. 'Which one?'

'A garden at night: taken through a doorway. Beautiful photo. Sorry, I didn't mean to look, just the next photo came up.'

He holds the screen towards her. The photo is dark, difficult to make out what it's of, but it's true, it is beautiful in a weird kind of way. 'I can't remember taking it.'

He looks back down at it. 'It's got last night's date.'

'Oh.' She takes it off him. 'Probably an accidental one – I was at a party.'

'It's a remarkably good accidental one, nicely framed.'

She stares down at the photo, the date and the time: the early hours of last night. It's been a long twenty-four hours. She puts her phone away; she really doesn't want to think what she's thinking –

'Are you OK, Tesya?' Zehra touches her hand.

'Yes – well, sort of.' She turns to Erwin. 'How easy is it for someone to get into another person's phone?'

'Depends what the lock password is, if it's just a straightforward series of consecutive numbers?' She nods yes. 'Then it's easy. You should change it.'

'Tesya?' Zehra looks worried.

'Oh, it was probably just someone messing around at the party last night –'

'People you know well?'

'It was a Thanksgiving party, the new people I work with.'

Hamid gets up and switches the kettle on. 'Coffee, everyone?'

Erwin and Zehra say yes to coffee, and get up and start clearing the table. It's like they've relaxed at the thought of a party of professionals, the kind of people they imagine she works with – the people she knows.

She takes the wine glasses, stacking them upside down in the dishwasher in a line.

She never told Zehra much about what happened at her last job, not to worry her – but she poured it out to Erwin late into the night last Christmas. He was angry for her, but at the same time he's a young black man who sees racism as a fact of life, being on the receiving end of lots of it. He's learned how to brush things off, get on with things despite it, but, well, she could see from his hands as he talked, the clenching and unclenching of his fists, he was frustrated to hear what she had been going through.

He'd said, 'Look, Tesya, racism is to be fought via the ballot box – you can't go getting upset about it like this, it's not worth it. They're not worth it. And it doesn't solve it.'

He continued by telling her yet again what the Socialist Workers were doing to fight racism, and she'd changed the subject. She was never going to join any party – politics, in terms of going to meetings, was just not her thing; the difference between them. She had once gone to a Labour Party meeting and found it excruciating, the procedures and minute-taking reminding her of academic meetings that go on for hours too. They had ended up raiding the drinks cabinet and drinking spirits while watching a film on Netflix, Spike Lee's *Do the Right Thing*, before crashing for the night far too late.

Zehra, scraping a bowl into the bin and then handing it to her stacking the dishwasher, says, 'Good you're socializing with people at work. It's all fine then?'

She nods; well, it's true … more or less.

'Talking of Thanksgiving, it's Christmas soon. Do you want to invite Jazz this year, if she's free?'

Which of course brings back last night, not just whether Jazz is hiding someone she'd prefer to spend Christmas with, but also that she's still not told Zehra about Holly. Not that Holly would come for Christmas –

Sometimes she feels like a teenager, having her best friend round for tea – when she's an adult, but is she ever going to feel like one?

'I'll ask her. I'd like her to come, thanks. What would you like me to bring?'

'I was thinking, let's go to the Heath the week before, so we can decorate the house, get some holly?'

It's only her name, of course, her name that's also the name of a plant with dark green leaves and hard red berries. The only colour in a wintry landscape – how does it go, 'the holly bears the crown'? Holly tucking her red hair behind her ears, revealing her elegant neck –

Oh, how she wishes she had a photo of Holly – though she can see her now: she's the one thing clear and straightforward in her mind's eye.

'Tesya?'

'Sorry, yes of course, I'd like that. I love Holly.'

10

WHAT IS LOVE?

AUTHOR'S NOTE

Is it possible to find true love in this technological era, the kind of love written about by Shakespeare in his Sonnets, or further back by the Ancient Greek poets, in the lyrical fragments of Sappho? Is it possible in this performative era with social media tracking our changing relationships, coupled selfies and red heart emojis – now love is primarily seen through virtual public avowals, is love more difficult to talk about in the private sphere between two people, without a running commentary on the internet?

The word love is overused on social media, people love books, movies and celebrities – 'love' in quote marks, the embryo of the word fertilized by the capitalist technology predicting or dictating our responses at the touch of a key. That gushing love has spread into the real world, overheard conversations on the bus or on the street, at the end of a call: 'Love you', two syllables incomplete without three in return, 'Love you too'; the hollowness of identical monosyllabic exchanges repeated like a mantra.

Does the proliferation of the word love lessen the power of the word in private, make it more difficult to say, to speak of love with another person alone in an intimate space? We live in such a wordy time, but it's the predictive wording of robotic automata. When our heart-beating bodies meet we're at the mercy of another's feelings, flailing to communicate, talking more difficult than texting, messy with unfinished sentences, half-said-half-thought utterances and non-verbal sounds – perhaps that's more real, more like the poetry of Sappho's fragments, delicate and only complete in the lover's presence: what love is.

Sometimes there's love without love, the word without the meaning, labelling an action or object – lovemaking or love-token. Capitalism harnesses the word, telling us to show love through material objects, presents, rather than relying on our live presence – although often we reveal more than we intend: our insecurities, and how delicate, shallow – or deadly – our love is to the lover. Love can turn to hate – and hate is a form of deadly self-love.

LESSON TEN

After the excitement of the new, the monitoring: I could pounce at any moment. Not until there's the chance of maximum impact though, loving the power, don't want to throw it away.

Yes, love and power.

Camera ready.

'Look over there, where the wind is picking up and the waves rock the boat from side to side, yet I'm still here, looking after myself, showing up despite the elements. Surviving on a boat in winter is a useful metaphor for biding our time, today's theme.

'Biding your time is about carrying on even when it feels like there's nothing to do to further your cause. Waiting for the right moment, you monitor evidence while stocking up for the harsh times ahead. Rather like what happens in long-term relationships, the bits when – if you're brutally honest – you don't feel the love you did when you first fell for your partner. You know. You're used to them, no longer turned on by them but not ready to ditch them; that's biding time, and let's add the emotion: love. No, I'm not getting sentimental, love is a complex matter, and especially during the biding-time phase it has a lot more to do with hate than marriage counsellors ever admit.

'Think about this time of year, the build-up to Christmas when supposedly loving couples come unstuck. The office Christmas do, and the coming home after one too many, or not coming home at all and waking up in the "wrong" bed. The arguments in that awful period when people are stuck together for days; think about love when the turkey's not defrosted in time, or burned, and Christmas is spoiled?

'Think about love as the Renaissance poets did, as a hunt between predator and prey, the consummation the kill. After capture the prey is tainted, the days of desire are finite once the flesh is consumed. In the middle of an orgasm the other person is forgotten, the ultimate goal is that moment in our own mind, alone. When it's over and they're still there in bed next to us, we have to appear romantic, even though we're not in the mood once we've got what we wanted. Love is like frozen food: like a slaughtered animal, love needs time to defrost and time to heat, to be edible for later consumption. For your project to be viable, your subject needs to survive, and you do too: so bide your time, and practise – that millennial word – self-love.

'So, let's break down the activity involved with biding time, taking a British Christmas as our example. Shops and transport are closed for days, so we order food in early, book the turkey, bake a cake a month earlier, and mince pies a few days before. Then cards and presents: writing a list of recipients, and the buying and wrapping. My favourite chore is the buying of a tree. You're probably thinking I've digressed, but no, I'll use the tree to show you how biding your time is a way of appearing to have digressed, so they'll hope you've given up and moved on. Biding your time gives a false sense of security, enabling them to forget, until you pounce again. They won't totally forget, you're lurking in their thoughts, without you lifting a finger, precisely because you haven't lifted a finger. Biding your time is holding back for the big day, like we do at Christmas. Waiting for the look on the recipient's face: priceless.

'Talking of waiting, I need to go and source a Christmas tree. I know someone who needs one, and I'm stronger; it's easier for me to chop one down and carry it there. Now, just need to find my axe, and gardening gloves.'

An axe, a tree and then a drop-off: an early Christmas present, anonymous of course, to show my love. My kind of biding time, my kind of love.

NOW

It's quite a long walk to the part of the Heath where they're more likely to find some holly. It's uphill too. Out of breath, they stop at the top of the lane leading to Kenwood House, the old ornate white building a stark contrast to the darkness of bare winter branches. Turning away from the grand house of Sunday visits past, with its gilt-edged old masters and busy tea shop, Zehra gestures towards the bushier wilderness area.

Tesya hitches up her rucksack. One path looks well trodden. Along the other path they might have to avoid overhanging branches, not to get scratched, but there might be more chance of finding branches with berries still attached. 'Let's go this way.' Ahead of Zehra, she holds back a branch, so it doesn't snap back.

They go slowly, the path winds around trees, down a bank and then up again – meandering like their conversation. Now, between the trees, they walk one in front of the other in companionable quiet, with just the snap and crackle of twigs and leaves underfoot.

Love is feeling comfortable with someone without feeling the need to talk.

With Jazz too, though they can talk for hours, they have quiet times like this – and sometimes they have prickly times like after the Thanksgiving do. She can hardly remember why now, well almost – and now they're back to normal anyway, hanging out when they can. Otherwise they have long phone calls after busy days at work, or at weekends, after whatever they're up to with their other friends, Jazz with her rowing and hockey crowd – and perhaps that 'no one really' – but they're both looking forward to Christmas together.

Love is accepting that others have their own private thoughts and worlds. We all need space to explore and dream, then we return to our friends and family, replenished with love.

The path widens, and they come across a massive fallen tree, its roots splayed out, leaving a gaping hole in the ground where it once grew. There's something sad about the dead tree and its dark crater of earth. They carry on past it, into the denser part of the wood, where there's no path and she can't remember having walked before.

Further on, at last, after the darkness of bare branches above their heads and dry fallen leaves underfoot, scattered across low-lying bushes of evergreen they find the bright scarlet berries. They open their rucksacks and place them on the ground, and then start to cut a few small branches each – just enough to decorate, and, as Zehra says, 'So it will grow back more next year. OK, that's enough. Time for a cuppa?' She gets out her flask.

'Mm, definitely time.'

They sit on the trunk of another fallen tree and take turns in sipping steaming tea from the flask cup.

'So is Jazz coming for Christmas?' Zehra asks.

'Sorry, I forgot to tell you. Yes, she said she'd love to come.'

'Great, it'll be good to have a full table this year. Last cup?' She holds up the flask.

'I'm fine thanks. You have it.'

While Zehra is pouring the last of the tea, she gets her phone out, on automatic. There's no coverage of course. She goes to put it away again in her pocket, then remembers Ben's party, or rather her phone – it still bugs her, but since then she's made an effort to keep her phone nearby; being out of range is like being without it. Holly's out of range, only the odd text every now and then about her hectic life – like she's pressed pause on whatever it is they have – but when she gets in touch she knows she'll be hooked again, dangling, like a fish at the end of a rod, not dead, not quite alive –

Gosh, that's a brutal image – there were men fishing in the pond at the bottom of the hill earlier – there is something brutal about fishing, a sport of killing.

'Tesya, what's wrong?'

'Wrong?'

'You're looking serious?'

'Oh, nothing really. Sometimes I can't stop thinking about silly things –'

'What sort of things? Not work?'

Zehra looks worried. She doesn't want her to worry, so she says, 'Work's fine.' Everything that's happened in London could have been accidents, nothing she'd report to Jo –

'Tesya, is it about someone new in your life?' Zehra nods towards her hand – she's still clutching her phone. 'Tell me – I mean if you want to.'

'Yes, I was going to tell you, but, well –'

She smiles encouragement.

'We don't see each other very often.'

'What's her name?'

'Holly.'

'Oh, how funny,' she says, then adds, 'I mean because here we are, with our harvest.' Zehra gestures to the rucksacks near their feet.

'Yes, it is, isn't it?' She looks down at the holly too. 'She's got red hair.'

'When did you meet?'

'In September, just after I moved back to London.'

Zehra re-screws the top of the flask and squeezes it into her rucksack side pocket. 'She's a Londoner then.' Before she can correct her, she continues, 'So, when will we meet her?'

That 'we': her and Hamid – or her and all of them, her waifs and strays – and friends like Jazz. 'Jazz hasn't even met her.'

'Oh?'

'It's complicated: she's got kids, and, well, she doesn't live in London. We don't see each other often; it's early days,' she says, though it doesn't really feel like it.

'Well, you know you're welcome to bring her round, anytime?'

They start to walk back, just as the sun is shrouded in the clouds.

'Thanks, Zehra, yes, I'd love you to meet her.'

Zehra leads the way. Ahead of her, she says, 'You could invite her to our New Year's Day open house, if you want. She could bring her kids too.'

She pauses, taking hold of the branch Zehra's holding back for her, but it springs out of her gloved hand and she quickly swivels away.

'Are you OK?'

'I'm fine thanks, don't worry.'

They walk on.

'Like I said, it's complicated. She's not out. I haven't met the kids. It's all new for her, too early for her to meet people I know.' It's also her; how she knows Holly, and how Holly makes her feel: that ecstatic island of hope between the covers. When every second counts, nakedly in love, it's like a fragile garment that might rip at the touch of too many hands. No, she can't imagine introducing her to other people, not yet.

They pass through the kissing gate onto the lane leading to Kenwood House one way and back to Hampstead the other way – the way they take, walking downhill to the car parked in a side street. Zehra gets her keys out, and they store their rucksacks in the boot, tucking the branches in so they don't get caught as she closes it.

Inside the car, Zehra continues, 'I do like the name Holly.' She opens her window and adjusts the wing mirror. Someone has knocked it – the street is packed, it's the last Sunday before Christmas and cars are manoeuvring in and out. 'She must be lovely.'

Zehra is wonderful; she thinks the best of everyone.

Her own name, Tesya, was given to her by the woman who gave birth to her, then gave her away. The only definite thing she knows about her mother is that she chose her name. She likes her name; she'd like her mother, because of her name she knows it – not that she's ever tried to trace her, like others she knows have done with mixed results, more rejection for various reasons, and the rare happy fairy-tale ending. She doesn't want her own fairy-tale idea of her mother destroyed – and it might be just that. Like she has a fairy-tale image of Holly and her kids – her playing with smaller versions of herself in a sunny country garden – even though life is often clouded with rainy days. Holly's a mystery, like her birth mother – but Holly is also a perfect fairy tale in the flesh.

'Just checking my phone,' Zehra says, and then looks up. 'You're quiet today: reflective?'

'Sorry –'

'It's fine, actually I'm feeling reflective too.' She puts her phone on the dashboard.

'Something on your mind?'

'Oh, nothing to worry about: end-of-year business stuff, that sort of thing. And Hamid – I wasn't going to tell you yet, I need to think about it – we've talked about moving in together.' She looks at her. 'It would be him moving in with me, of course. I wouldn't give up the big house, I need it for all of you when you come, it's what I'm used to –'

'Where does he live?'

'He's got a gorgeous old warehouse loft. You'd love it, it's your style – it's quite near yours actually. A few times I thought we might bump into you –'

'How funny, a role reversal, mum hiding her lover from her kids.'

'I didn't say hiding –'

'Just joking. I remember doing that with you, even though I didn't need to.'

They laugh, and she gets a sudden memory of the adrenaline rush of teenage years: a friend suggesting they go for a coffee, and nervously veering her the opposite direction to where she suggested so they wouldn't pass Zehra's restaurant. Then, after walking miles, going into a café hidden down an alley, they had sat in a booth right at the back. The girl said something like, 'Anyone would think you were hiding me away,' and then she kissed her. She liked the kiss; she was going to fall in love with girls forever. Not that life's turned out like that – yet.

Zehra puts her key in the ignition. Through the car window, a woman walks past, laden with designer carrier bags from clothes stores – like the labels sticking out of Holly's inside-out clothes, slung over the armchair in her bedroom when there's so little time but they're naked in bed, making love.

Zehra turns the key; the engine starts.

'Just remembered I have some last-minute shopping, something I need to post – last day is tomorrow, isn't it? It might be easier to get something here than near mine in the morning.'

'That's fine. Do you mind if I head off now?'

'Thanks, yes, I'll get the bus to yours, won't be long. I'll help you unpack the holly later, and decorate the tree?'

'Great, come round for tea, no rush; it'll just be the two of us.'

Love is knowing when the other person needs one-to-one time.

She hugs Zehra, then gets out, calling back through the window, 'Until later.'

She walks away but turns to wave back, like they always do, just like when she moved out to go to university as a student. Zehra waves back, then she's driving out into the line of cars, heading home. She loves knowing she'll see her later, knowing she'll always be there now. Unconditional love is infinite: 'til death us do part – all romantic love must be like that, with the right person – difficult though, the divorce rate in this country, all the love gone wrong.

She walks along the side streets of large Victorian houses. She'd read recently how so many were built off the compensation given to slave owners, not the enslaved. Their windows frame glimpses of families and Christmas trees, beyond high evergreen hedges. She turns onto the crowded high street past shopfronts displaying ties and socks, chocolates and lingerie. Her mind flips from the clichéd gendering of presents, to the workers who produce them – the issue of fair trade still there, in the twenty-first century.

There's a charity shop with cast-off clothes hanging decoratively around a full dinner service in the window; what people throw away: things they've grown out of, once cherished, now unwanted memories? Though is it ever really possible to give away the past? Marriages, and even divorces, are no longer permanent now people live for longer; they can leave each other, and even later on remarry. What couples must go through in leaving each other: shared possessions divided up; homes built together, sold; children shared part-time, or severed forever. What that must be like, missing a child: like not knowing your mother – but not if you've never known her, you need to know someone to miss them. Like missing a lover.

Love is so time-related: time together, time apart, and excruciating time, when it's been too long. Not seeing Holly since last month, with kids' school events in the lead-up to Christmas.

Window-shopping – what to get her? Not sure of her size, not even with those labels draped across the bedroom chair or tangled in the bedding; never actually having read the labels – only her womanly body, so different to her own.

In a women's clothes shop, the colours aren't at all what she's used to seeing Holly wear, her neutral barely-there colours, an array of beiges and creams – only when they first met was she dressed in funereal though chic black, after a work meeting.

There are the terribly obvious things people buy for Christmas presents, the one-size stretchy things, hats, scarves and gloves. No. There are accessories, bags and bracelets, necklaces and rings – expensive, over-the-top, or too obvious.

There's the sound of the door being locked.

Behind her, the shop assistant, a bunch of keys in his hand, says, 'Don't worry, we won't lock you in, you've got five minutes.'

She moves further to the back of the shop; there must be something. Then she sees it: a delicate bralet, the kind that is multi-size.

In her hands it's soft and silky, and the pattern of scarlet berries and dark green leaves on black is Christmassy but subtle. It's not obviously holly leaves, just wintry. It's elegant and expensive – she buys it without a second thought.

Sometimes love is knowing what to give because you know how it will be received. Holly getting out of bed; how she looks at her while fastening her bra, like she wants to take her back to bed, not leave.

When she's outside holding the carrier bag with its tissue-wrapped lingerie, she sees her bus approaching and runs for it, then makes her way up to the top deck as the bus lurches off.

Down the hill, they stop at a red traffic light. On the other side of the road there's a young couple kissing; from the distance they look still, like a statue of love. She looks away and gets her phone out. On the newsfeed there's nothing new, just the usual end-of-year round-ups and Sunday comment pieces on where the government has got to with Brexit – nowhere, of course – and the economy, sterling dropping against the dollar and the euro.

Glancing back as the bus sets off again, she looks for the couple, but they must have moved on. That phrase. Someone telling her, like a command, 'Move on, Tesya' after all the 'incidents' that to them may have just been 'accidents' – they had so many other things to deal with. Like she wasn't important enough to get to the bottom of it – that was it, feeling unimportant, not worthy of thought.

She feels the carrier bag on her lap – she'll wrap the present tonight, when she's home from Zehra's.

Love is making your loved one feel like the most important person in your life. Like those moments in the darkness, eyes closed, when Holly's arms circle her like a ring of love.

The bus turns left, past the police station. When she was facing Jo, registering what had happened the first time in her office, Jo's eyes were on her face, actively listening, repeating the phrases she'd used back to her, checking she'd understood. Jo was doing her job, but that day she made her feel that what had happened to her was important enough to record, and also to act on when anything new came up, any leads.

She should send Jo a Christmas card, to say thanks for her help. She'll do it tomorrow, when she posts Holly's present. The post office will be open late; it'll be packed, last day of posting. People standing in lines for hours, writing addresses on envelopes at the last minute –

She doesn't have Holly's address. She can send Jo's card to the police station. But Holly's – she'll have to text her and hope she answers before the post office closes tomorrow evening.

Funny, posting things to them both out there.

Her phone goes – Zehra: can she pick up some milk? She texts back yes; she'll stop at the all-hours corner shop.

Soon, a carton of milk in one hand and Holly's present in its carrier bag in the other, she's almost at Zehra's, the one constant in the past decade or so of her life, somewhere she feels at home.

What love must feel like, when you find it: like being at home.

11

PRESENCE

LESSON ELEVEN

No one around, the beauty of these short days.

There's a pall of melancholy hanging over the rows of trees, grown only to be cut down in their prime, decorate a house for a few days in the slow death of a family Christmas, and then be binned. Like battery hens and turkeys: stuffed and trussed, roasted and carved, eaten, and even in their final moments their skeletons gnawed at by small domestic creatures.

I check the angle, steady myself, draw the axe back, and then hack at the trunk. It falls, the branches bouncing back before the tree lies still.

A quick look over the fence, then I drag the tree, push it upright and then over. Climbing back, I fall down on its soft branches; a moment of that soporific scent of pine needles.

Then, hidden under the copse, there's the car. I arrange the tree, innocently at this time of year, sticking out from the boot across the back seat. The perfect wintry backdrop. Might as well angle the camera now, record while I'm driving; kill two birds with one stone.

Killing birds. That's an idea. Right terrain, and I've got the equipment. Drive slowly. There: a whole yard of them. Happily, for me at least, ready for the taking. Turn the engine off. Wait until they forget me.

Now quickly, if a little bloody, into the boot by the tree: perfect.

No more detours, time running out. Record in transit: no point losing the moment.

'A Lesson today about tapping into the uncanny, that strange mixing of the familiar and the unfamiliar evoking an unsettling presence. The familiar lulls the receiver into a false sense of security; false, because you choose something that relaxes their senses, taking them back to a time when they felt good. Like the smell of a Christmas tree evokes the perfume of perfect Christmases past.

'And then the unfamiliar, what makes the familiar uncanny. Familiar things looked at in an unexpected light become peculiar. A doll not in the nursery but in a ditch, its skirt torn and bundled up around its waist, with its lower torso naked and stuck in the mud.

'What taps right into our worst fears is when something that's usually alive is dead when seen close up. Think of the purring barking twittering animals we pet and coo over. Or the dead, once-living creatures on a plate, cooked or cured, that without a qualm we readily put a knife and fork into and consume. Now think of a severed head, a cut limb, a leg, a wing, with the goosebumps of freshly cut flesh and a pink-red blood colour blushing beneath skin. Isn't there something uncannily familiar yet unfamiliar, reminding you of something closer to you? Don't you shiver like someone's walked across your grave? What a strange expression that is, but how exact: a premonition of what will become of us when we're gone, what we can't and yet also can imagine, even though we don't want to.

'So, the mingling of the familiar and the unfamiliar: think about shape and form, and a fusion of what you desire and what the recipient might fear.'

Funny driving the route I used to every day for years after work, past the neighbouring houses in the village. Ah, almost took the usual way, just in time, turn off, steer the car down the overgrown lane at the back of the houses, leading to the woods.

They won't be home yet. Enough time to shovel up some earth and put the tree into a pot from the pile outside the garden shed. Leave it here, where the security light will shine on it when it's triggered.

Now bring the bird, and place it on the tree's lower stronger branches.

Not bad. Glad it's not a turkey or anything so clichéd. Not a partridge in a pear tree, but a headless chicken on a Christmas branch.

There's a car engine, the other side of the house. It cuts out, there's a moment of silence before a door slams shut. Definitely time to go.

NOW

It's a miracle: she's on the phone to Holly – almost the first time she's actually picked up and not left it to go to voicemail. Holly's saying, 'I'll call you when I leave, but probably be at yours just after eight –' when she suddenly stops. There's just her fast breathing.

'Holly, you OK?'

'Wait –'

There's a scream in the background, then a child's voice, 'Mum?'

'Sorry, better go see what's wrong, I'll call you,' she says, and hangs up.

Lots to get on with: wrapping presents, and making a nut roast to take to Zehra's. She switches on the radio in the kitchen; the deep voices of a male choir are in full flow singing the solemn carol, 'Once in Royal David's City'. She sets to grinding the nuts, sautéing the onions, and soon the dish is prepared, ready for roasting on Christmas Day.

On the coffee table the wrapping paper and the last few items to wrap are all laid out, and soon that's finished too. Then, even though her phone's been sitting silently, she picks it up – and of course when the food processor was on, or the radio, she missed the arrival of Holly's text. It just says, 'Sorry, really sorry, I can't call back tonight. Kids are hyper pre-Christmas, plus an old friend just dropped by. I'll call you soon.'

It had been only a possible last-minute thing, but now they won't see each other until after the New Year, her kids off school for the holidays.

What's the point?

She picks up a half-open bottle of wine from the kitchen counter, when from the other side of the room the radio sounds the six pips for the PM programme, then, 'It's 5 p.m., and here are the headlines –'

She switches it off; she's already seen today's headlines on her phone, all the increasingly racist Brexit blustering, how 'immigration has destroyed British culture' – and the other side of the coin, another boatload of refugees drowned in the Mediterranean, the photos of their lifeless bodies lying on picture-postcard beaches more usually seen in tourist snaps on Instagram.

She pushes the bottle back with the other bottles on the counter. She should do the washing-up. Holly must be in the thick of it, icing cakes and dealing with what really did sound like her hyper kids. She can only try to imagine how it is. And tonight she'll stay sober, rather than drowning her sorrows – a good idea too, before the excess of Christmas.

She runs a bath, and afterwards chills out on the sofa, the TV remote control in hand to see what's on. There's a romcom she's seen before: a feel-good movie set at Christmas, ending with two happy heterosexual couples. She starts watching, but after a while switches off, dissatisfied. It's a Hollywood version of London and England without multiculturalism, in an all-white, white Christmas – even global warming is erased in a children's picture-book idea of the seasons. Here she is wearing a t-shirt in December –

In the bedroom, she irons and packs for going to stay at Zehra's from tomorrow – avoiding the big Christmas close-down on public transport and time-and-a-half taxi fares to avoid drink-driving. She texts Jazz, checking when she's picking her up tomorrow – her reply comes ages later, she must be out. She notices that she has noticed that, and feels suddenly terribly alone. This endless repetition of texting, missed calls and evenings home alone; the cycle of getting up in the morning and going to sleep at night, over and over again; the repeated task of trying to occupy oneself sufficiently in between, so you don't notice you're alone. Perhaps it's just her, though she notices other people alone, looking at their phones, seated in cafés and pubs or walking around the supermarket with ready meals for one in near-empty trolleys, picking up a pint of milk, or a can of premixed drink – like her. Perhaps she will have just one drink before bed, might help her sleep.

And then it's the morning and everything feels better when Jazz arrives earlier than she'd said she would.

'Late night?'

She's still in her pyjamas. 'No, just a lie-in until the heating kicked in.' She keeps the heating on manual: you could never tell whether you'd end up over-warm, despite it being winter – and then of course this morning she'd woken up to a wintry chill.

She pours Jazz a coffee, and puts some toast on. There are carols playing on the radio, the festive and jolly sort, and through the condensation on the windows even the sun's shining. 'I'm so glad you're coming.'

'Me too,' she replies, as the toast pops up. 'It's so nice of Zehra to invite me.'

Putting butter and jam on the table, she tells her, 'She's mentioned it before, but it was when you were working abroad.'

'I was away so many Christmases. Now I've changed jobs, I never want to be away this time of year again.'

Sitting down opposite her, she wonders but knows not to ask, and changes the subject. 'You're up early?'

'Home so late that I'm up early rather than crash – just the hockey lot, their Christmas do.' Then she changes the subject. 'Is there anything I could get for tomorrow, besides the cheese?' She'd already offered to supply a cheese board from the organic market they planned to visit en route.

'I usually get Zehra flowers from the market. She'd be happy with anything you'd like to bring.'

*

Soon they are in the packed market with other last-minute shoppers, picking up the cheeses and a beautifully arranged bunch of wintry foliage and berries. Then they look around the other stalls, and Jazz queues up to buy a bottle of sloe gin.

There's a bunch of mistletoe hanging up on a stall, and she goes over and buys it. Catching up with her, Jazz raises an eyebrow at her purchase.

'Zehra will like it – and Hamid, I'm sure.' As they cross the road to get back to the car, she adds, 'Now I've got to know him more, I can see he's good for her, gets her to relax.'

On the other side of the road, a postman is emptying the post from the box into his red cart. Holly's present should have arrived by now. No news since the curtailed call of yesterday –

'Watch where you're going.' Jazz pulls her back to safety – away from a car speeding past, its exhaust fumes blackening the white mist of the damp day. 'You were miles away. Where on earth were you?'

The car was close – she's got to start living in the present, otherwise –

'You could have been killed, Tesya.'

Soon the moment's forgotten; they find the car and store their purchases.

When Jazz starts the ignition, the radio comes on, Heart FM – a cheesy number from years ago. Jazz starts to sing along, and she finds herself humming too, and then, as the track changes, 'Do you remember that Soho karaoke bar we used to go to?'

'How could I forget – our late-night out-of-tune duets?'

That silly happy time, singing when you think you can sing, but really you're just drunk and having a good time with friends.

They're driving bumper-to-bumper up the Holloway Road, so many two-by-two – each car with a couple of passengers like a human Noah's Ark. She's glad she's with Jazz, it's Christmas Eve and they're en route to Zehra's – the first time she's taken anyone there for Christmas. Is she a failure at relationships? All the Christmases when whichever girlfriend she was with went back to their parents – and they didn't invite her, and she didn't invite them, despite Zehra saying, 'You know you can bring someone?' Will she ever be at that stage in a relationship?

They arrive; the door is on the latch, so they carry their things inside. There's Hamid's unmistakable presence, a pair of smart suede men's shoes on the shoe rack, and next to it there's a khaki-coloured kitbag, more Erwin's style.

There are all the homely intermingled smells of brewing coffee, freshly baked mince pies, and something garlicky roasting in the oven. Above the clatter and sluicing sound of the dishwasher, Zehra calls from the kitchen, 'I'm in here.'

She calls back, 'We'll take our things upstairs, get them out of the way.'

'Great, then come and have coffee and mince pies.'

Jazz says, 'It's beautiful' – through the open lounge door, the tall Christmas tree they decorated on Sunday is sparkling with white lights dangling among the dark green branches, and on the mantelpiece beside a row of nightlights there's a sprig of holly.

She starts going upstairs when Jazz asks, 'Whose is this?'

She turns back. Jazz is pointing at the kitbag. 'Erwin's, probably – he's staying too. I don't think any of the others are.'

Jazz's face is serious. 'He's not –'

'What?' Then: the khaki colour. 'Oh no, don't worry, he's just a total gym freak – it will be his overnight bag. Come on, let's drop our things.' Soon that moment's forgotten – and there are so many other moments that start to make up this Christmas:

To begin with, that morning, when they came downstairs, Zehra putting down a tray of coffees, noticing the bunch of mistletoe on the table. 'Oh, how wonderful. Shall we hang it over there, in the doorway to the garden?'

Then, with Jazz holding the stepladder, she climbs up to hang the branches, just as Hamid arrives, closely followed by Erwin carrying a box of bottles. They all get stuck into the preparations, and the next twenty-four hours go quickly.

*

It's the late afternoon of Christmas Day. There's a moment when she's coming out of the bathroom upstairs, and from downstairs there's the sound of the TV, a romantic song from an old Judy Garland movie. If only life was like the movies, all happy endings.

She hovers at the top of the stairs, and then goes back round the banister to the guest room she's sharing with Jazz. She checks her phone on the bedside table: a few texts from friends, wishing her Happy Christmas; a daily news email she subscribes to, announcing a Christmas Day temporary ceasefire in the Middle East. That reminds her of Jazz's question about Erwin's khaki kitbag; she should go down and see where she is.

Downstairs, the song stops, actors' voices start speaking. It's funny how film dialogue is a semblance of normal speech but at the same time it's not really like it at all. Real conversation stops and starts, and descends into silences without you realizing it, until it's been some time and it feels uncomfortable.

Sitting on the edge of the bed, she picks up her phone again.

Downstairs, the doorbell rings. Zehra's voice, 'I'll go.'

The TV sound is lowered.

She sits up, peering down through the window. It's Erwin, back from a post-lunch run, out of breath, his tall frame leaning on the garden wall, waiting for Zehra to let him in.

She has a flash of memory, opening the door when Holly arrives at hers – her petite frame by the large heavy loft door. What's Holly's house like, old or modern, or something in between, post-war?

Before she can argue herself out of it, she dials – and anyway it's the first time she's had the room to herself, and probably her last chance today. It rings, and rings. She's about to hang up when there's a 'Hello?' but it's not Holly's voice; it's a young girl.

'Hello? Can I speak to Holly please?'

'Holly? Wrong number.' Then the girl hangs up.

She checks – it was Holly's number, her mobile. She doesn't have her landline; she'd said ages ago, 'I'm always in and out; it's easier to get me on the mobile.'

Perhaps Holly's got a new phone, changed her number – but wouldn't she have told her? She only spoke to her a few days ago. She's puzzled, irritated: why is everything so difficult?

She calls back. It rings once and goes abruptly to voicemail, like someone's switched it off, silenced it. The message is the pre-recorded one set by the phone company, one lots of people have, the same Holly's always had – it's never been her saying her name and telling the caller to leave a message.

Perhaps the child said 'wrong number' because she calls Holly 'Mum' or 'Mummy', forgetting her mother's got a name that other people call her – though that's ridiculous, she didn't sound that young, perhaps eleven or twelve; weren't the twins secondary-school age?

Jazz pushes the door open and comes in. 'There you are. I fell asleep in front of the telly.' Then, 'You OK? What's wrong?'

'Oh, it's nothing,' she replies, but her face must give away what she's feeling –

'It can't be nothing; what's up?'

'It'll sound silly,' she says, and then she tells her.

'It's probably just her kids playing around – you know what kids are like. It's Christmas, they've opened their presents, they're probably bored.' She's sitting on the armchair between the twin beds.

'The kid said wrong number almost immediately when I asked for Holly.'

'Kids do silly things. Believe me, at work sometimes it makes me crack up, the things kids say that they think we might believe.'

'I guess –'

'She'll call you, she always does eventually – otherwise you'd have moved on by now, wouldn't you?' She looks at her intently.

'Yes' – she wants to answer her seriously, because she's partly right – 'Holly does always get in touch, eventually.' It's true that's why she's not moved on from her, but also because she's hooked: Holly's like a drug – when it's been too long, she's desperate for another hit. 'But today, this wrong number or whatever it is feels, well, a bit freaky?' Like Holly's disappeared in the invisible spiralling lines of however mobile phones work. Before, she was hovering in the ether, almost present; she might text or phone anytime. A wrong number is like she's gone away and isn't coming back, or an imaginary figure who never existed.

Like her old office door, without her name card: as if she had never been there.

'Tesya?' Jazz looks serious. 'What is it?'

Perhaps she's being overdramatic. 'Oh, Jazz, I don't know, I feel confused to be honest.'

'Tesya, you do know her behaviour isn't normal, all the cancelling, and whatever else is going on that you haven't told me? I sometimes wonder whether we put up with things that other people wouldn't, because of our childhood … We didn't grow up seeing how normal couples treat each other, did we?'

'Oh, Jazz … it's difficult isn't it, trying to understand other people –'

'Sounds like you need a rest from thinking about her over the break.'

'You're probably right. Thank goodness I have you –'

'You'll always have me –'

From downstairs, Erwin: 'Hey you two, games time?' accompanied by a cork popping.

'Coming.' She stands up, and smiles down at Jazz.

'Games?'

'Board games – it's what we started doing together, since we've shared Christmases. Come on.' At the door she turns back. Jazz is still sitting, looking down. 'Jazz?'

'Coming. Sounds like fun.' She gets up, then adds, 'Something to take our minds off silly stuff.'

Then they're walking downstairs. At the bottom, in the hall mirror she glimpses Jazz behind her, and a sadness in her eyes – then she's annoyed with herself, selfishly thinking of her own stuff, the opposite of Jazz always putting her first. Not that she can deal with it now – Erwin and Hamid are coming out of the kitchen carrying glasses, followed by Zehra with the Christmas cake. So they are plunged into more drinking and games and, on the surface, what should be the perfect Christmas evening – but it's not, not when she feels the presence of something else, silly stuff that's actually really serious.

Games – such an innocent child-friendly word. And fun too, even as an adult, the fun of playing, the winning of paper money at Monopoly, going up ladders and sliding down snakes, picking up sticks and playing tricks with five stones, tossing them into the air and seeing how many you catch. Fun – until she remembers how games at school were cruel, all about power and gain for some, and weakness and losing for others.

It's late. Zehra and Hamid went upstairs ages ago, now it's just the three of them, with the contents of board games played and discarded spread around them. Chatting, sitting on the rug between the sofas and armchairs, there's a lull in the conversation while they finish the last of the many bottles opened.

She picks up a piece of the Monopoly set and starts to pack away the game, and Jazz picks things up too; they're tired now.

Then it happens: what she would never have asked Jazz, as it's clear she doesn't want to tell –

Erwin asks, 'Why did you leave the army?'

'Why do you ask?' Jazz bats back immediately, no pause, all defence, gathering a stack of Monopoly pounds into a pile and snapping on an elastic band to fasten them tight.

'Erwin –' She tries to stop him, but –

Jazz says, 'No, let him answer –'

'We've all drunk too much, Jazz –'

'Sorry – what have I done?' he asks, mortified.

'I'm sorry too. I'm tired – and yes, we've drunk too much. Shall I put the kettle on? I could do with a coffee to sober up.' Jazz turns to her.

She nods, touches her arm; Jazz nods back, like she's saying she's OK – she's not though, she only snaps like that when she's pushed too far.

The door closes behind her, and soon from the kitchen there's the running of the tap.

'Oh Tesya, what did I say?'

'Don't worry. She's never even told me, and it's a couple of years ago now – let's change the subject? I'll go and help her with the coffee.'

'OK, but I think I'm going to crash now. I'm exhausted.' He gets up.

'We've had a great day, haven't we?'

'Yep. Zehra's fab cooking.' He grins, and then hugs her. 'Say night to Jazz for me?'

'Yes. Don't worry.' She can see he is though; he likes Jazz so he's kicking himself, but he'll be fine, it's Jazz –

She pushes open the kitchen door. There are three mugs of coffee steaming on the counter, and beyond that, Jazz is standing in the open doorway, the garden behind her – and she's smoking.

'Gosh. When did you start again?'

'In the Middle East. I gave up when I came back, but now and then –'

It's weird how there's something so attractive about smoking, perhaps because it reminds her of her favourite films, like *Casablanca*.

'Can I have one?'

Jazz points to the packet, on the counter next to the coffees.

'Thanks.' She takes the packet, then picks up the milky coffee waiting for her; Jazz knows how she likes it. It's awful she doesn't know what happened to Jazz, so she doesn't know how to help her – and at the same time she feels like she knows: something you can't put into words. 'Jazz –'

'Don't –' Jazz looks away.

'I wasn't going to –'

'Sorry, I just –'

'Yes, I know, sort of, that's what I wanted to say: if you ever want to, you don't have to hold it in on your own.' Then, what she's only just understood, 'It was that last Christmas, before you came back, wasn't it? Tell me to shut up if you –'

'No, you're right.'

'Oh, Jazz, I'm so –'

'Let me tell you, then let's never talk about it again, OK?'

'Yes, of course. If you're sure?'

'I want to, I think, I'll try.' She moves outside into the open air, sitting down on one of the garden chairs.

She follows, then takes a cigarette out of the packet. Jazz flicks the lighter for her, and then stares into the darkness of the garden.

She waits. Her mind flickers and discards thoughts, then there's just the darkness of the sky.

'It was a night like this, almost pitch-black, how it is outside cities, in the desert. Christmas evening at the clubhouse, we were playing games – not board games – cards, pool: pub games. All drinking, all there is to do. It's cheap out there, everyone drinks more, and in the heat it goes to your head fast.' She stubs her cigarette out, then tears a corner of foil from the fag packet and screws the stub inside it in her fist.

'I left early. It got boring, you know what it's like, people you work with who you have nothing in common with, all drunk, talking nonsense. I left to go to bed, to read a book, fall asleep. I was walking away from the clubhouse …' Jazz stops.

She holds her breath; she doesn't want to hear what's coming, but it's the least she can do. She has to hear what happened to Jazz.

'Then. Two of them, shouting racist homophobic stuff, hitting me, beating me up – not my face, they were careful, didn't want to get caught. Faces are proof, aren't they? Then … you can imagine. I fought back, but two against one. They took me to one of the out-houses and they –' She pauses, picks up the lighter; her fingers flick it on and off. 'I was lucky, one of the women from my dorm came looking for me, just then –'

She doesn't say the rest; it's obvious.

'Oh, Jazz.' She puts her hand out to hold Jazz's hand, and puts her arm around her, and then Jazz leans in to be held.

They sit, holding on to each other, until Jazz suddenly says, 'Shall we have another drink – I mean a drink-drink?'

'Absolutely, just what I was thinking; I'll go.'

At the drinks cabinet she pours vodka into two tumblers, and adds tonic and ice from the fridge. Outside, she passes Jazz the glasses. 'I'll be back.' Then she brings their coats and hangs Jazz's around her shoulders, covers herself too, and sits back down.

'Thank you.'

'You know, Jazz, I'll always be here for you?'

'Yes, I know. Me too – for you I mean.'

She holds out her glass. 'To you, Jazz, you're the best person I know.'

'Oh god Tesya, I'm not, but thank you anyway.'

Then they drink, and when exhaustion finally hits, one of them says, 'Time for bed.'

A little unsteady on their feet, they stand up and get to the doorway, holding each other up. It's sort of funny, one of them laughs, perhaps both of them as the bunch of mistletoe above brushes their heads, and they look up at its white berries and soft green leaves, and then they look at each other, like they're trying to work something out. They stop, and holding each other up turns into holding each other there, in between the outside and the inside, in the dark, with their clothes and hair smelling of smoke, and the taste of alcohol in their mouths. And then she doesn't know anything else, only who is in her arms. One of them moves closer, or perhaps it's both of them, then there's no one else in the world and there's nothing else to do but kiss.

If this was a lesson on a play or film, she'd say – like Chekhov's classic example of a gun – that if you start a Christmas story with buying mistletoe, someone's going to use it eventually. She just didn't guess it would be her, or that she wouldn't feel terribly guilty either. She isn't who she thought she was –

She's falling asleep. Jazz is in the other single bed against the opposite wall, her eyes closed, her breathing slowing, how it does when sleep comes.

She turns on her side.

There's a snippet of raucous carolling from the street, people drunk, singing about reindeers and Santa Claus, animals and imaginary humans.

She turns over again, opening her eyes. Jazz's eyelids flicker, then still, she sleeps on. She turns back the other way, facing the wall.

Jazz's kiss – Jazz just an arm's reach away. What she –

She closes her eyes, inside the thought, under the cover of darkness, savouring the moment. Slowly, how she knows Jazz, the longest she's known anyone. The safety in each other's presence; how they really trust each other. Not just the easy hours of talking and drinking, like with other friends, but being able to cry and be serious, and then afterwards laugh and –

It comes to her: if Holly's little girl was playing, she would have giggled or laughed when she said wrong number – what kids do when they're messing around. She said it straight; she was just answering a call. Holly must have been listening; she couldn't contradict her, if she's really called something else. Does her name matter? What else doesn't she know about her though? Other than what she likes about her, does she know her? Does she like her – or has it only been sex, all this time?

She turns. On the other bed, Jazz is asleep, sprawled out, the covers shifting across her form.

Her limbs relax, she starts to drop off –

When she opens her eyes, sunlight is filling the room and falling across the bed next to her. The duvet's pulled back, and the sheet's smoothed over and tucked in, no traces of the absent body. She sits up, remembering last night.

12

FUTILITY AND GUILT

LESSON TWELVE

She is, I can tell, guilty.

The way she looks over her shoulder, then down again, like down is all there is. How she's dragging the tree; she can't get rid of it soon enough. Now she's dropped it, and she's thrust her hands in her pockets; from the cold, for her lighter? Bet she'd like to light the bonfire now, but she'll wait until the kids are home from school, keep them occupied, looking into the flames, stoking the fire, while she falls into the black hole of another new year, thinking about me.

There was a Bach concerto playing on the radio this morning, that heartache of straining strings; what music does, unlike people. People let you down. Nothing lasts; everything is futile, almost everything, but not quite, one thing lasts. The opposite of futile is fertile; need to think it through, the futility of guilt? A Lesson on how guilt gnaws away, making us impotent, killing the fertility of the imagination.

She's a portrait of futility: her guilty irritation sucking on an illicit cigarette by the bins, overflowing with bags of post-Christmas rubbish. All the smelly decay of flesh and bone, the flammable debris of torn cards, ripped paper and the twisted cellophane wrappings of long-forgotten-but-new toys, and no doubt my gift of a dead bird. She'll never see a Christmas tree again without remembering a headless chicken.

Now she's stamping out her fag; she'd like to stamp me out, if she could, but she can't: I'm a fixture. She stares into the rubbish of Christmas when it's New Year, with all its clichés of fresh starts, that by this time next year will become what she should have done; the ever-present participle of guilty thinking.

I told her before Christmas, 'Work with me, or I'll –'

'Absolutely no idea what you're on about.' She'd glared back, forcing herself not to look away, like she wasn't lying, though her clenched hands gave her away, followed by her slamming of the door in my face.

Though she really is the one who has no idea. The amount of what I know; what I could do.

Better go. Come back later, when she'll have lit the bonfire. Watch her thinking she's burning away the past along with the tree. She won't see me, on the edge of the wood through the smoke and the January twilight.

This backdrop works: the darkness of the spindly tree trunks against the wan light. Steer the car a bit further away. OK, brake on. Position the camera. The light is fading, which makes the point, like a Chekhov play or a Bergman film; all the great art about lost opportunities, and the pointlessness of delay. If you leave something too long, you'll lose what you've always wanted.

Red light flashing:

'A Lesson on the futility of guilt, and in contrast, the fertility of thought.'

NOW

She feels guilty.

Jazz hasn't alluded to it; she's been her normal self. It's almost like she's imagined it – almost, but not quite. She hid it away over the rest of Christmas under an extended hangover, soaked up by Zehra's turkey curry and rice, and lots of water, while trying not to drink, but failing. Alcohol numbed her memory, until it wore off.

They had drunk too much, and what Jazz told her was so awful. Not that that was an excuse.

She can't forget their kiss, though she wants to, sort of. It's that guilty feeling – then she's confused about which of them to feel most guilty about: her supposed lover, who's hardly in touch but who she assumes – not that they've ever discussed it – thinks they're monogamous; or her best friend, her total rock, who she doesn't want to hurt – or lose. But Jazz is acting like it never happened anyway.

She wants everything back to normal. Even the frustrations of Holly would be better than this. When things with her are back at their normal pace, perhaps she'll be able to forget what they did, or rather what she did. She has to take responsibility for what happened.

She feels guilty about wanting to plunge back into her feelings for Holly, using her to take her mind off what she's done. She hasn't tried to contact her since; guilt holds her hand away from her phone. She'll still be busy with the kids – or have schools gone back? Most workplaces have. Not like universities. The term doesn't start for ages – she should get on with her marking though, and go in. At home there are too many distractions – like her guilty post-Christmas thoughts she wishes she could shift away like this year's Christmas cards she's taking downstairs to the recycling bins.

The street is so quiet.

Upstairs again, her desk is tidy, ready for her marking, but she's procrastinating. She'll start tomorrow, early – not lie in, like she has the past few mornings, lying low since Jazz dropped her off.

In the kitchen she opens the fridge. She's run out of milk. Not feeling like cooking properly, she's been snacking on toast along with mugs of tea, when she's managed to leave the sofa. She should stock up. She hasn't been out since New Year's Eve drinks – Jazz there too – at Esther's, a mutual friend from their clubbing days. Esther's more career-oriented now, going by her new swanky apartment, so different to her last houseshare, the location of over-the-top all-night parties.

Jazz was cool, like she was avoiding her – or perhaps it was just there was never a moment for them one-to-one, people talking in small groups, drinking wine, standing around the kitchen island or perched on the arms of the sofas – no one sat down properly. It was a rather networking crowd, people mingling then moving on – not to miss making other more useful contacts. Like dating, out in bars: getting stuck with someone you find you're not that interested in, but it's difficult to move on if you're sat down.

Perhaps Jazz was avoiding her, lying low for a bit too; perhaps they both were.

When she was making an early night of it, she asked Esther where Jazz was, to say goodbye.

'Jazz? Think she's left. Might have been going on somewhere else.'

She had walked home alone. In bed in the early hours of the New Year she shifted, trying to get comfortable after those nights over Christmas sharing a room, their twin beds side by side.

An outsider, watching, would think she's the one playing it cool: she hasn't even texted Holly 'Happy New Year' greetings – though neither has Holly to her. No, she's just in hiding from everything – even work, with its reminders of before, that things go wrong.

Time to go out, stock up – and face the world.

Later that afternoon, when it's dark outside and she should be putting the blinds down, her mobile rings. It's Holly.

'I'm coming into town. I know it's terribly short notice, but can you meet me?'

And an hour or so later, not far from the station, they're walking along a side street, in the cold early evening air.

'Where are we going?'

Holly says, 'Really want to take you to this place –'

'Where?'

'Wait and see.'

It's exciting not knowing where they're going – Holly's elegant heels clicking along the pavement, and her hand touching hers briefly as they walk briskly between rows of red-brick Victorian mansion blocks. There's no one around – just a lone city fox, scavenging bones from split bin bags lying on the skeleton of a Christmas tree, its green spines scattered across the ground ahead of them. It's Twelfth Night; Christmas is over –

'Happy Christmas and Happy New Year, and –' Holly pulls her past the bins, through an archway, into a narrow passageway cutting underneath the building.

It's dark, but she can make out bikes locked up on metal bars on the wall – then Holly kisses her, and she closes her eyes. Held tight, her back against the hard brick wall, she breathes in her floral perfume and sweet powdery scent on her skin, feeling the urgency of Holly's kiss, but –

She doesn't like it here, in the semi-open between stationary bikes and burst bin bags. Someone could walk in on them – 'Let's go to mine?'

Holly whispers, 'I haven't got time. I just needed to get out for a bit –'

That 'needed' startles her. She pulls back. 'What's happened?'

Like she realizes what she's said, Holly's face softens, smiling. 'Nothing serious. I just wanted to see you after so long. I haven't got much time though –'

She's not sure what to say; what does she want?

They're looking at each other still, close but distant, awkwardly stuck somewhere strangely between desire and uncertainty – then the passageway darkens momentarily in a whistle of fast movement, the rhythmic thwack of a pair of trainers jogging past.

Alone again, in the subdued semi-darkness, the moment's lost.

Holly reaches out. 'You're shivering.'

'It's cold.' She'd left quickly without a scarf or hat, just pulled on the nearest coat, the one she'd taken off in the early hours of New Year's Day, with its lingering scent of last year's party.

'Come here –' She puts an arm around her shoulders, and they walk back out onto the pavement.

A few minutes from the station they peer through the steamed-up windows of a pub, see if there's anywhere to sit. There's still time. It's packed with office workers and commuters, between day and evening, but there's space at the back.

Holly looks at her watch. 'You go and grab a table – I'll get the drinks. What would you like?'

She puts her glass down. She's drinking too quickly, it's only half full now – though Holly puts hers down too, and her glass is almost empty.

Holly notices her gaze. 'I was thirsty; I should have got water too –'

She stands up. 'I'll go and get some –'

'No, don't. I need to go soon, otherwise I'll miss my train.'

She sits down again. 'It's always so rushed.'

Holly looks at her. 'I'm sorry. I'll plan better next time.'

'Sorry, I didn't mean –'

'No, you're right though.'

She doesn't say anything; Holly can't help it. Her mobile buzzes in her pocket. She doesn't get it, she's with Holly – across the table though, Holly's getting her phone out, to check a message, or her ticket home?

She glances at her own phone: a work email. She looks down. On the ground there are sticky dark stains of spilled drinks. Someone wearing trainers and tracksuit bottoms walks past. She thinks of Jazz pulling on her tracksuit, to go running with Erwin on the Heath at Christmas – and her teasing her, 'Come on, Tesya, a run wouldn't kill you!'

Holly's fingers still on her phone –

She remembers Erwin getting his breath back outside – just before she called Holly on Christmas Day –

'Holly?'

Holly doesn't look up; she's texting fast.

She thinks of Christmas Day, wrong numbers, and hanging up – and how playing games with Erwin led to a difficult conversation stopped, and then restarted in the darkness outside, and what happened afterwards, when they were really drunk and there were no words left, only –

She's making excuses; what would she feel if Holly –

Suddenly hot and thirsty, she empties her glass, then puts it down next to the scrunched-up snack packet wrappings and empties left by earlier drinkers – all the grubbiness of the pub after the glitter of Christmas. Tired and hollowed out – but yes, she should tell Holly that she kissed Jazz at Christmas, which was last year –

Not that the year changing wipes out the past. Everything's still waiting for her: work and everything else she can't face –

She looks at Holly.

Sometimes she feels alone, when they're together. Holly's often somewhere else, like now. She's texting fast as though there's some emergency – if there was, would she tell her? Are they really in that kind of relationship – the way it's been?

Telling her would rock the boat, and it always feels like they're on the cusp of a storm the way it is. But a kiss is a kiss. How would she feel if –

Holly pushes her phone into her handbag then shuts it, and looks up. 'I had to answer, sorry, and sorry, I really do have to dash.' She buttons her coat, kisses her quickly on the cheek, then she's slipping past the throng of suits –

They haven't said when they'll next meet. She calls her, 'Holly?' – she doesn't hear, she's the ghost of her pale-coloured coat through the frosted glass of the pub window. She's never seen her off at the station; she should have offered. She struggles through the crowded pub, to try to catch up.

Outside the station she can't see her, then her eyes search the crowded concourse inside. She's nowhere to be seen. She scans again, then glimpses a red head looking up at the platform indicator board – is it her?

Blocked by bulky bags and shoulders, slowly she threads her way through the crowd. She veers towards where the red head was – yes, there, she's facing away, but surely it's Holly almost, but not quite, within touching distance? Only one person between them now – she calls, 'Holly?'

Holly doesn't turn – doesn't hear.

People push past; but she edges along, closer –

Then Holly's putting her ticket into the gate – there's no point calling, it's noisy – the barrier closes behind her, and Holly strides away along the platform.

She feels suddenly dizzy – drinking on an empty stomach, and all the fatty fast-food smells from kiosks along the concourse, along with the commuters pushing past, with their sweat and breath of winter coats and too long since morning. She leans on the side of the ticket barrier. The doors slam shut, one after the other: the train's about to depart – but still her eyes search, despite the futility of seeing Holly when she's already on the train, getting on with her life. Like she should, but somehow can't; she's in limbo. The engine starts, the carriages slide away, picking up speed, then Holly's gone.

Walking away – through the crowd heading in the other direction, catching trains – she wants to rewind today, take it again slowly. She should have kissed Holly again, before she left – but there was something grubby about the city commuters' pub; like the bike store, near the bins: something sordid about kissing with urgency, among the skeletons and bones of Christmas past.

There's the sweet talcum smell of roses as she passes the flower stall in the street outside. A man in an end-of-the-day crumpled suit is buying the cliché of a bouquet of red blooms – she wonders what he's done, then sees the balloon attached: a birthday or birth. She feels guilty: why think the worst? She is guilty – for hours she hasn't thought about her mistletoe kiss.

She does up her coat as she criss-crosses through the gridlocked traffic to the bus stop the other side, where she waits for ages, trying not to breathe in the fumes; trying not to wonder what if Holly told her she'd kissed her best friend on Christmas Day. Her mind circles; the queue gets longer; the traffic is stalled; everything's stuck –

But when she's almost given up trying to tune out her thoughts, the person in front of her in the queue, speaking into their mobile, says, 'So, how was your Christmas?'

The phone is on speakerphone, so the reply is amplified despite the traffic. 'You'll never guess what happened?'

'Oh, do tell?'

'Can you guess who was with me?'

Then it comes to her, what she'd say to her dissertation students: think about the question you haven't asked – that's your missing piece of the puzzle. Holly hadn't asked her about Christmas, and neither did she ask Holly – so she doesn't know how she spent Christmas. They didn't have a conversation where she would have told her Jazz went with her to Zehra's, and reminded Holly who Jazz is, 'my best friend'. Wouldn't she have blushed, or avoided her eyes, at what she wouldn't have said? She didn't proffer how she spent Christmas, because she feels guilty, not because they had so little time – the question is whether Holly had a reason to not tell her too.

A bus arrives, not the right one. The last time she was here at this bus stop was after seeing Jo at the police station; that long packed journey, with the peace and quiet of the countryside through the window. What it must be like near Holly's. But what is she like there – how different is the London Holly from the home one?

She's freezing, and it's been ages. She's been longer at the station and in the queue than she was with Holly in that awful alley and grubby bar. How time runs away: how it masters her.

Finally the bus arrives. Her mobile buzzes as she's following the queue, getting on. She climbs to the upper deck and gets a seat at the back. Then, in the warm and the light, she reads the text. From Holly: 'Sorry I had to dash – and I forgot to give you your present. At least horrible hectic Christmas is over, and now it's a whole new year. We'll have longer next time.'

Time: her timing is perfect, her words work like the champagne she usually brings, lightening the darkness. She didn't mention receiving her present – but she's had a horrible Christmas. And they feel the same: that's all that matters. The bus sets off, and she relaxes back. Everything's going to be all right again, and it is a whole new year.

AUTHOR'S NOTE

I've had so many times over the years when I've thought optimistically that things will be all right, though in retrospect how futile things really were – when you look back you can often trace the roots of the end right at the beginning. Optimism hears hope – and looks away from the clues to where hurt will eventually emerge: people always reveal themselves, even if they don't mean to, and even if we can't see it because we're hoping this time they're the one.

It's what I've always done in my work life too: it was the perfect job, it would work out – despite the evidence staring me in the face when I'd get there on a Monday morning.

Perhaps there is no perfect job, no perfect lover. There's just work, and there's love. Sometimes there are moments you feel you're near perfection – when you lose yourself in your work, or in someone's arms, and you forget the time, you just are. At other times, when the days drag, and there's the silence of being alone in a place full of people, or when you're facing the person you're supposed to love but you sense they don't love you how you love them, that it's not love, you're aware how the clock is ticking, how finite your time; how finite your life is on this earth.

13

THE DEATH DRIVE

LESSON THIRTEEN

Monday morning, the quay deserted. Gone the blaring stereos, and indoor bodies quaffing champagne along the quay. Now just that thud, thud of the weekenders' empty yachts bobbing against mine on the tide, and the horizon a smudge of sea and sky: the semi-darkness of turn-of-the-year daytime.

Finish my tea then get started. Difficult though. Forget sometimes why I started this. Whether there was a point, where it's all leading. Then I remember what I felt: like a boat unmoored. Why it's worth carrying on until the end. This boat has saved me: my sanctuary from what got me started.

OK, log in. See what's going on.

We're all doing the same thing. Funny that. Sitting at our desks, finishing hot drinks, opening up documents, continuing where we left off. Trying to get through our daily lives, our daily deaths? That hour-by-hour, day-by-day grind towards where we'll end up. That's it: the death drive. It's about time to signal our destination.

'Here we are, the thirteenth Lesson, a number ominous for those of a superstitious bent, but what's unlucky for one is incredibly lucky for someone else.

'Lesson thirteen is on the death drive, one of the most interesting of Freud's works, not that we have time for more than what concerns us now: everything leads to death, right from birth, even sex.

'Our minds are geared towards death. Being aware of our own mortality, we are in competition with others' lives. Life is a rehearsal of death through symbolic mini-deaths in our interactions with others. Life is a disappointment, not a dream. Even if you're one of the lucky ones that gets it all – the romance, the career – once you've got it, it loses its value, the dream dies: there's always something or someone else.

'Think of your relationship history. You'll fit into one or the other pattern: you went with those who were easy, so to speak, but secretly lusted after the hard-to-get ones; or you let the easy ones go, and fought for the difficult. The in-between mutual feeling is relatively rare – if people are honest, which they aren't – hence the rocketing divorce rate. Either way you'll have ended up in the same place: you didn't get what you really wanted, or even if you did, it wasn't what you wanted, when you got it; nothing is, and nothing means no one. Despite that increasing awareness, we repeat our worst experiences, reliving our childhood traumas.

'Think of a beautiful woman at a party, someone you'd like to take home, marry until death. Doesn't she evoke a distant mother, off to an adult party, the sweet perfume of the quick kiss goodnight, then leaving you crying for hours behind a closed door? Which is what she'll do to you in an adult relationship – once she's got what she wants – especially as what she wants might ultimately be to hurt someone exactly like you.

'Think of a handsome man, a father at the head of the dining table, until one day his place is empty, he disappears from the family home, leaving bills and the downward spiral of domestic bliss gone awry. He too reappears later in life, in another guise: the trap of the steady-looking older man you'll fall head over heels for, and move in with overly soon, accepting his ring on your finger, despite friends' warnings. Until one day he disappears, like the father.

'There are many attractive people, so you don't stand a chance. Neither do they, eventually. These scenarios get repeated; death is hot-wired into human nature.

'To give one further, more specific example away from the domestic sphere, I'll share with you something I haven't done with you yet, a personal experience –'

Pause the tape.

That day, a different time of year, under a blue sky, it was easy doing what I felt. What was mine had been taken away, my whole life overturned, leaving only nothingness. That premonition of death awaits us all, but the aim is to be the giver, not the receiver. Should have said that.

No need to give myself away, get personal; don't want to rock the boat. Better the audience concentrate on their own lives.

Erase that last bit. The white blur of rewind, then press delete. Some days the best work is to start again, while you still can.

NOW

Monday and the deadline looming means the only thing to do is buckle down. Online marking is supposed to be quicker, but there's precious time taken tangling herself in knots, trying to type something positive into the pro forma despite the criticism – OK, another paper done.

Between the four walls of her office, in the quiet, she's getting it done faster now. She logs the mark in the Excel spreadsheet. Her stomach rumbles and her throat feels dry, but better get another one done before lunch –

There's a knock at the door.

'Come in?'

Ben's head appears in the doorway. 'Hi. Happy New Year, Tesya.'

'Hi, Ben. Happy New Year to you too.'

He steps inside. 'Gosh it's dark in here.'

It's like dusk outside, yet it's only midday. Ben flicks the light switch, and the too-bright fluorescent light flickers on above their heads.

'How was your –' she starts to say, but he interrupts. 'Do you have a minute?'

'Yes, of course.'

He shuts the door then sits down on the other chair, where students sit for tutorials – though the way he's looking it's like she's in the student chair.

He gets straight to the point: 'Sorry, so much to catch up with after the break, but when I saw this –' He looks down at the spiral-bound notebook in his hand and takes out a folded white sheet of A4 paper, straightens it, then holds it on his lap.

From upside down it seems like some sort of pro forma: black lined boxes containing neatly typed paragraphs. He scans it, his eyes darting side to side, slowly to the bottom of the page.

What is it? Has she missed something? Her Outlook diary is open: nothing. The marking? She's on schedule.

So stuffy under the strong light, her skin feels itchy underneath her roll neck.

'Tesya –' he begins, but stops.

'Yes?'

'I'm sorry. It was sent over Christmas, and with the backlog of emails I've only just read it –'

Annoyingly, he looks down again at the white paper in his hand – why can't he just tell her? How bad can it be? Her mouth goes dry, but she manages to say, 'What is it?'

'A complaint about a seminar you held last term.'

All the seminars had gone well. In fact, in the recycling bin at the side of her desk are a bundle of Christmas cards thanking her, from her now not-so-new students. Who could have complained – and why? 'None of them have said anything –'

'I'm not at liberty to name the student – there's a protocol. The student alleges you spoke aggressively during a seminar.'

She's speechless: when?

He looks down. 'Here it is.' He reads, '"She obviously didn't like what I said when we were discussing the play *Othello*, and I said what I thought about him strangling Desdemona. That's when she was aggressive to me, because I'm white – everyone else thought so too."'

She relaxes. 'OK, I know what you're talking about: it was the last seminar on *Othello*. One student did say something about Othello, making a sweeping generalization about black men and aggression.' When the student finished speaking, she wondered whether one of the other students might say something, but they remained silent. So she had gently pointed out the cliché then broadened the discussion to where these clichés come from: away from the play to contemporary racism, the Black Lives Matter movement, and all the unexplained deaths of black people in police custody in the UK, how none of their assailants had ever been prosecuted. Rather than generalizations about ethnicity and gender, she'd brought their attention to power and status – returning to the characters in the play. 'I wasn't aggressive, I was assertive, and of course I corrected the racist cliché, and –'

'Sorry, like I said, Tesya, I have to follow through: there's a protocol. The first stage is me telling you, then I'll set up a meeting between the two of you.'

'But it was simply –'

'Look, we'll sort it out quickly, don't worry.' He gets up. 'Got to go, senior-management meeting. I'll send you a date on Outlook.'

At the door he turns back. Under the light his pinkish healthy face is whitened by the glare. He looks down. 'I know you're still in your probationary period, but we'll sort it. It's just one of those things we all go through.' Then he leaves, and the door clicks shut.

He's right: there are loads of complaints now students are consumers – but he thinks when he goes through a student complaint it's the same, though it never would be: he's white; he doesn't know.

Had he ever been accused of being 'aggressive' when he'd only tried to reason with a student?

Oh god. Can't face this all over again – everything was going so well. Just like then –

What she remembers is how it was always when she relaxed a little that something else happened.

Then it was just after a lecture that had gone well, with lots of interesting questions from students afterwards. She was feeling good, walking to the lift, along the institutional-blue carpeted corridor, between the staffroom and the suite of management offices, when Seb stopped her – or rather pounced on her, appearing suddenly on the threshold of his office, as though he'd been lying in wait. 'Ah, Tesya, there you are.'

'Hi, Seb.' She'd probably have smiled, still in the glow of enthusing the students about whichever text it had been – only to be crushed by what he'd probably have said next:

'If you have a minute?' – not coming to the matter straight away, dragging it out.

The more she thinks about 'there you are' or whatever he said, 'here you are' or 'ah, Tesya' – phrases that mean someone has her in sight – she imagines a manager opening the online timetable, scanning it for her initials, then smiling, 'just a minute' until the break – time to go in for the kill.

Over the top, perhaps, perhaps managers feel bad then – though it never looks like it, inside their offices, behind closed doors.

Then, wasn't it just after Christmas too – though what happened and when gets mixed up now, all her years of research-assisting and post-docs, then three years from the Golden Spires to the New Build to the Red Brick, one thing after another, tension by tension – but, like all the Boxing Day hunts just after Christmas, it was probably just after when students look at their marks, rather than admit what they've not put into their work themselves – and managers check added value scores against profits.

'Take a seat.'

The manager focuses on their screen, hidden from the interviewee chair angled away from their desk.

What's that about? Looking anywhere but into another person's eyes, just before telling them something they're not going to enjoy? The fear of one day being in the other person's shoes – being accused too? More than that though ... That phrase, 'look me in the eye' – the person who can't do that in these situations, are they feeling guilty, even though they're the accuser? The guilty not-able-to-look-you-in-the-eye person is always the one in charge of the situation, the white, usually male, manager about to deal with her: the rare ethnic minority employee.

But then of course there's the point when the accuser does look you in the eye – and performing the power of their position, it's an I'm-not-your-friend-now look:

Seb – or, actually has she got it confused? Who was it in a long line of managers and deans, and various other job-titled people above her in job after job, suddenly looking at her directly, saying, 'A student has accused you of treating them unfairly over the marking of ...' and reading the module number aloud, then waiting as if in a court of law, lips closed in a straight line – like a child might draw someone looking serious – waiting for her to plead guilty.

Of course we're all guilty until proven innocent; people like her, with her skin colour – you're only innocent until proven guilty if you're white.

What was unfair about how she had ever marked?

'The student in question has received a first for every other assessment on every other module –'

'OK, I think I know who –'

'Tesya, we can't name names. There are procedures –'

It's funny how easily we can name some names – ethnic minority-sounding ones, like hers – but not others. 'I know, but this is a simple case of –'

'We have to treat everyone equally, so if a complaint has been made – in this case over marking and equality – I have to follow procedures.'

It was weird how equality was so often used to retain the status quo of racial power structures, but is she mixing up Ben with Seb, Seb with Ben, or one of those other short three-letter friendly-sounding names of people she is – was – on first-name terms with, until the friendliness disappears and the white manager starts playing the supportive authoritarian figure for a white student, against the kind of lecturer they don't expect to be lecturing them, or judging their work: the ethnic minority lecturer?

She imagines the manager with a student who's used to getting top marks. The student won't admit that she or he hasn't worked as hard at this module, or why – that there was something about this lecturer they didn't like, so they didn't listen, or do the coursework, or attend many sessions. They won't say it's because of the colour of their skin – though the lecturer knows. It's how some people look at you, or rather don't look at you, when they've decided something about you – based on your skin colour, and all the clichés they know they can use against the lecturer, because it's common knowledge that ethnic minority people are aggressive and hate white people; look at all the terrorism. All the clichés accepted as facts by white staff, used to terrorize ethnic minority lecturers – and work against justice.

In the chair of judgement over an ethnic minority tutor, the student spits it out, while the manager with the friendly-sounding name nods, taking notes, and the student fires off accusations, one after the other –

All easy to rebut, when she finally is allowed to respond. 'All marking is anonymous, it is second marked and finally externally examined; academic judgement applies.'

Just as now she would say, 'In seminars, just as when we mark end-of-term assessments, academic judgement applies' – what she's understood from her undergraduate to her postgraduate days, what she respected and thought everyone else did too.

It's weird now she's no longer a student and has the highest qual-ifications, she has less power – and feels fear. The places she loved as a student have become places she feels scared –

Hold on, no, here at the Red Brick she's not scared – it was then. So confusing, between then and now, between all the different but similarly white managers – because, she supposes, there's always a point when the manager stands up and says, 'Tesya, perhaps you could wait outside for a moment?'

Outside, she waits, nervously walking up and down at first, then, as the time goes on, she stands, staring at the noticeboard on the wall next to the manager's office, not reading the notices about lectures, rules and regulations, just seeing all the lines of typed words – and as her eyes well up, the words dissolve into each other, until she's just facing another wall.

Then the door opens, the student is ushered out and, head held high, pointedly looks the other way and marches offstage –

Yes, it's like one of those early twentieth-century drawing-room plays, everyone knowing their place in society, waiting to be invited in –

The manager turns to her, 'Ah, Tesya, would you come in again for a moment?'

That word: moment. If she could get back all the moments of her life wasted on moments like that and this, this and that. What she would have done with those moments: had time to think, to stand up and go, not sit it out as she did – but it's taken so many moments of time to work that out. Incidents and complaints consume time, filling her mind full of fear to the point she starts to question herself: what they said, as if it was true, as though they knew more about her actions, words and thoughts than she does herself –

'The thing is, Tesya, you can't –'

'Yes?'

'Tesya, listen to me, for once in your life …'

That phrase: 'once in your life' – like a slap, and meant to make her mind smart. How many times has she had that thrown at her by white men or women? When you haven't known someone all of their life, why would you say that? What do they know about her life? What does anyone know about anyone else's life? Such a patronizing phrase usually used by people who she never ever wants to see again, though usually has to see day in day out at work.

Yes, those reddening faces, and bulging veins colouring the whites of their eyes too – the bodily red flags – what does it do to their health, that power? Where else and who else would they talk down to like that? Only someone they see as inferior –

She listens politely to the spelling out, or rather spitting out – she moves back from the long breathy outbursts: 'Students are paying a lot of money …' or 'At the end of the day, the student is boss.'

'But it's been second marked and agreed externally.'

'Sometimes we have to change marks –'

All those newspaper headlines, querying massive university grade inflation – students paying thousands for once-free degree education. In the marketplace of higher education, the consumer is the marker and the manager the judge. 'Only doing my job' – judging her and her job, if she wants to keep it.

Unsure what to say, if anything – this is just the way it is, a battle she can never win. Everything leads to the same place: this exhausting nothingness. What death must feel like, when you're fighting it: wanting to live but knowing you don't have enough power to survive, that this is how it ends.

The time has disappeared; it's dark, and she wants to go home. An Outlook message pops up on the screen, across the marking: Ben's meeting invitation regarding the student complaint. Next week. She accepts, then logs off and powers down. Sometimes she wants to power herself down like a computer: stop thinking, and really switch off. Impossible, when stuff like this happens.

She gets her coat down off the hook on the back of the door and then checks her mobile, on silent while working. Nothing. It's times like this, if she was in a normal relationship, she'd call her partner as she's leaving work, tell them about her day, ask about theirs, then pick up whatever was needed on the way home. A home they'd share.

She sets off into the darkness.

The red of a bus goes past, destination Piccadilly Circus; she thinks of the Monopoly board at Christmas, Erwin or Jazz throwing the dice, then counting the squares and moving their marker to its next position, then to her, 'Your turn, Tesya.'

Who won? She can't remember now, and it didn't matter then, it was just a game; fun together. Funny how chance is relaxing, when it's with those she trusts.

As she crosses the road, it starts to rain. And at the bus shelter, there are too many people – she's half in, half out, and the rain is slanting. She tries to keep herself under cover.

Should she get advice about this meeting, from the union? Could it be that bad? Not at the moment, surely – but it might spiral like things do, coiling round and round like they are now, tightening the knotted thoughts of then and now, now and then.

She manages to get on the next bus but stands – it's packed, and terribly hot. Nauseous – she hasn't eaten or even drunk much water all day, not after Ben's knock on her door. Horrible day. Horrible then. Horrible now. Her head aches. She heaves – she's going to be sick. She rings the bell and gets off at the next stop.

A blast of cold air; breathe in, and out.

She gets her bearings. Old Street roundabout; toxic fumes from the traffic rumbling past. She draws her scarf up. She can walk home, but stop in here first, get a bottle of water.

That's better, now just need home – and then she's almost there, turning the corner – and Erwin's on the doorstep.

'I was thinking of you – nice surprise.'

'Just passing on my way home, thought you'd be in by now?'

She hugs him. 'First day back: long day. How about you?'

After mugs of tea are made, she says, 'Stay for dinner, just some-thing simple?'

'Love to.'

She puts a couple of potatoes in the microwave, and then they stand side by side at the kitchen counter, her rinsing lettuce while Erwin grates some carrots for a salad.

He asks, 'So how was it back at work?'

She drops the lettuce in the salad-spinner. She wonders whether to tell him, and then does: 'Rather horrible actually, marking still, and a student complaint arrived.'

'How awful for you –'

'Don't worry. Hopefully it'll be dealt with quickly.'

'But after all that stuff at your last place – you never found out who was behind it?'

'No, but – oh, I don't want to think about it; when I do, my mind can't stop mulling over and over it all. How was your day?'

'Same as usual. Great thing about working with computers, they're not people – well, not yet anyway.'

They laugh. The microwave pings. Then they're sitting down, tucking in, when Erwin stops eating suddenly, like he's just thought of something. He looks at her.

'Jazz is really nice.'

'Yes, she's lovely.' She looks at him curiously, wondering what he's going to say next.

'Zehra said you're dating someone new, but it's a bit difficult for some reason?'

'Yes, but just difficult as she's not out, so we don't see each other much.'

'You and Jazz get on really well though, don't you?'

'Well, yes, she's my best friend. You don't mean –?'

'I think Zehra's always wondered whether you two would get together – ages ago she said something, it just came back to me this Christmas.'

She doesn't ask why; did he see them kiss? He slept in Zehra's study downstairs, he might have woken up thirsty, come into the kitchen – though did it matter if he had?

'Zehra likes Jazz,' she says, and then, changing the subject, asks him about his love life.

He launches into his ongoing millennial tale of apps, virtual dating and the horrors of being ghosted –

'Gutted. I was really into her.'

They're clearing up. She's got her hands in the washing-up bowl, but she turns around. His eyes look pink around the edges, as if he's about to cry. He's the most sensitive, gentle man she's ever met. 'Oh, Erwin, there will be someone out there for you soon, I'm sure – someone gorgeous like you.'

'Oh Tesya, I hope so.'

When they're in the hallway, as Erwin is about to go, he brings Jazz up again: 'You know you could think about it – Jazz, I mean.'

She wonders whether to, and then she decides to tell him. 'Actually, it's funny you should ask about Jazz and me: we kissed at Christmas – but then afterwards we didn't talk about it. I guess it was just a drunken thing. We got talking about some deep emotional stuff that night. Anyway, I'll admit it to you, I've tried to forget it – I feel guilty, sort of … You know I have Holly, even if I don't see her much … And I don't want to lose Jazz's friendship. It's complicated.'

'Sounds it.'

'Call me soon? Nice to go for a ramble one weekend – get out of the city, country air?'

'That would be nice; you could ask Jazz too –'

'Erwin, you're such a matchmaker.' She hugs him, feeling comforted by talking it through with him. Now, though – as she waves him off – he's left her feeling she should make a move. But life isn't like playing a game, with the random fall of the dice directing moves from set rules. Though sometimes it feels like that –

When she suggested a ramble, she'd been thinking of Holly and her mythical countryside house, and the sun shining as they'd stroll hand in hand, or if it were cold they'd huddle together over a real fire; whatever the weather it would be perfect. Even as she thinks this – as she's drying the plates, putting things back in the cupboard – she knows it's a dream: Holly is tied to her domesticity.

Was Erwin right about Jazz? If she made a move, their friendship would surely survive, even if romance didn't work out. They go back so far. But human love affairs are a game as random as chance. Jazz had probably forgotten it already – and if she made a move, it might totally ruin their friendship. There is no certainty in human relations.

She packs her bag for work tomorrow, checking her diary – remembering that Outlook meeting request. Yes, human contact is a minefield.

In the bedroom she chooses an outfit for tomorrow, a bland professional-looking white shirt and black trousers, and hangs it over the wardrobe door, ready for whatever is thrown at her. She must look professional, despite what's thrown at her.

She sits on the edge of the bed and pulls her phone towards her, starting a message, 'What about a ramble in the countryside one Sunday soon?' In the address box, she types J for Jazz, and then stops. No, just because she's had a nice time with Erwin, and she's frustrated, doesn't mean she should blow it all away with Holly – or toy with Jazz's feelings. She deletes the J and types in H.

She gets into bed.

It's just a walk in the countryside.

She turns out the light, wishing Holly would answer soon – while wishing away the week and work, that wretched meeting, and the student's word against hers. The question as always was whether the student would eventually tell the truth – but students are humans, and humans are wont to exaggerate, to expand, to lie, and once a process based on a lie is started, the power lies with sticking to the lie. Systems are based on believing people tell the truth rather than taking into account the delicacy of human feelings – about oneself, and beliefs about other people. Students remember criticism, rarely praise – but that's true of everyone, like her worrying about that meeting. It's the ego, and its fragility; self-esteem is easily fractured, it takes time to heal, and there are always cracks that break again at a push. It's difficult to remember the good when your mind is tuned to what's gone wrong; you live in the past tense, and that unsettles the present, almost killing the future before it has a chance. She's been mulling over a kiss of seconds rather than savouring the heavenly hours she's spent with Holly –

Closing her eyes, almost dozing off, she's roused by a vibrating flash of light: a text.

Holly: 'I'd love that. How about next Sunday?'

Quickly, she answers – as though the offer might disappear if she doesn't. Once she's pressed send, she turns her phone off; she'll be able to switch off now too.

Just as she's almost dropping off, imagining walking hand in hand with Holly, she turns a corner and faces a cliff edge: a ramble near Holly's means a ramble back near –

The thought hovers over her, like the shadow of a bird of prey on a country walk –

She sits up, takes a deep breath.

In the corner, by the wardrobe, her trainers are neatly lined up on the floor; she's not worn them since a ramble on the Heath over Christmas. They're clean as new; she scrubbed the mud off when she got home. She lies back down.

Humans and experiences aren't like objects; you can't brush away the parts you don't want. A walk in the country in the opposite direction to Holly's, with Jazz and Erwin, would have been fun, and no added anxieties – but she's got what she asked for, time with Holly, so why is she having second thoughts? What happened there then is over; she's safe now, safe with Holly. Perhaps that's it. She's used to feeling unsafe. Missing someone, or not having someone, feels unsafe, and for some reason that makes them more desirable – to her. But she does feel safe with Holly. Like light obliterates the darkness, Holly bleaches out the past when they're together, and all she feels is love, or – as she rolls over, wrapping the duvet tightly around her – actually what she really feels when she sees her is massive can't-get-enough-of-her attraction.

14

COINCIDENCE AND COEXISTENCE

AUTHOR'S NOTE

Often I work late at my desk, here above the city. Afterwards I'll mix a drink and watch the moon rise across the rooftops, and glimpse, in the windows of the flats opposite, the silhouettes of other people's lives in motion. In bed, I read into the night – I enjoy time to myself with fiction, but also time with the real people I love.

Some conversations stay with me, like a song or a psalm – suddenly hearing another person voicing similarities in our shared coexistence on this planet, simple human stories of love and loss that chime with mine.

After other conversations, I'm happy to return home to my own thoughts, pondering the distance between humans – our different planets. It happens in relationships: you're seemingly committed, sometimes sharing a bed and each other's bodies, even the word love. Then there will be something that feels odd – and you ask a question. It turns out there 'never was a promise to be exclusive' – that you can't assume anything about other humans. Our ethics are diverse, like different species.

Sometimes the ethical cliff face is early on, and you're forced to look down into that chasm: the other person says, 'You've got such lovely skin' – how they're looking at you: they want to try out the 'exotic' for a night, like tasting a new food, or sampling another species. Or they think they're showing an interest in you, and ask, 'How often do you go home?' – assuming you weren't born here, despite sharing an accent and this country. That's when I scramble away, climbing out of the chasm, home to safety.

Sometimes I've tried not to listen and held the white hand taking mine in theirs. I've closed my eyes as I'm kissed, accepting the embrace and the coincidence of our coexistence.

What I'm saying is I sometimes give people a chance, despite what they tell me in their words or actions. I am ever hopeful of other people's humanity, like I am ever hopeful that love will last.

LESSON FOURTEEN

'Today: coincidence versus synchronicity. Synchronicity, like beauty, is in the eye of the beholder: when our minds make meaning from apparently random things, we feel like something was meant to be. For example, when we're thinking of someone we like, and we bump into that person, and they say they were just thinking of us too. That's the special feeling of synchronicity. We wouldn't think they're saying it because it's what we want to hear.

'Humans are narcissistic creatures, so it makes magical sense when what happens is what we desire: synchronicity. However, when it's the opposite, something we wish had never happened, we see it as an unlucky coincidence. For example, bumping into an ex we can't imagine now ever lusting after. The fact that you actually did have sex with them in the past is repugnant, claustrophobic even. That's a feeling rather like being strangled, another sometimes-random event, although

more often not, and with potentially coincidental properties
for our minds: we can have sex with each other, or we can kill
each other. That random human face-to-face coincidence is
about sameness, and it's horrifying: underneath our clothes
we are the same-bodied species, but we're better, aren't we?
We don't always want to recognize the other person as another
human, and we never really want to feel ourselves in another
person's shoes.'

A bit convoluted. Something more on manipulating emotions, making
people feel that it's just chance?

NOW

It's weird how it all started with her text, suggesting a country ramble,
almost sending it to Jazz, then at the last moment sending it to Holly.
If she hadn't, she wouldn't have got something else she wanted too:
Holly inviting her to stay the night at hers, to be up early for their
ramble on Sunday.

It was short notice; Holly's text arrived late Saturday afternoon.
She finished what she was doing, quickly packed to stay over and
dashed to the station. Then miles and miles of darkness – she arrived
late evening.

The station was deserted – there was the station sign, beneath it
a bench, and nothing and no one else – and opening the door, gosh,
it was so much colder than London outside.

She left the station, walking past a few shops closed up for the
night, and soon she was on the edge of the village. She'd fantasized
about visiting Holly for months – Holly opening the door to her home.
She hadn't thought about the specifics, what she was discovering now:
how far from the station, how dark – and the rural silence surrounding
her – whether it was safe. She got her phone out and checked Google
Maps, then set off again.

She turned down the lane leading to Holly's, between high bulky hedges – like a maze from which she might never work out how to escape. She looked up at the darkness above, and then as if by magic she became aware of the stars shining millions of miles away above the earth. She remembered how the glittery light of stars is only an illusion, the ghosts of their past light. How weird we see things that don't exist.

She tripped, and then flashed her mobile torch ahead on the uneven ground, scared to trip again on the tufts of weeds growing out of the gravel lane.

It was quiet, just her boots on the gravel and the intermittent rustling of invisible reeds or leaves – and her heart beating, though she tried not to think of what might be hidden under the cover of darkness, surely it's safer than in the city – until her memory inevitably booms out at her: what happened last year, not far from here? Though not so near – and it was never this sort of silent, no sign of anyone around. It's people she fears; she doesn't believe in ghosts.

Further on there were gaps in the hedges, giving glimpses of the dark outlines of large imposing olde worlde houses, with thin glimmers of light leaking between thick curtains. It wasn't late, just felt later in the quiet – it was about ten: time for the news. People across Britain watching journalists in flak jackets embedded in the never-ending wars in the Middle East, or politicians safe in well-lit London studios, talking about how talking about immigration isn't racist and how there are too many immigrants taking British jobs – and then the weather, always the weather. The safety of knowing how the news will end. People in places like this, who voted overwhelmingly for Brexit, sitting on their sofas with a nightcap, far from cities where people live side by side, hearing neighbours through walls and interacting in shared hallways and stairs, and life's ups and downs, not hidden from each other like here –

Round the corner, there was a house, the last house. It was like a gingerbread house made of sweets in a child's tale – and like a child's drawing, symmetrical, the front door in the middle lit by an old-fashioned lantern. And there was Holly opening the door –

She'd like to remember everything, but of course she can't, all she remembers now of that night are fragments: after the darkness, the relief of seeing Holly in a halo of light. Finally inside her home, in the dim light, Holly's pale hand led her upstairs through the moonlight falling from a window, a candle in her other hand held ahead of them – like a character from an old novel, not a live woman in the twenty-first century. Even in Holly's bedroom, she was a Victorian heroine in her long white gown, until she unwrapped herself and disappeared under the covers.

She undressed in the flickering candlelight – the window was open and rattled slightly, and there was the silvery rustling of leaves, and the long shadows of the branches outside fell across her naked body as she finally walked across the room. Then, between the covers, at last, there was Holly's sweet perfume on her neck as she kissed her there, and then she held Holly like she'd been holding her breath, but now she breathed out at last, unleashing herself, to be leashed again to Holly –

Her delicate lashes flutter against her face like butterflies, and yet when Holly holds her down, her lips and hands silence her into submission: she has no defence against her strength, she's lost – until she finds the sound of her, and then they are both lost together.

When morning came, it was early, with hot steaming coffee and the crackle of toast being buttered. Afterwards, walking boots pulled on and tied firmly, they walked out in the hazy light across muddy fields, through the wood, towards the sea and the palest of blue skies.

One brief stop on a rock-strewn beach, breathing in the salty air as the tide crept in with seaweed on its foamy tide curling towards them and catching on the rocks, then slipping back and forth, lapping gradually closer and closer – and there they kissed, slowed down in the sea-taste and cosseted by the sea air around them. Then she knows, now she's tasted it, this is what she wants, love and the natural world –

But as usual the moment was broken, and when she opened her eyes Holly was looking at her watch.

'It's that time again; we better go.' She looked back towards where they'd come from, the house hidden behind the woods. 'I'll drive you to the other station, that'll get you back to London quicker.'

She didn't want to get back quicker; she didn't want to leave. But it wasn't up to her; never is. Like the teenager she once was, she wanted to lash out: so unfair, too soon. She didn't though; it wouldn't be fair. She buttoned up her feelings, like her coat – it felt colder as they walked back through the wood, not talking.

Yes, they ran out of time, as always, so it's almost like it's not happened, and Holly's love is a figment of her imagination – except for in the hallway, by the closed door, one hand on the lock, Holly's other arm held her tight. Then the smell of the sea mingled with her sweat and the tease of her perfume, and they kissed, until Holly let go – and opened the front door, to the cold air and daylight.

When she climbed into the car, Holly's keys were already jangling from the ignition. She said, 'Fasten your seat belt,' and started the engine.

She clicked her seat belt in, then as Holly steered the car out into the lane, she glanced back at the house. In the daylight, she could see the ivy clambering up over the house and around the windows – the rustling leaves in the night. The front bedroom window was still open – the window swayed with its curtain of ivy in the breeze.

'Holly and the ivy.'

'What?' Holly was concentrating on manoeuvring between the hedges, along the narrow lane.

'The Christmas carol.'

'Yes?'

'And your name. I do love ivy –' and almost said I love you too, but didn't – sensing their moods dividing: Holly wanted her gone, with the kids back soon. Who was looking after them? She should have asked, shown an interest. She felt a tinge of guilt, how selfish she is to want more. She should enjoy the moment together – and savour it afterwards.

'Oh yes.' Holly's eyes flickered to the rear-view mirror, but by then her ivy-clad house was out of sight. Eyes ahead, she replied, 'Ivy takes so much work. You can't imagine how it grows.' And then almost to herself, 'Holly and the ivy,' and she smiled, then after steering out onto the main road, she put her foot on the accelerator.

And that would have been it. She wouldn't have thought of it, or even remembered a window swaying in the breeze –

But waiting on the station platform, long after Holly had dropped her there – there's a delay for the train – she feels how warm it is, how still the air, no breeze at all. Across the other side of the rails, beyond the green slope and past a quayside pub busy with people drinking outside – there's the green-blue slither of the sea, and a line of yachts anchored in still waters.

Of course, near the sea the weather must change constantly, like the tide – but she thinks again of Holly's bedroom window loose on its arm, swaying with the ivy covering the empty house. The kids weren't back; there was no one else living with her, and though she might have a cleaner, surely not on a Sunday. It was just the unpredictable weather of the British seaside.

The train and – remembering falling asleep, seeing only Holly's peaceful sleeping form beside her – a long snooze, then waking, London's glass-clad tower blocks mirror and dominate the now cloudy horizon. But nothing matters apart from seeing Holly again soon –

Walking through the station, past the newsagent's with its display of Valentine's cards, a text message pings into her phone. She stops by the window, and reads Holly's, 'I'm free of the kids in a few weeks' time. We could go away for Valentine's Day, if you like?'

'Love to,' she texts straight back, and smiles, then sees herself, phone in hand, her reflection superimposed across the cards and red hearts in the window display. The synchronicity of that: it was going to be the most perfect Valentine's Day ever.

LESSON FOURTEEN
ADDENDUM

'Coincidence has to be built up to, so it looks naturally random. That takes planning. Easier with someone you know well. It helps to have the hardware pre-planned: copies of keys they won't think you still have, not knowing you made copies early on for when they'll come in handy.

'What's useful is to take a good look at their home environment when they're out. Get a feel of what's going on in their mind. Look at the obvious things, their diary, and inside desk and bedside drawers, or on the kitchen table, places they might hide things or have left things out in a hurry. Look for what they don't expect other people to see in the privacy of their home.

'If they return early, they won't expect anyone there. You haven't broken in, so you can hide almost in plain view, in the shadows, or just outside. We don't see what we're not expecting. From your vantage point, take a good look, especially if they happen to be with someone else. Watch what people do when they think they're alone. Then retreat until you're ready to act on what you've found.'

What synchronicity that was, almost as if by my design; now to ready myself for the next stage: what a coincidence, or so it will seem.

15

VALENTINE'S DAY

LESSON FIFTEEN

'Those of you who are older might remember lateral-thinking puzzles, used to be all the rage at dinner parties. Someone would recount a scenario, then everyone would try to work out what had happened. It would go on for hours. Nowadays people would just Google the answer on their phones in seconds.

'There was one about Cleopatra and Antony being found dead in a pool of water, with fragments of glass nearby, and Caesar strolling away. Because of the famous names, everyone would be off on a wild goose chase: could the lovers have fallen through a window into a pool in the throes of passion? Or Caesar, fed up with what the two of them were doing to Rome, had thrown a vase their way, killing them both outright? The teller of the puzzle could only answer yes or no. Hours later, finally, a child or an adult with a more creative mind would ask, "Couldn't it be that Antony and Cleopatra are something else, like not humans?"

'You'd see the cogs whirring around the room, then someone would get it: "It's two goldfish, and their bowl's been knocked over by a cat." Everyone would be kicking themselves, falling for such a simple tale.'

Except me: I always got the puzzle relatively quickly, although I'd listen on. So interesting how most people can't see what is right in front of them, until they have exhausted every other possibility. It takes my kind of mind, one who takes nothing at face value, but most people aren't like me.

'Assumptions about the meaning of words trick the human mind: we assume the absolute truth of a word, that things are as they're said to be, but words, like objects, mean different things to different people.'

NOW

It's finally Valentine's Day – and tipsy, tumbling along together in the night air, at the sea wall they stop. Across the shingle beach, through the darkness, the tide turns and twists in silvery snaking tendrils.

It's a genteel small town of arty gift shops, gastropubs, well-heeled pensioners and yummy mummies, but now it's late; besides bins overflowing with cans and chip wrappers, and the day trippers gone, the sea front is deserted.

Under a lamp post, it's just the two of them. Strands of Holly's hair catch on her jewellery as she glances across the road then back, raising her eyebrows along with the kiss of the word, 'Bed?'

She replies by drawing Holly into a kiss; their bodies angle, pivoting towards each other. When they draw apart she says, 'This is perfect,' opening her arms out to their surroundings, then recircling Holly.

Holly whispers, 'You're perfect,' and leads her across the road, between the stationary vehicles in the shadows of the sea-front buildings.

It's eerily quiet. Holly unlatches the pretty picket gate they first saw on the Airbnb website a few weeks ago, when they booked quickly before they might miss out on it. As Holly closes the gate downstairs, Tesya goes up first, climbing the iron stairs to their home for the weekend above the shopfront.

On the roof terrace it's dark; she makes her way slowly past the outdoor chairs and potted plants, then she's at the front door –

She stares down at the doormat, its 'Welcome Home' logo covered up by –

Behind her, Holly asks, 'What's wrong?'

With the keys in her hand, she points at the bulky object on the doormat.

'It's so dark – there should be an outside light.' Holly fumbles in her bag, then flashes her mobile torch light down onto what lies between them.

On the doormat lodged against the doorstep is, on the surface, just a brown-paper carrier bag stuffed with the debris of an Indian takeaway: brown-paper wrappings with broken pieces of poppadom poking out; a couple of crushed silver-foil boxes, their cardboard lids stained with the orange glow of curry paste; and an open bottle of beer poking out too – there's a strong beery smell.

'Just rubbish, must have blown out of the bins. Let's go inside, it's freezing.'

Holly is uncurling her fingers from the keys – but she says, 'Wait,' peering through the darkened kitchen window, checking –

'Tesya?'

Could someone have got inside? It's deathly quiet – she remembers the stab of surprise at a substance dripping down her door, and the silence accompanying the darkness spread over the door handle, then smeared across the whole surface; how stains spread, like fear –

Why now, when she's hardly thought about it for ages, when everything's perfect? Holly will think she's being paranoid. She should tell her – 'There was someone out to get me last year. I thought it was over – how on earth would they know I'm here?' – but she doesn't. She turns, and, blinded by Holly's torch, she touches her hand and Holly dips the light back down again.

In the darkness she can't see Holly's face, but she feels her fingers taking the keys out of her clutched fist, then she's unlocking the door.

Inside, the light switched on, Holly says, 'Come, sit down,' leading her to one of the kitchen stools. It clatters against the wooden floor as she sits. Behind her, Holly locks the door – a flimsy glass door, just one lock. She moves past – 'I'll open the champagne, we need a drink' – opening a cupboard, placing a pair of glasses on the counter, then there's the suction sound of the fridge door opening and closing –

But the front door: through the glass, under the bright overhead light, they're like actors spotlit on a stage – or rather she is. Where's Holly? There's a clicking shut: the bathroom door.

She stands and switches off the light, then peers outside.

Behind her, 'Why are we plunged into darkness?' A cork pops and falls somewhere on the floor. The glugging of champagne poured into glasses, then Holly's hand on her shoulder. 'This will make you feel better.'

On automatic, she says, 'To us,' yet she can't help glancing outside again as she takes a sip – she didn't look into Holly's eyes first, like she normally would, what you're supposed to do, and it's Valentine's Day. That's unlucky – this is unlucky –

The door rattles – but Holly's wrong, it's not that windy, no, the rubbish was arranged deliberately outside the front door.

The click of a lighter; a flash, then, 'There, that's better, isn't it?' A couple of night lights glow on the counter, next to a gift box tied with ribbons and a rose, and above it all Holly's red hair sparkles like firelight.

'Oh, Holly, that's so sweet – let me just –' she pushes open the door to the bedroom, and kneels on the floor next to her overnight bag, looking for what she's brought for her. The alcohol has gone straight to her head; perhaps Holly's right, it's what she needed.

Then Holly is opening her gift, pulling out the creamy silk scarf, draping it around her neck, stroking the fabric. 'It's gorgeous.'

She opens the box, and takes out an antique silver locket. She prises open the clasp. Inside, encased in glass, there's a tiny lock of black hair – the colour of her own. She looks up, curious.

'It's a Victorian hair brooch – they kept hair in lockets as mementoes. I wonder whose it was … You like it?'

'Yes, very much, thank you.' She closes the clasp – something sad about the memento of someone she's never met, someone who's dead; and yet it is beautiful.

'I'll put the pizza in the oven to warm up, then let's sit in the other room.'

She nods, and takes the bottle and glasses into the lounge. It's cold; she turns on the gas fire. It's one of those that are made to look like a real fire with orange-red flames, but it doesn't really look anything like a fire. Just like the rubbish didn't look at all accidental. At least they're inside, and it's cosy. Not like what she's about to tell Holly, the whole story, including why she left there, if she can – why she's so frightened of what's to come.

THEN

The last thing that happened was so small and normal, in one way – after all, the incidents were what she had become used to – and yet it was what was different about this one that made it massive, an absolute game changer. She couldn't trust anyone there afterwards – or anything: why it was so haunting.

It was the last week of the summer term; the long vacation was in sight. That Monday morning she headed into work, relaxed. Nothing weird had happened for ages, the more time passed it made it almost possible to put it out of her mind – almost, though not totally. Everywhere there were reminders: walking through the foyer; collecting mail from her staffroom pigeonhole; going along the corridor to her office – but now she'd almost got through her first year there. Used to the work, used to the walk, she enjoyed the cool green light beneath the trees – she thought about buying a new bikini for a holiday soon, and books for pleasure, reading on a lounger by a pool.

Approaching the campus, and the security guards patrolling the perimeter, she swung her staff-card lanyard around her neck. In the lift, her mind was on her last seminar, dealing with student panic about assessments and fielding last-minute questions. She flitted to hopeful thoughts, squeezing in some journal work before the marking arrived, and perhaps next year she could devote more time to submitting to conferences and journals.

There was a moment – coming out of the lift, glancing through the window at the rays of sunlight outside – of glimpsing the summer ahead. A trip with Jazz, a spontaneous package and the adventure of not knowing where they'd end up until a few days before: mountains and lakes, or the sea. Oh, wherever they went they would have such a good time; they always did.

Then, keys in her hand, almost at her office –

A blankness, a door without her name – oh god, not again.

On automatic: digging in her bag for her mobile, calling Seb.

Then heart beating fast, like running a race, but still, facing her office door that now had nothing on it to show it was her office – her name card had completely disappeared.

'Hi.' Seb had his phone ready to take a photograph, but it wasn't going to be much of a picture: just a white door with the transparent perspex holder empty of its usual contents.

Seb's face, between her and the door. 'You all right?'

She felt sick. 'Just need to sit a moment.'

Her keys were in her hand; it was still her office, and she was opening the door. He followed behind her. She flopped down onto her chair and put her bag on the desk, her desk. Her things were all around the office, accumulated as she'd tried to make it a home from home: books, DVDs, pens – a cardigan hanging up on the back of the door, from when it was cold.

She looked past Seb in the doorway.

'Tesya?'

Then she saw it: a tiny little metal thing, opposite her door, high up on the wall: the CCTV sensor.

'Gosh, Seb, the CCTV camera –'

He caught sight of it too. 'God, you're right. I'd forgotten they put it up a few weeks ago, didn't they?'

'This means –'

'Oh yes, we'll have them on tape. It'll be the end of it.' He looked down at his watch. 'Almost time for morning seminars – meet you at lunchtime to take a look at the footage? Facilities Office about 1 p.m.? I'll email him to expect us.' He went off down the corridor, humming with the accomplishment, solving it just before the end of the year: perfect.

The thought of that tiny camera on the wall. Seconds later she set off for her seminar too. In the seminar room, waiting for everyone to settle, she wondered who would be on the tape; not long until she'd find out.

At 1 p.m. she went straight down to the Facilities guy's office. Seb arrived just as she did. The door was open.

Andy looked up from his screen. 'Come in, make yourselves at home.'

The office was dimly lit by the light from the screens, and there was a stack of cardboard boxes addressed to Finance or Administration, taking up a lot of space. They shifted a few boxes, but there wasn't room to set up the folding chairs, so they gave up and leaned against the back wall.

Andy said, 'Sorry, no one's picked up their deliveries yet today; bit of a logjam.'

'No worries.' Seb leaned forward, an elbow on the pile of packages. 'You found it yet?'

'Hold on.' After a series of clicks, the central screen divided into nine black-and-white square images, areas around the Arts block. In the centre was her closed office door, just as it looked when she arrived that morning: no name card, and the slight shadow of the empty perspex holder.

'That's the one.' Seb asked, 'Tesya, you weren't in over the weekend?'

'No, not since Friday morning. It was OK then.'

'Right, so we have a couple of days –'

'Don't worry, it won't take ages, hardly anyone's around at weekends, and only a handful on Fridays. The CCTV is triggered by movement,' Andy reminded them, swivelling around. 'I'll rewind back to Friday.'

When he pressed play, there she was on the screen: unaware of the CCTV camera, holding her bag awkwardly under her arm, she unlocks the door with her right hand and disappears into her office; the door closes behind her, leaving the door with her name card in the centre.

The screen fast-forwarded, then the next movement played: her exiting her office in the middle of the day, locking the door – more relaxed, leaving for the weekend.

It flipped forward a few hours, to the same day in the afternoon: on the screen Enrico comes vacuuming his way down the corridor and then appears on the other screen, getting into the lift, the coiled vacuum cleaner by his side.

The screen fast-forwarded, then played: hours later, the corridor is dark, then the lights are activated, like the CCTV, by movement – the tall male lecturer, the one Alice had gone on about at the welcome drinks, slopes down the corridor carrying a bottle and holding onto a young woman. They swerve past her door at the end of the corridor, then turn –

'Play that again? His office is near the lift; why are they near mine?'

The whole sequence played out across the screens: like in a silent black-and-white movie, the guy enters the lift with the woman on the ground-floor lift screen, they get physical in the lift – then let go of each other as they exit on the corridor, and walk unsteadily to his office door. He gives the bottle to the woman, she swigs from it while he looks in his pocket – he's mislaid his key. They argue, roaming unsteadily up and down the corridor – some wine spills on the carpet in dark splotches. They go back past her office –

'Your name card is still there, Tesya.'

'Yes. It's not them.'

Andy fast-forwarded to the next movement, covering the awkward silence by saying, 'A few of the lecturers kip here if they've had too many pints. You know, avoid drink-driving.'

Neither of them replied. It looked consensual, and it felt voyeuristic to have watched them. They weren't guilty – not of what they were looking for.

The CCTV played again: there's her office door, with the name card, then it flips on fast-forward until a few hours later, early Monday morning, that morning – there's her office door, but without the name card – like when she arrived. But there's nothing in between – and there isn't anyone there.

It's impossible –

Seb said, 'How did that –?'

Andy rewound the tape, then played it again, but it was the same. It had recorded the name card change – that it was there, and then it was no longer there – but it hadn't recorded the person taking it in between. What they were looking for wasn't there.

The screen started moving: she comes into frame and sees the door, without the card.

'Stop it, please?'

Andy paused it; the image of her in front of her office door distorts into a rash of white lines, like she's been scribbled on –

Like when she rewinds DVDs in the seminar room and pauses on key scenes, white lines distort whoever's been framed by the mostly white male directors, recording women's movements up close –

She managed to speak. 'How is that possible?'

Andy spoke slowly, like he was working it out. 'It's either a malfunction of the camera or the software – or whoever did it covered the camera with something, before they came into view. There's a black spot on that corridor between the lift and your office.'

She saw what he meant. The lift/corridor shot covered more than the shot on her door, but between them they didn't cover the entire corridor. Someone could access the cameras, covering them temporarily – then they wouldn't get recorded approaching her door.

Seb got up. 'I've got another meeting soon. Tesya, we'll sort it. Thanks, Andy.' And then he was gone.

She looked at Andy. 'Who has access to the software?'

He looked back at her. 'I do, and one other person, the other Facilities guy.'

She had to ask, 'Do you think he …?'

He knew what she was asking; he answered, 'No, I don't. And it's not me. The software anyway records all the changes made. We could do a printout; it would exonerate both of us –'

'Sorry, I didn't mean –'

'It's all right; don't worry. I know you need to sort this out. But I don't think it is a malfunction. The system is relatively new. No, it's someone who noticed the camera and chose to cover it. It's not an accident.'

What she'd known all along: of course it wasn't an accident.

He turned back to the screen. Her image was still paused, scribbled over in white fuzzy lines. He pressed a button, then the screen went blank. Like she'd been deleted.

She felt like screaming –

She couldn't stay any longer; not if what they wanted to do was to –

Have to get out.

Andy said, 'Sorry, I don't know what to say.'

At least he was honest. 'Thanks, you've done more than anyone else really.'

And within weeks she was gone.

NOW

She feels the presence of then, even now. Was that what they intended? To make her scared, so she'd leave – or was there something more they wanted to do to her? It was like a warped love affair. In a romance you want the other person to be near, and be in touch – but this was someone who stayed close yet never revealed themselves, and their actions were messages of hate. It was an affair of hatred – could she have unknowingly done something to provoke that feeling?

The sun is rising slowly across the sea, a pink sky: shepherd's warning. She takes her shoes and socks off, and walks into the dark blue waves rippling towards the shore.

She's been gone for hours. She should get back before Holly wakes, and say, 'Sorry, I didn't tell you before –'

Holly will answer, 'I'm glad you have now, but Tesya, this was just an accidental thing, rubbish –'

She will stop her with a kiss, and take her back under the covers, make love, the only place where she can hide from this storm of hate – though it will only pause what's happening, like she's a character on a screen, at the whim of someone else's fingers to press play, pause – or delete.

Holly doesn't understand. She'd never have known anything like this before; it's why she's such an oasis of peace, untainted by hate. Despite everything last night, she's still her perfect Valentine.

16

FAMILIARITY AND FEAR

LESSON SIXTEEN

Mustn't give anything away at the last moment. Check the viewfinder: OK, no shadow. A spring day of hazy sunshine, the dead leaves are gone and there's new greenery. Romantic: a fitting end, in a way.

Sad it'll be over after today, but time for something new, somewhere less familiar, to start again.

'This is the last Lesson, and perhaps the most difficult to learn. I'm going to phrase it as a question: How are you going to take care of yourself in the extremities of where you eventually find yourself in your project, and not be put off from getting on with the final act when you're comfortable in the surroundings, and with the people involved?

'Familiarity diminishes your natural ability to pick up on aspects that would usually make you fear someone. Just as others don't know everything about you, you don't know everything about them, even though you've been following them physically and virtually.

'Think about it like this: someone looking at you for slightly too long might mean they can't take their eyes off you, or that there is something about you they're uncertain about, like the possible duplicity of your feelings. Remember perhaps your mother, one moment overloading you with affection, the next shouting when you came too close and she couldn't be bothered with you? Feelings twist in a heartbeat.

'Love is closely tied with hate; sometimes we don't know which it is, and we will never know. All that matters is getting what we want. So finish what you planned, don't be put off by any feelings erupting. Their final reaction is the only way to tell love from hate, though at that point it's immaterial, just nice to know at the end.

'Act on your gut instincts, and when the time is right to strike, do it. When it's over, walk away before you're caught; move on.'

It's working out. The perfect end to Valentine's weekend: the perfect crime. Not long now, then time for me to go.

NOW

Calmer in the morning haze, with the calls of gulls on the wing above, and last night's shadows banished – a moment of elation, a new morning, to be alive.

At the top of the beach, she sits for a moment on a bench and brushes the sand off her feet, and slips her shoes back on. The sea slips closer inland, such a picture-postcard place, timeless – if she doesn't include herself, the colour of her skin, it could be years ago. When Britain ruled its global empire, people like her would have been subordinates – what some still want now, in the twenty-first century.

Perhaps she should call Jo, let her know about last night – but it's Sunday, the duty officer would answer … and until there's a suspect –

Where are they now? Hidden behind the faded velvet curtains of the obviously once-grand Victorian hotel, resting behind the floral flounced drapes of one of the B & Bs, or up and out – planning their next move?

Holly last night caressed away her anxiety, so she forgot it for a while, in bed, giving herself to that exhilarating desire, like riding the crest of a wave –

An engine revs up behind her. She gets up, making her way across the street, then opening the gate – it squeaks loudly – that question: how do they even know where she's going to be, somewhere temporary, for a weekend?

Now she's at the front door, on the doormat with its 'Welcome Home' in old-fashioned curly lettering – shabby chic: why they chose it –

The website must have had the lock symbol at the top of the page when she paid. The email confirmation arrived: she forwarded it to Holly. Days later, Holly's text message jolted her awake, telling her which station she'd pick her up from, then she bought her train ticket online –

She'll ask Erwin to check her phone. Perhaps she's missed a security update; she's always behind with things like that.

She opens the front door. There's the smell of coffee – a half-full cafetière on the counter, next to a mug with a coffee-stained rim. The bathroom door is open, the windows steamed up – and there's the metallic hiss of hairspray from the bedroom. Holly's looking at herself in the mirror, arranging her hair. Dressed, she's ready to check out – no snuggling back into bed then.

'Oh, there you are.' Holly puts her hairspray away in her holdall.

She hovers near the bed – Holly moves to the bathroom, bringing back her toiletries bag and zipping it away in her holdall too.

Puzzled – why the hurry? – in the doorway, between rooms, unsure what to do, she offers, 'Shall I put some toast on, scrambled eggs?'

'That would be lovely.' Holly turns back to the mirror and starts her make up.

The checkout isn't until midday, but Holly's in a brusque get-up-and-go mode, so she doesn't ask why. In the kitchen she slices bread, cracks eggs and puts butter to melt in a pan on the hob.

From the bedroom, Holly's mobile sounds a text alert, then there's the snapping shut of her handbag, and she's in the kitchen.

By the front door, she drops her holdall down, placing her hand-bag on top.

'Sorry, I should have told you: while you were out I got a call – the childcare seems to have fallen through.'

'Oh.' She glances towards Holly, then turns away – she doesn't want the eggs to stick in the pan; she doesn't want to show what she's feeling –

But a hand on her arm, then closer, Holly whispers, 'Smells delicious,' and she threads her arms around her, and holds her tight.

Perhaps it's going to be –

Holly kisses her neck – then moves away, laying the table, weaving around her, until they dish up their meal.

When they're sitting close together at the table, Holly pouring her a coffee from a fresh pot, she has a vision of a future: living and being together, like couples do –

Until Holly looks at her watch – she wants to say, don't say it; don't rush off – then she looks at her, glances at her bags ready by the door, then she smiles and, taking her by the hand, leads her back to bed. Past the metallic spray, perfume, without all the layers of cover – then naked, yes, everything's perfect when Holly's holding her, they're making love on a Sunday morning, and she's about to come –

Then, time again; time to get up. Holly pulls away, dislodging the sheets, leaving her naked in the cold air.

Soon they're washing the dishes and tidying up. She takes the rubbish outside, and when she opens the bin, there's the scrunched-up bag of takeaway cartons from last night on top – Holly must have dumped it when she wasn't looking.

'Tesya, what are you doing?' Holly's by the door –

Soon, earlier than planned, they're in Holly's car driving away past a mood board of pretty pastel-coloured cottage doors, old black and white pubs, leaving a bed made up with linen sheets – just like the photos on the website.

There's the whizzing past of intermittent cars, overtaking – Holly's eyes flicker to the rear-view mirror, then looking straight ahead she puts her foot down, accelerating past them, her hands tightly clutching the steering wheel.

Holly asks, 'Are you all right?'

What was there to say? Rather than try to talk above the hum of the engine, she says, 'Yes, I'm fine,' like they're strangers or acquaintances – not lovers after a weekend break cut short. She looks the other way, where the sea glistens, a silver snake following them, however fast they go it's always equidistant. They're on an island surrounded by the sea, what you lose sight of in the metropolis –

Holly's silent, somewhere else already, making a smart three-point turn between difficult subjects like last night, dropping her lover off and picking up her kids. Keeping things separate; like sorting rubbish from the recycling –

Holly hadn't understood – her 'Tesya, why on earth would anyone be out to get you?' But at least she now knows some of what happened then. She had started to tell her over their pizza last night – and she listened, before leading her to bed: what she does, what she loves about her –

But now they're outside the station, and out of time; the engine's still running. On the kerb, she leans back in, picking up her shoulder bag, and goes to kiss Holly – but she just touches her hand briefly: there are people around, taxis stopping and starting. Her hands back on the wheel, she says, 'That was lovely; we must do it again soon.'

Like they've been away on totally different weekends.

'I'd love that,' she replies, like a character in an English drawing-room play, terribly polite, rather like how she waves her off – but Holly's looking ahead, and then her car disappears at the bottom of the road.

She looks down. All the bits of rubbish in the gutter: screwed-up snack wrappings, cigarette stubs and chewing-gum wads. Covered in saliva and DNA. Rubbish sums it all up: what's happened, including the stuff that's happened since that may or may not be related – but there's her gut instinct: it is related, it's racist.

She looks back the way Holly drove off, remembering last time, the only time she went to Holly's.

'Excuse me?' Someone with a huge suitcase –

She moves aside, then goes to check the departure board. The train isn't for ages.

Someone goes past with a takeaway coffee in hand – further down the platform, inside, the café's warm with the steam from an old-fashioned tea urn, and the smell of toast and fried breakfasts.

A cheerful woman behind the counter asks, 'What can I get you for, love?' A friendly reminder of Hackney, nice adults, random dinner ladies at school who'd know when she'd had a bad day and give her an extra helping of pudding with a 'There you go, darling' – or the lollipop ladies at the school crossing who'd stop the traffic to let her across, while blocking trouble they'd noticed behind her – a head start away from the bullies.

'A white coffee, please.'

'Here you go.'

'Thanks.' It's hot and frothy, and she sips it, looking for a seat, between the busy tables. Then, turning round the corner at the end, there's no one sitting, but her eyes are drawn to a frame above the empty fireplace. It's an old black-and-white newspaper front page, a photo: a row of men's and women's faces stare ahead; police photos. One woman with a stylish hairstyle looks something like Myra Hindley, her attractive face masking her other, evil side – the side that worked with Ian Brady. She turns away –

Back near the door, she sits by the window to keep an eye out for the train.

The door opens, and a couple walk in and buy teas then carry them round the corner with a gentle toing and froing of conversation; people who love each other. She remembers the romantic assignation in another station café, the wartime film *Brief Encounter* – how did it end? She tries googling it, but there's little coverage – and she's almost out of charge. She reaches down for her weekend bag –

But it's not there.

She gets up, looking around the café – no, she hasn't left it anywhere inside.

'All right, love?' the woman behind the counter calls out.

'Just left my holdall somewhere –'

Outside the café, a train whooshes in on the other side of the tracks. Doors slam back, there's a flurry of movement, more slammed doors, and then the train departs – like Holly's car disappeared at the bottom of the road, that last view of the back of her car registration, the boot … where she put her weekend holdall next to Holly's – and never took it out.

Her mobile is still in her hand – only one bar.

Behind her there's chatter, people leaving the station, now heading past her, down the road. Before she's thought about it, she's following them, and once she's walking it feels right: why bother Holly to drive out when she's perfectly capable of walking to hers?

It's good to be walking – like extending the weekend away – and through a pretty country village. In the light she can see the cottages with their carefully tended gardens, and the little church, where people are shaking hands with the vicar and then walking through the graveyard to the kissing gate out onto the village green. All the old granite headstones, green with moss – only a few newer ones, white stones with flowers faithfully arranged; one of those must be tended by Holly and her kids.

Not far now. There's the lane leading to Holly's.

And there it is now, Holly's car parked in front.

The front door is wide open, so she walks in. She's about to call out to Holly, let her know she's here, when she hears a voice, not Holly's. From the back of the house, there's an unmistakably angry male voice, slow and steady, like someone used to getting his own way. 'Listen to me –'

She moves back into the porch, not sure what to do.

There's the tone and hiss of an argument – she can't make out more words – until suddenly shouting, it's Holly. 'Oh, do what you want, you always do anyway.'

He backs out of the kitchen, a hand feeling for something in the pocket of a coat hung over the bottom of the banister. She ducks behind the porch door – though not before she glimpses him, or rather his clothes, the familiar cord jacket and jeans of so many men she knows.

There's the click and spark of a lighter, and footsteps –

Then Holly's voice, more normal now, 'Oh, go and have your fag in the garden. I'll make coffee, and we can play happy families for a bit when the kids come home – then you'll have to leave us in peace.'

'And the other thing?'

'I already told you.'

'If it wasn't for me you'd never have even –'

'You don't know that.'

He laughs. 'You always win, don't you?'

She laughs too, then, 'Garden, fag?'

There's a kettle coming to the boil, followed by the clink of mugs being set down. Soon the water is being poured, there's the aroma of coffee brewing, then the glugging of milk, the whispery unsealing and opening of a cellophane packet, and the chink of a spoon against china, sugar being stirred. She remembers the morning, Holly's hands pouring her a coffee over breakfast then taking her back to bed – where she knows her. It's just a Holly she doesn't know, who's having an argument. Everyone does sometimes. Perhaps it's her brother, her kids' uncle – that 'happy families'.

Why's she hiding?

Down the hallway, she walks into an empty kitchen. Past the half-full cafetière on the end of the counter, across the room, through the half-open patio doors – standing at the end of the garden, near a pile of firewood, Holly is passing a mug of coffee to the man. As he takes a sip, Holly gestures towards the countryside beyond the end of the garden, chatting –

Then suddenly the man's arm jerks, the coffee from his mug is thrown upwards, staining Holly's white blouse – she moves back – he's keeling over, now he's down on the ground, writhing violently. Then he's still –

Seconds.

Holly's looking down, watching –

Lying on his back, his limbs are askew – no, he's not moving. Must be a heart attack – is he dying, or –

They should call an ambulance. She feels for her phone, then remembers her lack of charge. Holly's mobile? She scans the kitchen for her bag, then glances over the counter, the jar of cooking utensils, spice rack, coffee and tea canisters, one for sugar – oh yes, there's the digital display of a landline base – but there's something else –

Next to the cafetière and an empty mug, there's a coffee-stained spoon, beside a small open cellophane packet. She looks closer – just a packet of ground almonds, for baking and savoury meals too, yes, but –

Confused, sort of – and yet not – the realization sinks in slowly, like tiny minuscule specks of nut swirling, stirred into hot coffee, like sugar. There's the sugar canister, closed; and here's an open packet of –

She feels sick –

Down the garden, Holly steps over the man's body, then stands staring through the trees at the end of the garden, a glimmer of light on the horizon.

Have to get out –

Down the hallway, out of the front door, shutting it behind her – what comes back clearly is what he looked like, twisting round, looking up at Holly: his face distorted in agony – the black polo neck and jeans, cord jacket, that classic so familiar arts-lecturer look of male colleagues.

Fast – out of there – her heart kicks with fear along with flashes of him, still as a corpse, and Holly looking down, like she's waiting for him to –

What did he do to deserve that – she catches her thought – does anyone deserve that, whatever they've done?

It couldn't be Holly, her familiar perfect girlfriend, the one she made love to – last night, this morning – couldn't it be her twin sister, someone who looks like her, anyone but –

Past the graveyard, finally back at the station, on the kerb where Holly dropped her off, suddenly nauseous, she throws up there in the gutter.

In a while, in the old-fashioned station Ladies' toilets, she rinses her mouth and splashes cold water on her face. Through the mirror, behind her is the closed door to the outside world, the world she must call – but her hands are still shaking, she has to stop shaking; think. She's holding onto the old-fashioned tap, like something from before the war, *Brief Encounter*; all the romance and tragedy of train stations: *Anna Karenina*, of course; no happy endings: all romance ends in 'til death do us part or the death of love – or when something is done to one of the bodies. The human condition: birth and death, nothing else is certain, even love.

After the ecstasy of Holly's bed in the dark that one night – in the morning, through the ivy growing around the window frames, she glimpsed the dark skeleton of a climbing frame, the sadness of cut-back flower beds, a pile of garden refuse ready for a bonfire – and a wall of trees on both sides, and at the end. The garden wasn't overlooked. No one else would have seen –

Heart drumming fear, she takes out her phone and turns it on – perhaps there's enough power for one call? As the phone powers up, she looks down. On the floor is an over-full waste bin. That rubbish by the door, last night; her fear of what that person could do –

She never imagined Holly, with her beautiful eyes and sweet lips, and her elegant white hands, more usually handing her a glass – like she handed her a coffee this morning –

A half-empty cafetière on the counter, and in the garden Holly holding a mug of coffee out for –

Phil. That was it.

At least he looked just like him, the lecturer in Arts that first day in the New Build, who came and introduced himself – not that she ever saw him again, not until –

Why was he at Holly's?

That day she hadn't heard him come in, she jumped – then he'd introduced himself. He was close – she would have stepped back, nearer the open window. For a moment – now she thinks about it – didn't she feel scared, her back to an open window, with a strange man standing between her and the door?

Could it have been him, nearby ever since, right up until yesterday – but why was he at Holly's?

She opens the door, and in the fresh air, she stands on the London-bound platform.

Someone walks outside to smoke in a garden, and someone else makes a quick decision and stirs something that someone might be allergic to into the darkness of hot coffee. A body writhes, and then lies still.

Stab marks mutilated her face and hands – in a photo; milky coffee dripped down a door across her name; the smell and stickiness of curry paste on her office door handle – and the black-and-white CCTV footage recording something having happened, but no presence of a human.

Didn't it start that day, a few hours after Phil introduced himself, when she returned from the staff induction to the coffee stain across her name on her office door?

All along, it must have been him last year, recently in London, and finally yesterday. Though what it's got to do with Holly, a whole year before they met, it can't –

A train roars past, not stopping.

Her phone is in her hand. One bar left, enough to quickly call Jazz; who else?

17

ANOTHER LESSON, AND ANOTHER ENDING

'She's done what?'

'I know, it's unbelievable –'

'Too right – have you called the –'

'Jazz, my phone's about to crash.'

'Almost with you.'

En route home from one of her sports weekends on the coast, Jazz's car pulls up to the kerb.

'Get in. I'll park somewhere, then we can talk.'

Once they're stationary, she sighs, 'Oh, Jazz.'

'Breathe. Take it slowly.'

It tumbles out fast, what she'd already blurted out on the phone again – what she'd seen – and now, 'I think the man is, was, behind what happened to me last year.'

'We have to call the police.'

'What would I say?'

'What happened – you haven't done anything wrong, what are you worried about?'

'I just … I have a weird feeling, like, what else is she going to do?'

'Exactly. That's why we should call the police.'

'OK, you're right.' She thinks of the only police station she's visited, and – 'Jo – I'll call her.'

'Here, use my phone.'

She keys in Jo's number. It goes to voicemail; she leaves a message to call her urgently. 'What now?' She turns to Jazz, just as Jazz's phone rings. She picks up. 'Hi, Jo.'

As the police backup vehicles head towards the front of the house, the three of them set off on foot, between the wood and the houses on the edge of the village – their shoes getting muddier and muddier as they trudge along the track. The wind hisses through the trees, there's the shivering rustle of leaves, and shrieking kids larking about behind the high hedges.

Almost there, there's the dense smell of a bonfire – and above the trees, the white outline of Holly's house: a chimney, and a gable, where she'd once stood at one of the bedroom windows, looking down –

Now behind the garden shed, hidden in the shadows of trees, she leans a hand against a trunk and peeks through the branches.

Scarlet crackling flames twist and spark in the dimming light. Two kids squeal and frolic, throwing twigs and branches into the flames – damp branches, throwing smoky black clouds back.

Further away, there's Holly, gazing into the depths of the bonfire, her pale face flushed red from the heat. It's not Holly – and yet it is. She's seen her like that, under the covers together, close up – oh, Holly –

A hand on her shoulder, Jo signalling: move back.

Now she sees what Holly was staring at: past the flames, and the logs piled up and burning black and scarlet, there's something bulky underneath. Wrapped in a thick hearthrug, its fringes sparking, there's something long, burning slowly, becoming charred and unrecognizable –

The kids, backing away from the fire, turn away from the smoke in their eyes – then she sees their faces. How familiar they look: like him. He's someone Holly once loved, or desired – and he's someone she killed and then burned away in cold blood on a wintry Sunday afternoon in an English country village.

She fainted, so that's all she remembers. Some things are better left unknown. Though in her mind, she's often there, between the trees, watching her lover staring into the flames –

Had Holly actually told her he was dead, or was that her assumption because of how Holly looked – and what she didn't say – when they first met? Did Holly play on what she showed she believed – is she guilty too: did she put the idea into Holly's head, kill him in her imagination first?

And what was the connection between what he did to her and what Holly eventually did to him?

So many unanswered questions –

Yet when she returned home that night, one answer was clear: something she'd never faced but had been there all along – there was no trace of Holly anywhere. Real lovers leave toothbrushes and stray garments, reminders of their human bodies. Had their love affair been only a projection of her dreams, like celluloid, and Holly's love like a cinema heroine – a consummate performance, but too perfect to be real?

That night, she'd stripped off her clothes, reeking of smoke and sweat, then naked, she started to cry: Holly's scent was there, still on her skin since the morning. If only – if she'd never met her – but her heart beats, and she cries, then she gets under the shower spray and washes Holly away.

A few days later, Jo called. Some things had been found that she needed to show her.

When the buzzer goes the next day, she's on the sofa, huddled under a soft throw, trying to work but failing –

She walks slowly to the entryphone, where she used to rush, to welcome Holly arriving all aflutter at the last minute, like a bird that might fly off at any moment. She doesn't want to think about Holly, yet like a ghost she appears out of nowhere still, her eyes and lips, her hands, and her body when she lifts the covers – she's mourning Holly, like she would if it was Holly who'd died, or rather been –

Jo's face on the screen; she buzzes her up.

Sitting down on the sofa, Jo asks, 'You're not staying here alone?'

'No, Jazz comes after work every evening. And Zehra and Erwin are taking it in turns at lunchtime.'

'Good.' Jo opens her briefcase and takes out a file. 'We've been inside the house, and also a car and a boat that belonged to him – he was living along the coast.' She watches her. 'We need you to identify a few things. Nothing scary, just evidence he was following you.'

She nods. 'OK.'

Jo takes out two photos: one, her induction letter for the New Build job, addressed 'Dear Tesya' – the missing letter; and the other, her name card, taken from her office door. 'These are yours? Sorry, I have to ask, even though it's –'

It's her name, Tesya; she nods, speechless.

'These were in the house, in a locked study where most of his stuff was stored – since he was living on the boat. They were going through an acrimonious divorce, and he'd left the family home, around the time you got that job –'

'Phil was her husband,' she says, not as a question; she knows.

'Yes. Tesya, I'm sorry, but there's more. Probably best to know it all now, as much as I have. In the study there was a letter from the university to him – he had applied and didn't get the job, I mean the job you were appointed to.'

'But – he was on the website; he already worked there.'

'Yes, temporarily the year before, then he applied for the perma-nent job – which you got. He kept his staff pass, the interview guest pass, or he took someone else's – we don't know – but he accessed the building that whole year you were there.

'Something else, before you hear it in the press, or when we get to trial: in the boat was a laptop, and a series of videos he'd made and uploaded to YouTube, though he hadn't yet gone live with them. It's a series of lectures – no, he calls them lessons – it was like he was planning something big that last day, but it's not clear what. I'm just warning you in case more comes out when we interview Scarlett –'

'Scarlett?'

'That's Holly's real name.'

Was nothing about Holly true? 'I don't understand. Why me? Why did she – he – were they … they couldn't have been in this together, could they?'

'We don't know, yet. She must have seen that letter and your name card in his study – she knew of you well before you knew her. Her digital record includes searches for your name. The thing is, she's refusing to talk. We might never know the whole truth. Often barristers get psychiatric reports backing up clients' silence, using mental-health records. I'm sorry.'

'But I met her on a dating website –'

'Her searches predate that. She's an IT specialist, she'd know how to see beyond what you posted; she knew the profile was yours. We don't know why she was searching for you. He might have left your letter out in his study, so she'd get interested in you – they had a complicated relationship history. We may never know why. It's best to – I know it's difficult – but to try putting it behind you: what you've been through, what you've seen. It's going to be hard, but to prosecute her we'll need you to speak about this – although not for a year at least. In the meanwhile you must get back to your life –'

There's the front door being unlocked, the door opens: Jazz has the spare key.

Jo gets up. 'Hi, Jazz.'

'Hi. Won't disturb you, I'll go unpack this' – in her arms, a rucksack of groceries.

'Just finishing.' Jo picks up her file. 'Call me whenever you want.'

'Thank you.'

She sees Jo out and then comes back – Jazz is through the archway, in the kitchen. She holds up a bottle. 'Too early?'

She joins her and gets the glasses out. 'Never too early, and it's Friday.' She holds their glasses, and Jazz pours.

When they both have a glass, Jazz says, 'To you.'

'Me?'

'To the future.'

'Oh yes, you too, to the future.'

They walk towards the sofa and put their glasses down on the coffee table and turn towards each other, like they're going to talk about their days, as they've got into the habit of this past week – Jazz telling her about funny things kids do at school and her talking about whatever she's been procrastinating on for work, where she'll return soon –

Then for some reason she gets the courage to do what she's felt like for days: she leans forward and kisses Jazz – the only way she can blot out the past, it's what she has to do, kill off Holly, metaphorically speaking. Jazz is kissing her, and the longer they kiss it's a rather nice feeling. They lie down on the sofa making out, and then after a while she takes her by the hand and leads Jazz into the bedroom, and –

Now it's nothing to do with anything but the fact she's wanted to make love to Jazz ever since they came home.

Since then they've laughed about how it all ended – sort of, it's not the kind of thing she'd normally find funny, but now she has to. How she believed in the perfect lover, and all of Holly's fiction, even her name evoking the natural world – until she saw what she could do to another human being –

That's the thing, he was human, and humans do bad things. They hate, lie, and also sometimes kill, what she'd feared ...

It's been confirmed now. What the police and Jo labelled it as, it was: serious racial harassment was his intent – his computer record showed far-right white-supremacist reading increasingly over that year, confined on his boat.

She almost feels sorry for her harasser, his failure to get the job, his ending by a drink from Holly's hands and in the bonfire at the end of his family garden – almost – though if he'd succeeded in whatever he was planning, she wouldn't be writing this.

It's complicated: why we write things down, thinking things through, how we show humanity.

Now she wants to think about the other lesson: the lesson about love, not hate. It all started when she was grappling with putting her life together, back in London, starting yet another job, and spending more time with Jazz after living away. What she's learned is that sometimes dealing with difficult things actually pays off. Like facing up to her gut instincts, not just her insecurities about what Phil would do next – before she knew it was him – but also her gut instincts about Holly, or rather Scarlett. Now she knows when something seems perfect it probably isn't what it seems, and when things feel awkward, like they have recently with Jazz, it means there are probably more conversations to be had, and more potential depth in the relationship than she had ever imagined possible – like swimming in the sea, where she's gone before, then out of her comfort zone into the ocean, and finding the island of her dreams.

She's got the sea on her mind. They're off to Brighton for the weekend tomorrow, and then they have their lives ahead of them. The complaint in her new job has been withdrawn, and now she's busy with work, but she has a feeling there are some things that just keep happening when you're a minority in an almost all-white workplace, in an increasingly racist world. When things happen, she knows that she will have to keep speaking out and not take 'but it's probably an accident' for an answer. She has to try to make the workplace a better space for speaking about the experience of racism, while underlining she's not problematizing the workplace but trying to treat it with hope, understanding, and love of what an educational establishment could be – or rather should be.

There she is again, mixing up the crime of racism with love. Perhaps that's the final lesson: when we're unhappy with what we're told is perfect – the workplace, a lover – it's a sign something's not right, and it's not a crime to ask questions, or to expect answers and the truth. We have to be comfortable and love our work – and we also have to be comfortable and work at love. She has a suspicion that these lessons are going to continue for the rest of her life.

THE KILLING OF A
ONCE SACRED INSTITUTION

AUTHOR'S NOTE

I hadn't realized I'd been holding my breath, not knowing what was coming next, until I stopped typing and sat back, shocked at what was on my mind without me knowing, until it appeared on the page: the unexpected aggression of a white woman against a white man. That by whom, and against whom, I note plus what I've skirted over – the details; why – the stuff of white fiction I've studied and read, white characters in love and in hate.

That was the beginning of the epilogue, in my first draft. I remember my shock at the aggression welling up from somewhere deep inside me, and how my fingers lashed out at the nearest character. But with the distance of time and redrafting, I see what is inside others is inside me too, at least in my fiction. People lash out without thinking, and end up accidentally or intentionally wounding, or even mortally injuring others. It's different writing a book: we redraft, rewrite, delete and add, we can bring characters back to life or kill off others. In *Lessons* I always knew who would be killed off, I just didn't know until it came to it who would do it, and how – although of course the author is always the real murderer; the lives of the characters are ultimately in their hands.

Writing through and out the other side of what has happened to me, my growing aim was to explore the relationship between racism in childhood and adult life, which is why this hybrid novel is constructed from a critical race memoir of growing up British despite racism, and through fiction inspired as an adult trying to love while living through hate crime. Racism impacts on all aspects of our lives, so my ending for a fictional perpetrator – like my protagonist and antagonist characters when talking about Freud – has revealed my subconscious desire: I wanted a loving ally, someone to kill off – metaphorically, of course – whoever was behind the racism in my real life, because love, when I feel it, momentarily destroys the hate. Of course, my fictional ending projects closure of the crime, and a romantic return to the friend who the protagonist trusts – in the happy-ever-after ending of genre fiction.

Then there are the Lessons, my lessons. Whether from my protagonist or antagonist, these lessons are mine. I've feared hate up close, and I've been in the arms of love, where I've learned lessons for life.

As I've reshaped this narrative, some sentences have remained in each draft, like these which remain in this epilogue:

> It's time for heroines and heroes with darker skin, in stories of the hate we experience, despite our love. In this era of hate, our stories of this contemporary moment might contain white characters who hate us, perhaps want to murder us, and whose apparent love might be only camouflage for hate.

In this final version there are glimmers of hope for intercultural relations in the blended families and friendship groups of multicultural society – what I know from London, my extended and blended family, from friends, and my queer family. My genre ending rewrites the often melancholic endings of gay relationships in fiction, projecting a future of queer hope.

In reality, there has been no revelation of who was behind the incidents of serious racial harassment against me. I still live abiding by the advice I was given by the police, even now. In the novel, there are elements of my lived reality: the anxiety, the everyday weight of the lack of resolution. Racist crime in real life isn't like a genre novel; it doesn't always get solved. Just like the happy endings of romance fiction aren't the solutions they're made out to be: in real life those endings are just pauses in the continuum of relationships. When people meet, or marry, their unions are never finished products; relationships have ups and downs, they're works-in-progress with repetitions and circularity as people get to know each other, loving more, or falling off, or apart. Love is a continuum, it's never static – except in fiction.

When I read back over what I've written in the Lessons, I'm aware of what I haven't done, and what I don't want to do: give voice to verbal racism. We are hardly aware that Phil is racist. Privileged people, people in the professions, are good at hiding who they really are, even from themselves – but their indirect or direct racism hurts more than the racism thrown casually in the street, impacting on livelihoods and lives. I'm thinking about Brexit – and the COVID-19 pandemic as I write – and reflecting my own experience.

I remember flinching inwardly when an acquaintance once voiced a racist term out loud. She obviously didn't think she was being racist – she voiced it as though checking what I'd meant. I'd just told her about a racist incident that happened to one of my relatives, without mentioning the racist term, speaking about the action of racism, not the words – its impact. My acquaintance said that racist word aloud, perhaps to make the incident real for her, to imagine racism. Whereas hearing that racist term aloud made me feel sick, bringing back when that four-letter word has been thrown at me – and when I found it written on my school coat, as I described in my introduction.

Afterwards, when I thought about that conversation, I couldn't stop hearing this acquaintance saying the racist phrase. When I hear racism, I can't unhear it. It made me feel differently about that person, and after a while I worked out why – when she said that racist phrase she wasn't just trying it out, she'd obviously used that phrase before: she said that word calmly and not as though she was saying anything wrong. Presumably she doesn't see herself as racist – perhaps she'd said that word in all-white company and no one called her out. Perhaps then she was recounting a racist incident she'd witnessed, but I don't think so. No, the calm way she said that word meant she'd said it before in a different context, when she meant it to be racist. At some point she has been racist to someone like me.

That sounds ungenerous of me, believing the worst of an acquaintance – like my antagonist Phil, rather than my protagonist Tesya. Perhaps I should come out of the fiction and get back into the critical race memoir. It wasn't an acquaintance: when I heard the word I was sitting up in bed naked, and I pulled the sheet up tightly around my body, covering myself – like I want to cover up that hate word that has been aimed at my body so many times. Hearing a hate word from someone you like or love is worse than from someone you hate. I want to be able to relax with and respect the people I love, but love is also an ongoing lesson of sometimes difficult discoveries and conversations: if you love someone, you learn to challenge them.

We see ourselves as individuals, but we are more similar than we think. We have the potential to do evil and commit crime, or not. What makes people individual is how we deal with our place in society: going along with the status quo, or being aware and reacting against what is wrong and inhumane whether in a society or institution. Now dark-skinned babies are killed on borders by white government officials, whole dark-skinned families are drowned in the sea rather than be taken in by wealthier nations, and closer to home some dark-skinned citizens are seen as less equal than their fellow white citizens, burned alive in tower blocks unfit for human habitation. Doing nothing to work against hate, and perhaps even benefitting, means being as much part of the crime as the racist thugs beating up refugees, or the politicians leaving them to drown in the sea. Humans allowing evil to happen, by doing nothing, destroy the very meaning of humanity. Humanity is drowning in the waves of nationalism sweeping the globe, but I'm hopeful we will swim against that tide, and try to save it.

Since the election of Trump in the USA, and the global rise of anti-immigrant nationalist parties, two twentieth-century novels are often cited, reflecting readers' fears of where we might be heading in the twenty-first century: Margaret Atwood's *The Handmaid's Tale* and George Orwell's *1984*. Margaret Atwood has said that all the atrocities in her novel have happened, or are happening, somewhere, that the unbelievable cruelty of the society in her novel is based on our world. In Orwell's novel, what resonated for me was his protagonist's need to share love and intimacy, in opposition to a regime that sought to divide people. In my novel, like Orwell, I have shown the character turning to love despite the hate she experiences, and I have also followed Atwood and portrayed the exact racist crimes committed against me, revisiting them through fictional characters and places.

Incidents of serious racial harassment against me ranged from the mutilation of photos of me, curry paste smeared on my office door, and the repeated destruction of my name on my office name card – besides the apparent tampering with or malfunction of the CCTV camera placed opposite my door, thus never recording the culprit. Yes, all of this happened to me while working in the UK, despite the best efforts of the management and other staff in my workplace who did what they could to support me, as appropriate to their roles, besides the police trying to find out who committed those hate crimes. Of course all the blame lies with the criminal, who was never identified.

I have moved on, and creating a resolution through fiction has helped. I have also worked without experiencing hate at a number of other institutions since then. So, although there have been times when the once sacred institution of academia had been killed for me, my experience of racism could have happened in any workplace. Despite my experience, I continue to believe in the power of education and literature for combatting the increasing nihilism of the current political trajectory.

My experience has made me more attuned to people's indifference to racism – I am often quite scared of what white people might intend to do to me and others I care about. The impact of the racism I have experienced is such that I have often felt like I'm living in a dystopian novel while wishing I were in a genre novel, one where racist crime gets solved, and where I find love.

ACKNOWLEDGEMENTS

Novels are born of long hours of writing in isolation, but they also emerge from life shared. Too many people to thank, but first my mother, who listened, encouraged me to write and move on to new adventures; thanks to my writing family, in particular to my friend Kirsty Gunn; for giving me a stage to read my writing, Farhana Shaikh and The Asian Writer, Paul Burston and Polari, Sophia Blackwell and the Below Stairs LGBTQ Poetry Night at Blacks, London, and Jiwar, Barcelona.

Books take time away from work; books are work. I acknowledge the generosity of The Authors' Foundation and the Society of Authors for their support of this work in progress.

Thanks to Jessica Craig, my agent and friend on this journey to publication since we met in Gràcia, and thanks to Mireia Estrada Gelabert who introduced us; to Indigo, Susie Nicklin and Alex Spears for their warm response and care with this novel, and Tamsin Shelton for copy-editing.

Thanks to Tessa McWatt, Stephen Maddison and Kate Hodgkin; all these years later nuggets of dialogue with my former tutors resurfaced. Thanks to Olumide Popoola, fellow student, now writing friend, and Sara Haworth too, keeping each other going on our publishing journeys.

This novel is in part about the workplace, so thanks to colleagues over the years for support, and now friendship, especially Alison Kenny, Jeanne Engel, John Gray and Mohamed Moustakim. Thanks to my queer family, unconditionally there for the fun times in Soho and the difficult times too; friends from NAZ, Kiss, and the Internationals. Grazie to Paola Cavallin, champion of my writing, sharer of the stage, walks and Italian dinners, reminding me to take a break from my desk and live like an Italian. Thanks to my late dear friend Perlita Harris, who sadly died before I finished *Lessons*, and her widow Chris Atkins who advised me on aspects of the care system. Finally thanks to Lisa and Tessa for offering sanctuary when things were difficult, modelling a long loving relationship, and offering a doorstep of creative inspiration, and to Katy for love and bearing with me through the writing of 'that book'. Now, here it is.